Books by Lisa Glass

Blue

Air

LISA
GLASS

Quercus

First published in Great Britain in 2015 by

Quercus Publishing Ltd
Carmelite House
50 Victoria Embankment
London EC4Y 0DZ

An Hachette UK company

Copyright © 2015 Lisa Glass

The moral right of Lisa Glass to be identified as the author of this work has been asserted in accordance with the Copyright, Designs and Patents Act, 1988.

A CIP catalogue record for this book is available from the British Library

PB 978 1 84866 342 8
EBOOK 978 1 84866 817 1

This book is a work of fiction. Names, characters, businesses, organizations, places and events are either the product of the author's imagination or used fictitiously. Any resemblance to actual persons, living or dead, events or locales is entirely coincidental.

10 9 8 7 6 5 4 3 2 1

Typeset in Perpetua by Nigel Hazle
Printed and bound in Great Britain by Clays Ltd, St Ives plc

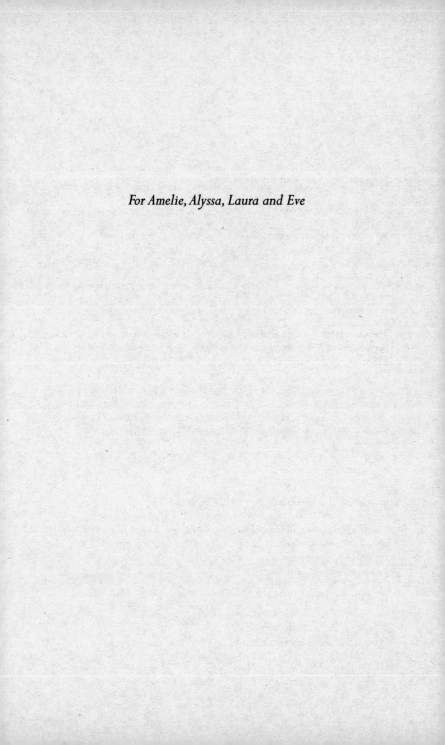

For Amelie, Alyssa, Laura and Eve

'There's music in the deep:
It is not in the surf's rough roar'

John G. C. Brainard, 1795–1828

everglades

Five in the morning and I was driving faster than was legal down the empty road that sliced through the Everglades. For once the chatter in my head was quiet. No more worry, no more stress. All I had to concentrate on was the road ahead.

I didn't think of my mum, Zeke or even the cute boy sitting next to me. Seb moved his hand to my thigh, ready to take the wheel if I veered off course, but I had it under control. I soared with the feeling of freedom; endless possibilities stretching out around me. I was free of the arguments, the jealousy, the pressure. I didn't need a boyfriend to make me happy. I could do anything, go anywhere, be anyone.

I'd hidden behind walls of doubt and fear my whole life, but at last I knew the only thing that had ever held me back was me. The old me.

In that moment, I thought I was invincible.

four days earlier

miami

monday 20 april

chapter one

Sprawled on the silvery sand with my face turned to the sun, I reached over and the back of my hand found the stubble of his cheek. Asleep at one fifty-three on a Monday afternoon. The sun beat down; the sea was shining like a gemstone and we were in Miami.

'Zeke,' I said, just loud enough that I would have caught his attention if he was already stirring.

No response.

I turned on to my side to make sure he was still breathing, my mind falling back into the cold water of the Cribbar, where I almost lost him.

Struggling in the swirl of sucking currents, scanning the whitewash until, finally, his surfboard had floated to the surface, tombstoning, its urethane leash snagged on submerged rocks. Hand over hand, I followed that leash down into the darkness, and my fist closed around his hair.

Now, on South Beach, his breathing was shallow and peaceful, seemingly untroubled by the fretful dreams that plagued my nights. Fast asleep, his face looked younger, and beyond the square jaw and stubble I caught a glimpse of the young boy he must've been just a few years before I met him; the Zeke I knew was deep-voiced and fearless.

Not just a surfer; an adrenalin junkie who'd chase any high. He wanted to explore every path, see all the different clouds and pretty sunsets, and try everything he thought looked fun, no matter the risks.

I teased him about having a severe case of FOMO, but it wasn't fear of missing out; he collected experiences and treasured them. With Christmas Day sun burning our backs, we'd paddled over a coral reef in Bali, swarmed by a thousand yellow fish, and he'd told me he'd keep that moment in his pocket the rest of his life and take it out whenever he needed to smile. I loved that he could do that.

Two o'clock and on he slept.

Behind us, the Miami skyline rose up jagged and stark; in front, an enormous cruise liner sailed by. Miami, it seemed to me, was built on water. Interconnected islands linked by roads carrying the vehicles of the rich and powerful. Shops were boutiques, cars were supercars and luxury seemed to come as standard.

For a second I let myself compare it to Newquay, and thought of my pre-dawn treks to surf a bump of swell at Fistral Beach, walking barefoot over sand dunes that were silent except for the snores of freecampers and the scuffle of foxes.

I ate the rest of my Reese's Pieces, drank my Dr Pepper and looked at him again. Giving in, I touched his hair, which had fanned out on his towel, and I wondered what the week would bring. Whatever the answer, I wasn't afraid. Travelling for so many months, so far from home, I'd got used to uncertainty. Before, I'd wanted to know where I was going, who would be there and what time I could leave. After six months on the road, as long as I had snacks and access to a working loo I was happy. In some ways, it occurred to me, I'd turned into Zeke.

My phone began to buzz. Zeke stirred a little and turned on to one side.

'You sounded rather American just then,' she said, when I answered with a whispered, 'Hello.'

'I said one word.' I got up and moved down the beach so Zeke wouldn't be disturbed.

'You'll be calling me "Mom" next, I suppose, and turning on a "faucet". How are you? How's Miami?'

'All right. Busy.'

'I don't like the thought of those six-lane expressways. It's not natural. Good lord, I can only imagine the road rage. And, of course, one-third of motorists in Florida carry guns in their cars. A third! You could pick up gunshot residue just walking down the street, and don't get me started on the serial killers.'

I looked around the beach and saw young families, pensioners and gym bunnies. Out on the water, people were paragliding, kite-surfing and playing around on jet skis. Hardly a crime scene.

'There's some Feelgood Festival going on here,' I said. 'We've come a week early, to take a few days to chill out and get baked.'

'You'd better not be getting baked, Iris Fox.'

'Not in the marijuana sense. Catching rays.'

'Iris, the ozone layer resembles Swiss cheese – you are using suntan lotion?'

Suntan lotion. My mum still called it that, despite me correcting her, the same way she called hot chocolate 'drinking chocolate'. She was set in 1978 and always would be, no matter how far into the future the rest of the world moved.

'Yes, I'm using sunscreen,' I said, walking down the beach and trying not to gawp at a ridiculously ripped bloke jogging down the steps from the lifeguard booth.

'Excited for your birthday? Only three more sleeps!'

'I can't believe I'm gonna be seventeen,' I said. 'Feels so old.'

My mum scoffed at this. 'What about this launch party? Will there be press? Can I see it on YouTube?'

Florida was splashing on to the scene. It was going to be a stop on the following year's World Surf League championship tour, and the official announcement, with all the details, would be wrapped in a huge celebratory media launch. A Miami socialite had organized this party

8

at a flashy hotel and apparently a few slebs who surfed were coming: Cameron Diaz, Chris Hemsworth, that Sam guy from *True Blood*. There were also going to be some supermodels and NBA stars I'd never heard of, plus the mayor, the governor, and tons of other Miami power players. Oh, and a bunch of scruffy surfers, including me and Zeke.

Florida had been home to some of history's greatest surfers, including the legendary Kelly Slater, who grew up on Cocoa Beach, so it seemed only right for it to be represented on the world surfing stage. I was looking forward to seeing how it all went down.

'Yeah, I reckon. And don't forget the contest on Saturday will be going out live over the webcast, so you can watch that too.'

Mum didn't say anything, probably not wanting to commit to doing something she hated, so I said, 'Hey, you should see our hotel here, Mum. It has linen art.'

'*Linen* art?'

'Where they twist your towels into swans or bears or whatever. Ours were alligators.'

'Good grief. You wouldn't want that near your undercarriage, would you?'

I was still grinning at 'undercarriage' when she went on with, 'Aunt Zoe said you did smashing in California. She watched every one of your heats. What was this camera she was telling me about – a hundred frames a second?'

'A *thousand*. Phantom cam.'

A zip wire had been strung across the line-up at Steamer Lane in Santa Cruz and the Phantom camera chased each surfer down the wave, catching every moment of the ride, to be replayed in slow motion for the people watching over the Internet.

'Did you see any of my heats, Mum?'

'I had a Mont Blanc of marking, more's the pity, but Aunt Zoe told me all about it.'

I don't even know why I was disappointed. My mum hardly ever watched me surf. She said it was because she didn't know what she was looking at, couldn't appreciate all the manoeuvres, but I knew that was rubbish. She couldn't bear to see me try so hard, only to lose.

'Third place is fantastic. Well done, darling.'

'Thanks, but, you know, it was out of only ten girls . . .'

'Fantastic — end of story. When did you say the contest was?'

'Saturday at New Smyrna Beach.'

'Is that in Miami?'

'No, it's a few hours away. We're going to get the coach there.'

'Well, I promise I'll watch some of that one.'

'Thanks, Mum,' I said, almost certain that she wouldn't. 'I'm a bit nervous about it. There are only two other contests after this, and if I'm not top of the board, I probably have zero chance of sponsorship.'

'Is that even possible? From fourth?'

'Yeah, everyone's expecting a lead-change, because me Beth, Leilani and Jilene are super-close in points. Any of us could take the title.' Which was as stressful as it was exciting, because it meant that the pressure was always on. Everything was up for grabs, and one bad day could mean the difference between taking the trophy at the end of the tour, and having a real shot at a life as a professional surfer, and getting nowhere.

When Zeke had encouraged me to run for the Face of Billabong UK, he'd told me it was going to be a huge deal. Billabong was looking for ten girls internationally, one from each participating country, and the winner would receive a cheque for five grand, magazine coverage and entry to a series of new girls' contests that would run parallel to the Qualifying Series. The idea was to use the same locations and dates as the main events, to guarantee an audience. They were apparently spending a lot of money, seriously investing in the future of women's surfing. But it felt like everyone, including Billabong, had been disappointed in the lack of interest from the surf community. Sometimes it felt as if our contests were an afterthought, something that had to be shoved in, but never when the best waves were breaking. A pity contest. I didn't know how much of that my mum had picked up on already, but I didn't want to be the one to spell it out to her.

'How do you know I'm in fourth?'

'Oh, I saw it on your athlete page on Facebook. I do like that picture of you and Zeke on the Hawaiian mountaintop with your arms in the shape of a heart. Very sweet.'

Facebook? Apparently my mum *had* changed in my absence.

'What happened to social media being *the downfall of civilization as we know it*?'

'Naturally I only joined for the hotties.'

I laughed. My mum hadn't had a boyfriend in the ten years since my dad left. Even if she was actually checking out blokes, I doubted she was talking to them.

'Why haven't you accepted my friendship thingy?' she asked. 'Kelly accepted within twenty-five minutes of me sending the invitation.'

My best mate was friends with her own mum. And her grandparents. She didn't care what they found out about her. The way Kelly saw it, there was no point trying to hide anything, because it all came out in the end. She was weird like that.

'I'll check for it later.'

The phone went silent and I thought we'd been cut off.

'Mum?'

'I'm here. Oh, before I forget: I need you to be available

for Skype on Thursday at 1 p.m. your time. They'll all be here, including His Highness.'

'Dad's coming over? Like, actually into the house?'

My absentee father, not quite a deadbeat but nearly, was the comedy nemesis of my mother. They walked in circles around each other, eyes blazing, waiting for the other to make the first move.

'I can hardly leave him outside like a garden gnome,' she said, adding under her breath, 'much as he deserves it.'

I stopped to adjust my new bikini bottoms, retying the knot at my hip and trying not to flash the young woman with a baby strapped to her chest. 'Good morning,' I said, doffing my baseball cap at her.

'Why the big thing though? It's not like I'm gonna be eighteen.'

'Your aunt and I have been planning this party for months. We're not cancelling, just because the guest of honour is too busy to attend.'

'I'd have come home if I could've,' I said, feeling guilty, 'but I have the contest, and Anders said we have to go to this media launch party, no excuses. And then Zeke booked us a fancy hotel to make a birthday present of it.'

Zeke had seemed so happy to surprise me with the hotel reservation. We'd stayed in a lot of grim hostels on our travels, and slept on the battered couches of friends and strangers. It wasn't that we couldn't afford to stay somewhere nicer; at some of the more remote beaches there weren't any better options, and we made do, just like all the other surfers who travelled with us. In Spain we'd slept in sleeping bags under the stars.

'I know. We miss you, that's all.' She paused and added, 'I wish you'd come and visit, if only for a week.'

I'd heard this a few times over the past months, mostly before contests with heavy waves that broke over coral reefs – the sort of breaks that could break me. I knew she missed me, and worried about me, but I was locked into a strict contest-and-training schedule, and when I wasn't training or competing I had publicity and advertising commitments.

'What are you doing today, Mum?'

'Pub quiz at the Red Lion. One hundred pounds in the kitty, and there's a meat raffle. Iris?'

'Yes?'

'You are safe there, aren't you?'

'Mum. Be real. I'm knocking around the Art Deco district and South Beach. Caffeine overdose and an empty bank account are the main dangers here.'

She stage-coughed, delicately, which was some kind of code that I still hadn't totally figured out, although I had a feeling it was related to her finely tuned bullshitometer. 'Be careful.'

'I will.'

At the water's edge I waded into the shallows, shuffling my feet to ward off any stingrays lying in wait. The wind was warm and I took off my cap and felt my hair swish out behind me.

'It's not like I'm here alone. I'm here with Zeke.'

'You are indeed. The only word I'll say on the subject is "butterflies".'

We'd first had the butterflies conversation a week before I left Newquay. She was worried I couldn't count on Zeke, thought his free-spiritedness made him unreliable.

'He's looking out for me. Actually, we're looking out for each other. Stop worrying. He's not a bloody butterfly.'

I kicked at the water and sent an arc of spray through the air, marvelling for a moment at micro-rainbows.

'Are you surfing today?'

'Maybe, but there's only a couple of feet of swell.'

'Do keep a weather eye open for bull sharks. They have more testosterone than a charging bull elephant.'

'Mum! Stop worrying!'

'I'm just saying. Anything with that level of testosterone needs to keep away from my daughter.'

I heard the faint ring of the doorbell and my mum shuffling across the room. She was probably still wearing her knackered raccoon slippers – a Mother's Day present from my sister, Lily. I pictured her twitching the net curtain to peer out of the living room window, and I couldn't help smiling.

'Must dash. Renie's waiting.'

Kelly's mum did not seem like the pub-quiz type.

'Why is Renie—'

'I'm setting her up with a new member.'

When it came to boyfriends, Renie was the opposite of my mother; she liked to have at least one on the go at all times. Said being single felt like going to work without lippy.

'*Are* you now?'

'Of the Historical Society. You get that filthy mind from your father.'

'Bye, Mum.'

I walked back to Zeke, who was still lying in the fetal position, sound asleep.

I read two pages of my book and, as a reward, logged on to Facebook. Some of my mates back in the UK were gearing up for a night out on the town and had tagged me in their selfies. Kelly pouted in electric-blue lipstick, our friends since primary school Rae and Maisie on either side of her; all three looking glam in slinky club outfits.

Cass, I noted with relief, was nowhere to be seen. But then, she was probably busy with my ex-boyfriend Daniel.

I wrote a few 'Wish I was there with you lot' comments and loaded up Spotify. I whacked up the volume and went back to sunbathing, but I couldn't get comfortable. The sweat from my face was running past my ears, pooling at the back of my neck and dripping on to my towel.

How was Zeke still out for the count? It wasn't like we'd had some rager the night before.

I sat up and stroked a tiny scar on his forehead, and thought about the other scars that littered his body; painful wounds delivered by unseen rocks, heads of coral, the needle-nose of high-performance surfboards. The knife of my ex-boyfriend.

'Zeke,' I said.

He didn't stir.

'Zeke.'

I felt panic rise and shook his arm.

Nothing.

I shook it again, more violently this time.

Still he slept.

'Zeke.'

'Zeke.'

'ZEKE!'

chapter two

I slapped him across the side of the face and finally he moved, opened his eyes, looked up at me and said, 'Whoa, that hurt!'

'Jesus bloody Christ, Zeke, you almost gave me a heart attack!'

'Huh? What's happening? You OK?'

'I was calling you and shaking you and you wouldn't open your eyes.'

He sat up, stretched his arms above his head and yawned. 'So I napped for a minute. *Geez*. I thought you were doing the yoga?'

A quarter-mile down the beach, a hundred people were engaged in a mass yoga class that had been going on for an hour already. The teacher was an elderly Californian guru, with grey hair down to his bum and pink tie-dyed shorts. He hadn't bothered with a shirt, and every time I looked at him all I saw was huge, hair-ringed nipples.

'Couldn't be bothered.'

'You said you wanted to be loose for the contest. There's not much time left to train.'

'I already did the t'ai chi and Pilates taster classes this morning. Plus my knees are killing from the capoeira. Whereas you've done precisely zero, you lazy sod.'

'Sod? Like, a pile of dirt? Besides, it's different for me: my next contest isn't for three weeks. Yours is in five days.'

Our New Smyrna contest had been arranged last-minute, to tie in with the Florida media launch. It was a two-day event just for the girls on my tour and would probably be ignored by the surf community, as so many of our other contests had been. I suspected that Billabong was getting a bit panicky, since their shiny new competition was failing to generate excitement or make any noticeable impact at all.

'Blah, blah, nag, nag.'

'OK, I get it. Your contest, your decision.' He yawned again.

'Did you take a sleeping tablet?'

'I was beat.' He touched his cheek, where red welts were already rising. 'I feel like I have finger marks on my face.'

'Sorry. Overreaction, in hindsight.' There were times, and this was one of them, where I was sure Zeke suspected I was ever-so-slightly unhinged. Slapping him while he was dozing on a beach didn't exactly do much to dispute that theory.

'I always was a deep sleeper. I once sleepwalked out of the house and woke up in a pineapple field with a bunch of new mosquito bites. My mom was sipping her coffee on the lanai when she saw me racing down the trail. You shoulda seen her face. I think she thought I'd escaped a kidnapper.'

Zeke's mum, Sephy, was one of the kindest, most laidback women I'd ever met, but raising three boys alone must have caused her a fair bit of worry.

'I shook you really hard, Zeke.'

'Would you quit wigging out already? I was just sleeping.'

He picked up a handful of sand and let it fall through his fingers. I had watched him do this on every single beach we'd visited on our travels. For him, this pleasure never got old.

I noticed some sand sticking to the damp skin of his chest and I brushed it off, which he seemed to find amusing.

'My mum called,' I said.

'What's new in the quay? Catch me up.'

'Not much. She's off to some pub quiz with Kelly's mum.'

'Bar trivia?'

'Yeah, and there's a meat raffle.'

'That doesn't sound so sanitary.'

Zeke couldn't bear the thought of dead animals, so a meat raffle was probably his idea of a horror show.

'Oh, and she wants me to visit home.'

Zeke met my eyes and I detected a guilty expression.

'You should go then,' he said.

'So should you. We should go together.'

Zeke sighed, in an exaggerated way, as if the suggestion that he go and visit his two brothers, his mum and his stepdad – who were all currently residing in my home town – was utterly ludicrous.

'Soon as we get a minute, we will,' he said, with absolutely no conviction in his voice. 'Anyways, you were the one who said you didn't want to go visit until you were doing better in the rankings. We could have gone home for Christmas but you didn't want that, remember?'

'I know, but it's been months.'

He threw his arm around my shoulders and pulled me in close to kiss me. The sort of kiss that I still found completely thrilling and disorienting, even after all this time. There was just something about his mouth, his warmth, his scent even, that made any sense in my head disappear.

Eventually, when the sun was significantly lower in the sky, we pulled apart and he looked at me a long time and my brain recoiled a little at the beauty of him, all high cheekbones, dishevelled hair and blue eyes. *How?* it seemed to ask. *How is that your boyfriend?*

I looked at his hair, which had grown longer – too long. A strand of it had fallen over his face and he batted it away from his eye.

21

'Do you want to borrow a hair elastic?' I asked, completely seriously. 'Stop it getting in your face?'

'A hair-what now?'

'You never tied your hair back?'

'Nope. What would I even use? It's not like I have a stash of hair accessories.'

In the list of stashes that Zeke had once possessed, I couldn't imagine hair bands among them. Weed stash: definitely. Meth stash: apparently. Pills? More than likely. But all that was in the past. On each of his competition surfboards he now had a sticker with the letters DFS: Drug-Free Surfer.

I slipped one of the beige hair elastics off my hairbrush and handed it to him.

He wound it in his fingers and said, 'So . . . what exactly am I doing with this hair tie?'

'Give it here,' I said impatiently. 'And sit down.'

He sat patiently at my feet like a little boy, even though he was nineteen and about a foot taller than me, and I looked at the top of his head, dotted with golden flecks of sand.

'Do you want a high ponytail or a low one?'

'Whatever you think will look good. Or maybe least bad.'

'Your head – your call,' I said firmly.

'You know how Owen Wright does the Samurai topknot thing for contests? Can I have that?'

Owen Wright was one of the best surfers on the World Championship Tour and built like a Greek god. A six-foot-three Aussie with shoulders almost as wide, he was one of the nicest blokes in surfing and I knew he was one of Zeke's idols. If a Samurai topknot was good enough for Owen Wright, it was good enough for anyone.

I hooked the elastic on to my fingers, scooped all of Zeke's hair up on to his head and then wound it into a tiny blond bun.

It looked hilarious, but Zeke didn't care. I watched him turn his head from side to side, testing it out and revelling in the freedom. 'OK, so this is awesome,' he said, jumping to his feet. 'Thanks.'

'If your hair annoys you so much, maybe you should do something about it.'

'Like what?'

'Like get a haircut?'

'Naw, man, screw that.'

'Why not?' Zeke didn't seem like the vain type, but maybe he was secretly proud of his mop.

'It's not just one haircut. It's never just one. What you're signing up for right there is a commitment. Get it done once and then you have to find someone to do it again, the next month. Shoot, I wish I had that kinda time.'

'Zeke, you spend six hours a day surfing, but you can't spare thirty minutes once a month for a trim?'

'My office is the ocean.'

'Someone must be cutting your hair, even if it is once a year.'

'Uh-huh. Me. I get scissors, grab some hair, take off a little, bam, done.'

I stared at him. I wasn't at all into the salon experience, but even I got someone to cut my hair for me.

'Do your modelling sponsors know you do that?'

He shrugged, like that wasn't a factor worth considering, and pulled on a grey T-shirt that had the words '*Eat, Sleep, Surf, Repeat*' printed on it in three-inch lettering.

Suddenly his phone started vibrating in the pocket of his board shorts.

'Hey, Anders.'

I groaned.

Anders was the surf agent who represented both of us. In his better moments he was sort of OK, but his anxiety level was always set to max, and he was totally paranoid about us getting disqualified.

My last argument with him had started when he'd insisted the new breed of sponsors were going to clean up surfing – get rid of the uke-strumming, van-living, pothead image – and rebrand it as a serious sport watched by the masses, like football. Anders got offended when I told him to dream on. But I couldn't help it; the idea of surfing going mainstream just seemed laughable to me. Zeke and I took our fitness and training seriously, but we knew there was no way the general public would ever consider surfing a sport.

'What?' Zeke said. 'No, nothing. Iris, can you check *Surfing* magazine on your phone? Something's happened to Arron.'

I loaded up the page and there, at the top of the news section, was a slow-motion video of a surfer wiping out on a giant wave. The surfer in question was one of Zeke's best surfer buddies, Arron Burns, otherwise known as Micro, as he was only five foot three. Micro was filming a segment of his latest webisode for Epic TV. Little had he known the footage would end up in every surf e-zine and beyond.

'Oh, man,' Zeke said, when he saw his friend free-falling, hitting his head on his surfboard and disappearing into the thick lip of the wave. The last few frames showed Arron's body floating face down in the whitewash, with a rescue jet ski bombing towards him.

'I'm gonna put you on speaker. Iris is here. Yeah, just Iris.'

'Hi, Anders. Christ, that looked terrible. How's he doing?'

'We're waiting to hear. He was pulled from the water unconscious. I mean, looking at the video, he's hurting or gone.'

'Jesus,' I said, fingers of cold fear closing around my heart. 'Who got him out?'

I could see the moment through the rescuer's eyes. I knew exactly how it felt to pull a person who seemed dead from the water; remembered the horror, the powerlessness.

'It was a right balls-up. Kalani was on one of the jet skis, but when he went to grab him, he timed it wrong and the next wave munched him up and spat out the ski. Kalani had to swim for it and Butler got them both before the fourth wave broke. They're bloody lucky they're not all dead.'

'Thank God Butler was there,' I said. I looked at Zeke, who was gripping his phone so tightly his fingertips had turned white.

'I'm gonna see if I can get hold of Burnsy's manager now,' Anders said. 'I'll let you know when I hear more. Say your prayers.'

'We sure will,' Zeke said. He ended the call, sat down on the sand and his put his hands together.

'Zeke?'

'Yeah.'

'Are you actually going to—'

'I need a minute.'

He closed his eyes, bowed his head and started murmuring something.

After a few minutes he opened his eyes and looked up at me.

I didn't know what to say. As far as I knew, Zeke

wasn't at all religious. In the time we'd spent together, I'd never known him to go to church, pray or even talk about religious belief.

'So, are . . . ?' he said, looking at me expectantly.

It was tempting to follow suit, to get on my knees and pray as hard as I could, but something stopped me; my sense of hypocrisy maybe.

'I would, Zeke, honestly I would, but I'm not totally sure there's . . . anyone listening.'

'You don't believe in God? For real?'

I shrugged.

'How can you surf a wave and not believe in God?'

'I don't really understand what you mean.'

Zeke stared at me wide-eyed. 'OK, my girlfriend's an atheist.'

'I never said that. I don't know what I am.'

'Wow, I guess you learn something new about a person every day.'

I tried to change the subject, get him talking about anything else, but he didn't seem to want to talk any more. Instead he sat with his knees close to his chest and his eyes on the horizon. It didn't occur to me until afterwards that he could've been thinking of his own near-drowning at the Cribbar, wondering if I'd prayed for him.

After ten minutes of this excruciating silence, Zeke said, 'I sure could use a cigarette now.'

'Hey. You're doing so well with the quitting – don't

throw it all away. I reckon Burnsy will be OK. He's one of the toughest blokes I ever met.'

Burnsy competed in Ironman contests, and his party trick, after about eight pints of lager, was one-armed press-ups, performed on his fingertips.

'He was held down too long,' Zeke said, 'and the wipeout from that wave looked super-violent. Even if he does survive, he'll be busted up. I mean, it's clear he hit his board. His spine, or his skull, could be broke.'

'He'll be all right,' I said, and it sounded so lame, so unconvincing, that I wished I'd said nothing at all. We sat in silence and I thought again about Zeke at the Cribbar, pulled lifeless on to the rocks. How cold he'd been. How heavy.

chapter three

Half an hour later, Anders called. 'Panic over. He's gonna make it. Puked up a whole lot of blood from ruptured capillaries in his lungs, poor git, thanks to some extreme breath-holding, but apart from a bust knee and a couple ribs ripped off his spine, the lad's right as rain.'

Zeke exhaled, thanked Anders for letting us know, whooped and did an actual somersault. Then he did another one.

When he'd returned to standing, and I'd gone from being elated that Burnsy was going to pull through, to amused that Zeke had apparently been hiding secret gymnastic abilities, I said, 'Thank God he's all right.'

Zeke raised his eyebrows and replied, 'Yeah, you said it.'

There was an awkward moment, where I knew I was being reproached. Zeke seemed to be waiting for me to say something more, so I went with, 'Since when can you do a backflip?'

'Since always, I guess. The airs I pull on waves – the big alley oops and rodeo flips? Basically the same thing, except there's a board under my feet.'

Zeke's aerial surf manoeuvres were legendary. Somehow he'd find the right ramp of white water, take off and, hallelujah, he'd spin through a big rotation and land it. It was beautiful to watch, that moment when he'd hang in the air, tail high, and then stomp it on the face of the wave without falling. It was like watching a snowboarder. Or a skater in the half-pipe.

'Well, now you're just showing off.'

I still hadn't got the hang of airs. Barrels, cutbacks, carving hacks, snaps off the lip and big tail throws weren't a problem, but airs I had not mastered. If I managed to stick one, it was generally a fluke; most of the time my board shot out from under me and I ended up getting worked. The problem was partly timing, but also my survival instinct. Airs can mess you up. All the air-game surfers I knew, including Zeke, were really susceptible to injury in the lower extremities, often seriously damaging their knees, hips and ankles. Which explained why a lot of older surfers in their forties had replacement knees – they'd totally battered their shock absorbers. One of the things I'd discovered on my travels was that my body was really reluctant to get hurt, and launching airs felt too much like asking for trouble, like picking a fight with fate, so at the last second I hesitated. Game Over.

'You wanna take the boards out now?' Zeke said.

We turned and looked at the little lime-coloured waves, which had faces of two feet at most, and Zeke said, 'It could be fun. Amber waves.'

'What waves?' White waves, green waves and blue waves I'd heard of, but never amber ones. Perhaps it was some weird wave traffic-light system, I thought, bored.

'Amber. After Chase's sister.'

'The guy we're supposed to be meeting today?'

'Yeah, when we were growing up, his sister would only surf waves like this. Anything over two feet and you could count her out.'

'Does she live in Miami now too?'

'She's some sort of swimsuit model here, I think. You'll like her. I think Chase is bringing her to the cabana later.'

'Great,' I said, recognizing the tension in my voice.

'Come on – let's get a few good ones before the wind picks up too much.'

'Fine, but I'm using the Shark Shield,' I said, unpacking it.

'Good idea.'

So we surfed, and by a few waves in I had almost forgotten the uncomfortable feeling that had been nagging at me for the past few weeks. I didn't even quite know what it was, but it was there, vague and formless, slipping away every time I tried to grab it.

chapter four

After barely an hour, the wind made what surf there was too messy to be worthwhile, so we paddled back in and made for our beach towel.

I was getting out of my rash vest and into a fresh bikini top, when Zeke blurted out, 'Iris. You ever wish you didn't meet me?'

'Err, of course I don't wish that, Zeke. Why would you even ask that?'

'Phew. You know you're the best thing that ever happened to me, right?'

I didn't know how that could possibly be true. Zeke Francis, one of surfing's most promising sons, had the world at his feet; how could I compete with the world?

But there was something in his face – a longing – that seemed to suck away all doubt, all air, reducing the distance between us to nothing.

I smiled at him, and he reflected it back at me; morning sun on the horizon.

'Aw, thanks, Zeke,' I said. Which was my way of saying, *You're the best thing that ever happened to me too.*

'If I ever die out there, Iris, you'll move on, right? Don't let me ruin your life.'

I looked at him sharply and said, 'Don't say that. Don't even think it.'

But he wasn't to be put off.

'Promise me.'

'All right, I promise.'

'OK, good.'

'And ditto.'

He rubbed sand out of his eyes, looked at the sea and said, 'Come on, we need to do something, get out of our heads.'

'Agreed.'

He looked back at me and, for a split second, I could once again see the boy-Zeke, a child of excitement and hope.

'Wanna surf a fast wave?'

'Uh, where? Because Amber waves or not, quite frankly I've seen better dribble in a baby's mouth.'

'Ha ha, follow me.'

'Where are we going?'

'You'll see.'

Zeke had a determined sort of stride and I struggled to keep up with him. From behind I could see that his neck was sunburned and I let myself worry about what my mum said about the ozone layer and made a mental note to check him over for dodgy-looking moles before the day was through. If anyone was likely to get a melanoma, it'd be the blond boy from Hawaii who'd surfed in board shorts almost every day of his life.

He turned and looked back at me, where I was struggling with my board and my overstuffed beach bag, and he took the bag from me, slinging it over his shoulder. The effect of my six-foot-one, scruffy surfer-dude boyfriend carrying this orange bag covered in an orchid print wasn't even comical; somehow he made it work.

When we finally reached the car park, sweat pouring off me, I saw a crowd staring up at a huge blue plastic monstrosity.

chapter five

'Told you,' Zeke said. 'Surf's up, yo . . .'

As he said it, I saw a small figure get sucked up towards the top of the FlowRider. Wipeout.

'Uhh . . .'

'You never rode a FlowRider before?'

I shook my head. Wherever there was a FlowRider, hundreds of people were sure to clump together and gawp. Today was a case in point. It was one thing wiping out a hundred yards offshore, but smashing my head on a lump of plastic in front of a cheering crowd? No, thanks.

'For real, I love these things,' Zeke said, handing me my bag, his phone and room card and walking straight up to the man in charge of the line.

He didn't even have to introduce himself; the man recognized him straight away and announced on the mic, 'Wow, put your hands together for Billabong star rider Zeke Francis, here to show us a little Hawaii style.'

In a flash, Zeke was out of his flip-flops and T-shirt and

on a shortboard, skimming up and down the FlowRider like he wasn't even trying, then breaking into deep carves and 360-degree helicopter spins. He looked super-bendy, as he maintained his balance through whatever the FlowRider chucked at him – I got a video for Kelly, since she had this line about Zeke being so flexible she was sure he'd been filleted.

I looked around me, and saw that pretty much all of the people watching had a look of awe on their faces, and I couldn't help feeling a tiny bit jealous.

Then the thing happened that I should totally have expected.

Zeke skimmed over to the edge of the FlowRider, jumped off his board, grabbing it in one swift movement, and got the guy in charge to hand him the mic.

'Iris, get up here!'

I kept completely still. No one would spot me, because no one would know what I looked like.

I considered backing slowly the whole way across the car park.

'Iris Fox, Face of Billabong UK, is in the house! Come on, girl!'

People started clapping and looking around, and then a middle-aged woman in a headscarf shouted, 'There she is.'

Before I even knew what was happening, I found myself being jostled to the front of the crowd and climbing the stairs to the FlowRider.

It was a weird sensation, more like skateboarding a half-pipe than riding a breaking wave towards shore, but I quickly got the hang of it, staying low and keeping my weight on my back foot so that I kept control, despite the sheet of water gushing towards me at thirty miles an hour. I hadn't even come close to falling off, when it happened.

The first odd thing I noticed was a couple of lads in the front row laughing. And then ripples of laughter spread backwards. Hands shot over faces, hooting started up, and several older gentlemen and parents with children walked away. I couldn't figure it out. I hadn't fallen. Both boobs were safely behind fabric, and I was kicking ass on the FlowRider.

It took Zeke to point out what had happened, with a wordless demonstration.

The fabric of my new bikini bottoms had stretched in the water, and the front panel had gathered at my leg crease. In other words, I had exposed a crowd of three hundred people to a perfect view of my undercarriage.

chapter six

I pulled my bikini bottoms back to their correct position and left the FlowRider, with Zeke right behind me.

There was no way to put a good spin on it. Even the guy on the mic was wiping away a tear of laughter, which was, I felt, deeply unprofessional.

Embarrassing myself like this was bad enough, but doing it in the coolest part of Miami, right in front of Zeke and hundreds of strangers, was absolutely excruciating.

It would have been better if Zeke had outright laughed, but instead he patted my back and gave me a look of pure pity.

'Tough break,' he said.

'Can we go? I think I've had enough now.'

'Chase is meeting us with a bunch of friends at six. We can't just blow them off.'

'What if your friends were in the crowd? What if they saw that? Zeke, I can't be chatting to people who've seen my pubes.'

'Hey, they weren't in the crowd – they have to work, remember? Don't sweat it. So a few people saw two seconds of you sorta naked. Who cares?'

I cared. My epidermis had cared itself scarlet.

'"Sort-of naked"?' Completely naked would've been better than just flashing my bush. 'Honestly, Zeke, I'm just not feeling it. I want to go.'

'You're making me crazy. We can't just leave – we got shit to do. You shouldn't care so much what people think.'

'Pardon me for feeling mortified.'

'Look, you gotta put it in perspective. I guarantee there are people online right now saying all kinds of mean things about Burnsy's accident. Calling him a wannabe, saying he shouldn't surf those waves cos he can't handle them, or he's too little, or whatever, but screw the haters. What are they surfing, except the Internet?'

'I know, Zeke, but—'

'But what? You can't control that stuff. Let it wash over you or you'll drive yourself crazy. Your first time and you were doing great up there. Maybe don't check YouTube tonight, but don't be embarrassed. It's nothing to the universe. Try and forget it.'

'OK.'

Times like this, it felt as if Zeke was on a different planet to me. How could you put something massively humiliating out of your mind just because you wanted to?

Finally Zeke broke the silence and nodded at one of the

festival marquees, 'Hey, you don't wanna be all stressed out when you meet my friends for the first time, right?'

'Exactly. That's why I'd rather we just called it a day now and met them tomorrow.'

'Not necessary. I got just the thing to make you feel better.'

'A time machine?'

'Ha ha, nope.'

'Does the plan involve alcohol?'

'There might be some lame-ass fizzy wine,' he said, looking dubious.

'I'm in.'

chapter seven

His warm hands worked their way across my shoulder blades. They circled around a tender spot in the muscle, finger rubbing hard into the knot, flattened palm sliding across coconut oil down to the small of my back.

'OK?' he said.

'*Uh-huh,*' I mumbled into the pillow.

'The pressure's good? I'm not hurting you?'

'No, it's fine.'

He'd given the massage therapist a hundred bucks to take a break and we'd taken over the therapy tent.

'You're super-tense.'

'No shit.'

'Just try to clear your mind.'

'My heart's still racing, Zeke, and all I can think of is YouTube.'

'This will help. I promise.'

For the first five minutes I was completely anxious. At the ten-minute point, my mind started to wander from stupid FlowRiders and the people who found them entertaining. Fifteen minutes in, I felt a bit better.

His hands got further and further down my spine and then he withdrew them, and I felt them on the backs of my thighs.

My breathing was weird and ragged, and I wondered if I was the only one here *really* getting into it.

'Turn over.'

'Turn over?'

'For your shoulders and the fronts of your legs.'

He'd seen me in the nude plenty of times, but somehow turning over seemed like something I just couldn't do. It was one thing to be seen naked by Zeke in the heat of the moment, but I didn't want to be inspected in bright daylight.

'Iris?'

But he wasn't looking for flaws. He was my boyfriend and he cared about me. I screwed up my courage, turned over and saw him looking down at me. As if reading my mind, he handed me a towel the massage therapist had left folded on a chair. He also hit Play on the sound system and the tent was flooded with meditation music.

'Cheers. I was feeling weird there,' I said. Not just weird. Exposed and vulnerable was more like it. Which was crazy, because this was Zeke, the least judgemental guy I'd ever met.

'Hey, don't apologize. If I overstep, just tell me, so I can take a step back.'

I closed my eyes, relaxed into the softness and took more deep breaths as Zeke moved his hands up and down my arms, soothing away the tension from training and surf sessions. He was working my hands, moving into the spaces between my fingers, and then circling my palms. I had flashes of tropical seas and a feeling of floating over water until I was flying in one long slow spiral towards a bright sunset.

I woke up with a snort, opened my eyes and Zeke was grinning down at me.

Oh God, oh God, oh God.

I knew I'd been snoring. Even worse, the side of my mouth was wet and a pool of my own drool had formed under my chin.

'See, you were tired too!' he said, grinning.

I put my hand over my eyes and willed my face to stop blushing.

Why? Why did my body have to keep humiliating me at every opportunity?

'Aaargh.'

'I'm kinda proud I made you so relaxed you crashed out. Feel better now?'

I was feeling better. Even though I couldn't have been asleep for long, I felt totally refreshed, and suddenly a bit of flashing didn't seem like the worst thing in the world.

Zeke touching me like that also felt super-romantic. Being with Zeke all the time had unexpected consequences: he was there when I was drowning in snot and sweat from flu, he was there after a dodgy curry wrought havoc with my digestive system, and he was there when I wanted to pluck the mutant hair out of my cheek. That sort of stuff wasn't exactly conducive to great romance, but being with him in the marquee absolutely was.

'Is there a fastener thing on the door?' I said. 'Like something you can tie?'

'I don't know,' he said, walking to the fabric doorway, which he started inspecting. 'I don't think so. We could put a chair in the way of it, like that time in Portugal?'

'Well, we *could* do that, or we could just chance it.'

I gave him what I hoped was a winning smile and pulled him on to the very narrow bed. He hesitated for a second, said, 'What the hell?' and kissed me.

I reached up and kissed his collarbones, and his body relaxed. He slid his hands under the towel, as I moved a hand further down his chest and his breathing got heavier.

When we first met, I felt awkward even holding his hand; ultra-conscious of my own sweaty palms; wondering if the way our hands fitted together was comfortable for him. His fingers were much longer than mine but almost as slim, and sometimes he caught me staring at them. I didn't even know I was doing it. Once those fingers had been inside my clothes, I wasn't able to look at them without remembering.

I had wriggled down and moved my mouth to his belly button, when a young guy wearing a weird hat walked in.

'Shoot. My bad,' he said, backing out. And then he said, '*Zeke?*' and failed to leave.

'Chase! Dude!'

'Friend, I don't know where to look. Put on underwear.'

By this time, I was wrapped in the towel and getting dressed underneath it, thinking that I should just give up any attempt to be dignified and accept a life of constant embarrassment.

Zeke pulled on his T-shirt and board shorts, and said, 'Wow, it's so good to see you. I thought we weren't meeting you guys until later. Don't you have work? This is my girlfriend, Iris, by the way,' he said.

'I see that.'

'Hello!' I said, aiming for bright and breezy, despite the ongoing mortification. 'Nice to meet you.'

'My dad gave me the day off to come to the festival.'

'Good guy. Are the others outside?' Zeke asked.

'No, they're coming later, along with a whole bunch of Amber's friends. I'm supposed to be grabbing a quick leg rub. Goddam capoeira.'

'Oh, I did that earlier while Zeke was crashed out!' I said. Chase had an olive complexion, grey eyes, and when he smiled at me, I became aware of excellent dimples.

'Can you still walk? Because my leg muscles are

45

somewhere between pulled pork and shredded crab. I guess the masseuse bailed already.'

'I paid her to take a walk,' Zeke said. 'She'll be back in fifteen minutes if you want to wait.'

'I ain't going nowhere near that table. What is it they say on CSI? "Biologicals".'

'Hey, there's no biologicals from us,' I said, offended.

'Except a little drool from when she was sleeping,' Zeke chipped in, and I punched him in the arm.

chapter eight

Chase waited outside while we finished getting dressed and Zeke filled me in on a bit of their history. Apparently, when they were really young, Chase had been like the fourth Francis brother, until his family had left Oahu for Miami. Zeke was already travelling the world at that point on the surf circuit, and he tried to stop over in Miami on the way back to Hawaii as often as he could.

We emerged from the tent and saw Chase standing to one side, biting his nails. He gave us a huge grin when he saw us, shook my hand, and then we strolled along the beach until we reached a waterfront hotel. My first impression of Chase was that he sounded like Michael Cera and had a very individual sense of style – anyone whose idea of a relaxed beach outfit was a waistcoat, green skinny jeans and a porkpie hat was OK with me.

Chase led us to the cabana and started chatting to a guy called Lucas, who stood at approximately seven feet. Also in attendance, each in a brightly coloured maxi-dress, were seven women. One of them, who jumped off a sunlounger and straight on to Zeke, was, I realized, almost certainly Amber the swimsuit model.

'Ezekiel! It's been way too long. You want shots? Let's get shots.'

'What rum do they have?' Zeke asked, looking around for a waiter.

'Hey, you remember that time we went horseback riding on the beach? I was just telling the girls.'

'Yeah – what were we, ten?'

'Your hair is wet – have you surfed today? Amber waves, right?' She paused for one second to take a breath, and then went on with, 'Where've you been the past year?'

'Surfing all over.'

'And who's this?'

'Oh, sorry, I should have introduced you already. This is my girlfriend, Iris. Iris, this is Amber.'

Amber was a radiant beauty. No two ways about it. Dark skin, perfect curves, green eyes. Sitting on her expensive-looking bag was a Yorkshire terrier, who was working a zebra print coat.

'Hi, Iris. It's so nice to meet you. How are you liking Miami?'

'It's lovely.'

'Lovely? That accent is lovely. You know Zeke taught me to surf?'

48

'He's good at that,' I said, smiling.

One of Amber's friends, a smiley girl with wild hair, said, 'And you taught him something too, right, Amber?'

Suddenly the cabana went very quiet, and Zeke's smile vanished from his face.

Chase frowned at Zeke and said, 'I hope she don't mean what I think she means.'

'Spanish!' Amber said. 'I taught him Spanish. Geez, Elsa, I'm not crazy about you making that sound so—'

'Like Amber stole Zeke's innocence,' Chase said.

'Please,' Zeke said. 'This girl right here is a sister to me.'

'You sweetheart,' Amber said. 'I love you, baby.'

'Ha ha. Back at you, always and forever,' Zeke said.

So my boyfriend was declaring his undying love for a bikini model. Even if he was joking, it still sounded weird to hear him say that. But the thing was, I could feel that there was absolutely no chemistry between them. Brother and sister, in feeling, if not in blood.

I couldn't, however, say the same thing about Amber's friend, who had been making cow eyes at Zeke since we'd got here.

She finally worked up the nerve to say something, 'Hey, Zeke, how's the surfing going? Saw you finished in the middle of the board last year. That's too bad.'

'Yeah,' he said, stroking Amber's dog. 'I missed a few

contests. Got myself injured pretty good. I had to take some time out.'

Because my ex-boyfriend whacked him over the head with a bottle and then stabbed him in the leg. I really hoped Zeke wouldn't tell her that.

'That sucks.'

'Then I surfed a big wave and got held down. Nearly checked out. I was lucky Garrett was around to help me out.'

I was also around, I thought, remembering the panic I felt as I dived down and untangled Zeke's foot from the surfboard leash that almost killed him.

'Oh, really? I never heard about that. Where'd it happen – like, Tahiti, or, like, Java?'

'No, the town that Iris is from, in England. Little place called Newquay.'

She looked confused. 'Nukey? You mean, like an atomic bomb?'

I shook my head in a way that I hoped signalled, *You are a moron of the highest order, lady.*

'*New*,' I said, 'as in not old. And *quay*, as in a harbour.'

'Well, I never heard of it.'

'It's so nice,' Zeke said. 'And it has some sweet waves. But, you know, obviously not the greatest in the world.'

Oh, really? I thought, feeling as if I had just been stabbed. I mean, technically he was right; Newquay didn't necessarily have the best waves in the world, but it was home and it hurt like hell to hear Zeke cast even a bit of shade on it and, because of that, my mouth geared up before my brain.

'Actually, Newquay does have the Cribbar reef break,' I said, 'which kicks up gigantic waves that could rival Jaws in Maui, or Mavericks in California, and pro-surfers the world over go there to surf it, so . . .' I said, trailing off.

The girl looked at me, face vacant as a yellow-lit street, and said, 'If you say so. It's great to see you again, Zeke. Man, I missed your face.'

'I'm a Face of Billabong,' I said, before I could stop myself. Super-lame. 'Oh God, I can't believe I just said that.' It was probably the most cringe-worthy thing I'd ever come out with, and of course it had to be in front of this girl who seemed to have an epic crush on my boyfriend.

'You're a model?' the girl said, looking at me with great scepticism.

'She's mostly a surfer,' Zeke said, butting in. I had the feeling he was trying to help me out, but it felt as if it just added insult to injury. 'She won a surf competition so she's representing the surf girls of England in this tour thing Billabong is running.'

'The UK, not England,' I said, since accuracy appeared to be the order of the day.

'Is that different?' asked idiot-girl.

'Uh, yep, quite.'

'So, I have to go to this work drinks thing tonight,

but I'm so glad I ran into you, Zeke. Send me a Facebook message if you have some time over the next couple days and maybe we can meet up for lattes?'

Zeke never drank lattes. *Five dollars for a cup of warm milk is crazy,* he'd say.

'Sure thing, Inga,' he said, and I watched as they kissed each other on both cheeks and she swung off through the hotel bar. She didn't even say goodbye to me.

Zeke, completely oblivious, got into another conversation, with the rest of them, about their various globetrotting histories. I was too shy to say anything, but I listened to them talk about the countries they'd left, the languages they'd learned and the careers they'd forged.

'You guys have plans for tomorrow night?' Chase asked.

'Nope. I guess we were gonna try and find some place for dinner and then check out some bars.'

'So you have to come to our mom's place,' Amber said. 'She's hosting this party for charity. Everyone's gonna be there.'

'What do you think, Iris? You wanna go to a party?' Zeke asked me.

'Can do, if you like.'

'Oh, you have to come. It's a pyjama party.'

'Yeah, we totally believe your mom is hosting a pyjama party . . .' Zeke said, rolling his eyes.

'Seriously. It's for some teen-depression charity.'

'I suppose pyjamas and depression do kinda go together,' Zeke said, looking at me to make sure I was OK with being railroaded into attending a party that involved slippers.

'Sounds cool,' I said. 'I'm in.' I wasn't totally sure I liked the sound of it, but travelling for months on end had taught me that some of the best experiences happened when you were least expecting them. And conversely, some of the worst nights were the ones you'd been looking forward to for weeks.

'Where's she holding it?' Zeke said, 'Her waterfront place on Palm Island?'

'No,' Chase said, 'the dry-lot in Coral Gables. You won't recognize it there. She spent like a million dollars on renovations. Blue marble floors, saltwater pool, exotic-wood kitchen, custom bar. She even got brand-new hurricane-resistant windows fitted. You need a ride?'

'That would be awesome. Man, that last party was really something.'

They exchanged a look that spoke volumes, and I wondered just what had gone down at the last party, and whether it involved Inga.

'Oh and bring your pocketbook, Zeke. Mom has the guests pay two hundred dollars each towards the charity.'

'No problem.'

Four hundred dollars to attend a pyjama party? Still, it was only a fraction of the $250K Zeke was making this year in sponsorships. It was for a good cause, but it was by far the most expensive party I'd ever gone to.

'Do I have time to buy new PJs? Mine are ancient,' I said.

'Good point – I don't actually own pyjamas,' Zeke said.

'So just go in whatever you do wear,' Chase suggested.

'Um,' Zeke said, considering how to formulate his reply, before I said, 'He'll buy some.'

The girls in the group had been chatting to each other and mostly ignoring me, but one of them, a girl called Marisa, asked me the question I always dreaded. I'd been hoping they'd heard my previous conversation with Inga so I'd be spared it.

'And what is it you do, Iris?'

I knew from eavesdropping that Marisa was the owner of a fashionable art gallery and appeared to have done pretty well for herself, judging by the Fendi handbag on her arm and the diamonds encircling her wrist.

'I surf.'

'To make a living?'

'Yep, although not much of one.'

'Not yet,' Zeke said. 'But one day. Just you wait. We have the next Steph Gilmore here.'

I smiled at him. He never gave up. My own personal motivational coach.

'You know, Zeke,' a Brazilian woman called Ursula

said, 'you have time to come down to the magazine and do a shoot for us.'

'Which magazine is this?' I asked, imagining a spread of my boyfriend in *Ocean Drive* magazine.

'*Ride*. You come too, Iris. You might get a kick out of it.'

'How long would it take?' Zeke asked.

'Honey, you're no rookie; two hours and you're done. You'd really be doing me a favour. Sergio wants a fresh face for the August issue. He'll probably put you on the cover.'

'You should do it,' I said to him, 'cover boy.'

'We'll have you on a motorcycle,' Ursula said. 'You still ride that bike back in Oahu?'

'Gave it to my brother.'

'To Garrett?'

'Wes.'

'Really? He never seemed like the type. Not to me.'

Zeke gave her a sharp look. 'Why not?'

It was an awkward moment, and I knew what Zeke was thinking: he thought this was a dig at Wes for being gay. As if gay guys didn't ride motorcycles or something, which was obviously ridiculous, but a few of the surfers who competed with Zeke on the tour had made snide remarks about Wes and his boyfriend Elijah, and Zeke always pulled them up on it.

'No reason. Did I say something?'

'I'll come down and get my picture taken but we're only here for a few more days.'

'So come Wednesday morning. I can have something set up for eleven.'

'OK, but Iris has to be in the picture too.'

'Zeke, NO. Ignore him.'

'Of course,' Ursula said, looking at me with a new expression in her eyes. Appraising me for the first time. 'A little make-up. A dress. Hair up. Sure, I can see the potential.'

I stood up. 'Thank you very much, but I'm not at all photogenic and I'd only ruin the pictures of Zeke. You know, I think I'll give you some time to catch up. It was nice to meet you all. Bye.'

I turned on my heel before I could get pushed into doing something that I really didn't want to do.

'Iris,' Zeke called after me and I waved at him, shouted, 'I'll meet you back at the hotel,' and then turned to keep walking.

'Wait!' he said, persistent, and caught me up, breathless and sweaty. 'Why are you leaving? We only just got here. I want my friends to get to know you.'

I was just going to answer that I really needed to find a loo, as I was busting for a wee, when his phone started ringing.

I could hear the deep New York tones of our publicist, and Zeke hadn't even put her on speaker.

Whatever she was saying had the effect of making him frown hard.

'No, no. Tomorrow. Definitely. Tomorrow. I have the email right here. You sure? They never sent another email, Whitney, I swear. No, no voicemail either. Seriously? That's like a half-hour drive, without traffic.'

'What's happening?' I mouthed. 'I thought we were free today?'

I secretly thought it was a bit cheeky of Anders to have made Whitney arrange any publicity during our Miami trip, as it was supposed to be a holiday. The media launch was one thing, as it was a major event in the surf calendar, but it sometimes seemed as if Anders couldn't bear the thought of us having any actual time off. As if every hour of chilling out was a missed opportunity to build our brand.

'I know we made a commitment, but I just told . . . OK, OK. Yeah, Iris is here too – she says . . .' Zeke looked at me, and I whispered, 'I've really got to find a loo before I pee myself.'

'She says hi,' Zeke said, ever the diplomat. 'OK, I'll remind her to edit that clip for the website. Speak later.'

I was already looking through my beach bag for cab money. 'How much time do we have?'

'Forty minutes.'

'To leave, or to get there?'

'To get there.'

'I just need a quick wee.'

'Iris, we gotta go.'

'I will also need to find a vending machine, as I'm bloody starving.'

Chase appeared at our sides and said, 'What gives?'

'We have to go to this mall signing that we totally thought was tomorrow. Could you drop our surfboards back at the Grove Hotel? The girls at reception will hold them until we're back later.'

'No problem. You'll be at the party tomorrow though, right?'

Zeke looked at me for an answer.

'It's up to Iris.'

I very nearly said, *'No, I've changed my mind,'* because, I suddenly had a really bad feeling about that party. But Chase looked so hopeful, and I'd just met him, and he was Zeke's friend and I didn't want to disappoint anyone.

'We'll be there,' I said.

chapter nine

Messing up the day of the mall promo was a seriously unprofessional screw-up on our part, but I trusted Zeke to lay on the charm and stop us getting a bollocking.

We had a two-minute loo-and-snack break, then caught a cab to the Dolphin Mall. Sitting in the taxi, with Zeke staring out the window, I had nothing to do but think, and my brain kept going back to the girls I'd met. Zeke definitely had some history with Inga. No doubt about it. And Amber had just taught him Spanish? Yeah, right.

Zeke kept looking at his watch, stressing. Even with the taxi driver weaving through the traffic like a pro, we still arrived at the mall fifteen minutes late.

It was just a poster-and-merchandise signing, but bona-fide surf fans were going to be there and we couldn't skip it, even if we did both reek of massage oil, sweat and sunscreen.

Most of the people that showed up – roughly 99.9 per cent, I guessed – would be there for Zeke. I knew this because we'd done around twenty of these events already, in various surf towns around the world, and the fan breakdown was always the same.

The queue for the Billabong store was out the door, snaking past a Dunkin' Donuts, a kids' clothing store and all the way down to Ron Jon's Surf Shack, which actually looked better than the Billabong store.

Zeke looked fine in his shorts, T-shirt and flip-flops. He'd shaken his hair out from the topknot and, like always, it had dried perfectly tousled, whereas mine was a bleached-out mess of frizz. My face was pink with sunburn, my T-shirt was creased and I had Cheeto breath.

As we walked past the queue of surf fans, I heard a bunch of people saying, 'There he is!' and 'Oh my God, I can't believe it!' Then another voice said, 'Gross! Who is *she*?'

I turned towards the voice, and made eye contact with the girl, who didn't even have the grace to look embarrassed.

When we entered the store, a local photographer in a Hawaiian shirt, shorts and white boat shoes greeted us with a big smile.

'Zeke and Iris, welcome to our store!'

'Thanks,' Zeke said, shaking his hand. I looked up at the back of the store and saw a bigger-than-lifesize picture of Zeke, standing in board shorts right next to

Dave Rastovich, Greg Long and Joel Parkinson: some of the best surfers in the world. The legends.

'And welcome to Florida. Y'all having a fun vacation?'

'Yeah, loving it,' I said, shaking his hand and trying my best to reflect his level of enthusiasm back at him. It had been pointed out to me that even when I wasn't being sarcastic, something about the inflections of my voice made me sound as if I was.

'Sorry we're late,' Zeke said. 'We thought this was tomorrow. We'll stay on a little to make up for it, if you need us to.'

'No need to apologize. We're just stoked to have you visit our little store.'

Several members of the store staff were staring at us, but none of them came over.

'Is there a rep from Billabong here?' Zeke asked, looking around.

'Right this way. You need anything else before you get started? A soda or something?'

'Do you want something, Iris?' Zeke asked.

I shook my head.

'Then no, sir; we're good to go.'

The photographer led us to the back of the store, past two junior male Billabong riders, and there, sitting at the back of the store, with her legs crossed and her red hair tied up in a glossy bun, was one of my favourite people on the planet.

'Saskia!' I said, rushing towards her. Zeke was right behind me.

Saskia was basically the reason I'd even made the tour, and I owed her everything.

'Iris!' she said, hugging me tight and sounding excited. 'Took you long enough. I thought you weren't going to show!'

'Had the wrong day. Why didn't you tell us you were going to be here?'

'Wanted to surprise you. How are you, darling?'

'Good. I really missed you!'

'I can't believe you're here!' Zeke said. 'We missed you so much.'

I stepped aside to let them embrace.

Tears that made no sense were pricking at my eyes, because I could feel it flowing through me – sheer joy.

'So you're working for Billabong since when?' Zeke asked.

'A few weeks. It's only an internship, but it's a start.'

'Congrats,' Zeke said. 'Anders was so mad you ditched him.'

'I couldn't stand being his PA for a minute longer. He's turned into a right little fascist these past few months. I know he's having personal troubles, but honestly, he was making my life a misery.'

'Personal troubles? Did you know that, Zeke?' I said.

'Yeah. Split up with his long-term girlfriend.'

Zeke knew Anders was going through something like that and didn't tell me?

'You didn't say anything.'

'It's not really my place to talk about someone else's personal life.'

The store manager came over and asked Zeke if he could start signing, since the people in the queue had already been waiting a while and were getting restless.

'Yeah, I'm so sorry. We just got caught up. I'll be right there.'

They walked away together and I couldn't help feeling a little bit embarrassed that the manager hadn't asked me to go with them.

'I should get a move on too, although I'll probably only have to sign one poster.'

'Don't do yourself down. I had a look at your Twitter. Thirty thousand followers is absolutely not to be sniffed at.'

'I tweet some sick surf pics, so they're probably following me for that . . . Anyway, congrats on the job. Stoked for you, mate.'

'No bugger wanted to sponsor me to surf, so at least this way I get to follow the tour. And even better, I'm going to be interviewing the surfers beachside for the webcast on Saturday. I'll have to do you too – so to speak.'

'Wow, cool job.'

'Not really. They're not paying me, and I'm sorting

out my own travel and hotels, so I suppose it hardly counts as a job at all.'

I winced. Saskia was working for free. Actually, worse than free. This internship must be costing her thousands in travel and board. She was from a wealthy family, sure, and probably had a fair bit in the bank, but if it wasn't for me, she'd have won the Billabong sponsorship and would have been on the tour, getting paid to surf. I owed her everything.

I looked over at Zeke and saw him signing a surfboard in black Sharpie.

'I've been wondering how you've been getting on,' she said. 'It's not easy at first – leaving home. Everyone struggles.'

She stretched her arms above her head, as if she was about to go into a sun salutation, and then thought better of it.

'Zeke never seemed to have a problem,' I said.

I looked over at Zeke again, chatting and laughing with the very pretty owner of the surfboard. The girl turned and held up her long hair so that he could sign the back of her neck. At least he wasn't signing a cleavage, which was a frequent request.

'Not true. He struggled too.'

'I doubt it.'

'Ha – I happen to know that the first time he took a flight on his own, to a contest in France, he got himself into a right pickle. He was far less confident back then – shy, even – and liable to panic. Poor thing couldn't speak the language, didn't know how to get to his event and couldn't find anyone to tell him. He'd been wandering the airport for an hour, and was so desperate for the toilet and so worried about his big-wave boards being nicked while he was in the loo that he gave up the whole thing as a bad lot and got the next flight home to Honolulu.'

'No way. That did not happen.'

Zeke, my world traveller, had missed a surf contest just because he couldn't figure out how to go to the loo without having his gear stolen.

'Promise you, it did. It's scary for everyone at first. You just fake it until you make it.'

Faking confidence was definitely a skill I was learning.

I gave her another hug and said, 'I'm really glad you're here. Let's spend some proper time together, all right?'

'Will do, kiddo. Where are you staying?'

'South Beach. Grove Hotel.'

'I'm in the Colony. The manager here said he'd give me a lift back after the signing. I'm sure you guys can jump in too. Save on taxi fares.'

'That'd be awesome.' I didn't want to rub it in by pointing out that Billabong reimbursed my work-related expenses.

She kissed me lightly on the lips and then went off to hover around Zeke and confer about Billabong's plans for total global domination of the surf market. I stood to the side of them, at a different table, and chatted to three eleven-year-old fans who wanted my signature on promo posters of me surfing J-Bay in South Africa.

It was always exciting to meet fans, and I tried my best to reply to their questions with interesting answers, but I couldn't concentrate, and couldn't stop grinning. I felt completely euphoric. I had a friend in Miami.

chapter ten

'That went good,' Zeke said, as we hit up the nightwear section of a department store in the same mall. The signing had lasted a couple of hours and the store was only thirteen minutes away from closing.

'Yeah, it did. So did you sign any nice racks?' I asked him.

'Not today. Some arms; one ankle.'

'And one neck.'

'You saw that, huh?'

'Sucks to be you, Zeke Francis,' I said, smiling through gritted teeth.

'How about these?' Zeke said, holding up some blue plaid pyjamas that looked as if they'd been designed for old men or toddlers.

'Er . . .'

'Excuse me, ma'am,' Zeke said, turning to the blonde girl who'd been hovering around us, eavesdropping, 'we're going to the Tanashian pyjama party tomorrow night and have no clue what to wear. Can you help us here?'

'You need a silk robe for sure,' she said to Zeke, producing a deep red silk dressing gown that wouldn't have looked amiss on Hugh Heffner, 'and the matching shorts.' Zeke took both of these items, and without looking at anything else in the store, or even checking the sizing or price, and said, 'Done. My girlfriend needs something too.'

'Yellow would be good with her colouring,' she said, handing me a slip.

'I can't wear that out,' I said, fingering the lacy cups and feeling quite sure that my nipples would be on show.

I turned away from her, and picked up a red striped shirt.

'It's not exactly fashion forward . . .' she said, seeming disappointed in me. 'How about this?' She handed me some stretch-cotton bum-skimmers and a matching vest, again in buttercup yellow, which came with an overshirt.

Zeke raised his eyebrows at me, and I nodded. 'She'll take it.'

I caught a quick glimpse of the price tag on the shirt alone — $149, which seemed insane — and was mouthing this sum to Zeke, when he put up his hand and said, 'I got this.'

The woman rang up our purchases, and charged Zeke's American Express with over five hundred dollars of nightwear, which Zeke appeared totally fine with, even though it seemed to me like it would have been better for the charity if we just gave them the money and wore our own clothes.

'Thanks, Zeke, but let me transfer the money into your account.'

'Relax.'

We returned to the Billabong store, and waited outside for the manager to cash up. Saskia came clip-clopping out in her super-high heels, ushering the two young lads in front of her, who were being picked up by their parents. She'd let her hair down, and it swung as she walked.

'Thanks so much for coming to our store,' the manager said, pulling down the shutter. 'You're welcome here any time you're in Florida.'

'We won't be back for probably a year,' Zeke said, 'but if you want us to come do another signing then, just get a hold of our publicist, Whitney, and she'll arrange it. I think I have her card here,' Zeke said, flipping through his wallet.

The manager led us to his minivan, and Zeke sat up front, to be polite, I guessed, while Saskia and I piled into the back.

'Are you good for a catch-up tomorrow?' I said, feeling really happy at the prospect of some girl time. 'Let me take you somewhere decent for lunch. Caviar. Lobster thermidor. Whatever you want.'

'Lobster thermidor?'

'Isn't that what you London people eat?'

She laughed. 'Never eaten a morsel of crustacean in my life. Not my thing.'

'Well, whatever you fancy. My treat.'

'Not necessary, sweetheart. I can pay my way.'

'You're doing enough of that as it is. Because of me. Let me do something nice for you.'

'You don't owe me anything, Iris, but Zeke invited me to the Tanashian party, so we can catch up then?'

'Deal.'

'You folks seen the sights?' the manager said, taking his eyes off the road to look at us in the rear-view mirror.

'We only got here last night,' I explained, 'so we've been mostly checking out South Beach.'

'You gotta go see Everglades National Park! My brother-in-law has an airboat tour down there. Here, I have his card.'

He riffled through the glovebox and pulled out a few business cards and passed them to Zeke, who handed them out.

I put it in my wallet to be polite, and Saskia did the same. When she looked up, she gave me one of her dazzling smiles, and said, very quietly, 'So, I have a boyfriend.'

'Ooh! Details! Anyone I know?'

'Yes, actually: Gabe Monterroso.'

Gabe was a Brazilian pro-surfer, with epic dreads,

who lived for two things: longboarding and computer programming. He was planning to retire from pro-surfing at twenty-five to start his own computer-games company. Zeke had known Gabe since they were groms, as Gabe's family had travelled around contests in huge vans kitted out with every games console on the market and all the lads on the junior tour had hung out there in between heats. He was absolutely not the sort of bloke I imagined Saskia shacking up with, but he did have a very cool, very large family, and I knew from the way Saskia talked about Zeke's family that she valued that, particularly since she was an only child who'd spent years in boarding school.

'Oh, I love him! When did that happen?'

'It's only been a couple of weeks. He's going to be at the media launch party on Thursday actually. What are you wearing, by the way?'

'Buying a dress here. What about you?'

'I have a vintage Valentino that used to belong to my mother. It's terribly revealing, however, so I might wear my new Prada.'

It was times like this that I remembered just how different Saskia's financial situation was from mine. I had two grand in a savings account and a few grand in my current account. Saskia had once let slip how much she had left in her trust fund, after burning through some of it on a lavish trip to the Caymans, and

I knew she was worth more than my mum and dad put together.

We dropped Saskia off at the Colony and the manager drove us on to the Grove.

'Y'all have a good night,' he said, as we climbed out. 'And don't forget to go do the gator tour!'

'Sure thing,' Zeke said. We gave him a wave and then walked up to the entrance of our hotel, where the doormen rushed to open the door for us. Zeke slipped them a few dollars and said to me, 'Hey, it's so cool that Saskia's here!'

'Yeah, she's the best. Did you know she has a thing going with Gabe?'

'No, but I can see that. They're both the same way.'

'Are they? They seem completely different to me.'

'No, they're the same. Super-organized. Driven to succeed. Type A.'

I was none of those things.

'And they both have a thing for cleaning. Gabe's condo is like a show home, just with a whole lot of computers. And you know Saskia is obsessed with interior design. Even the pillows on her couch have places.'

I felt a pang of disappointment in myself. I knew for a fact my constant messiness was getting to Zeke. He never said anything, but I could tell he was irritated when he had to move my stuff off all the surfaces to find whatever he was looking for.

We stopped outside the lift and Zeke said, 'I think I'm gonna call Anders – see if there's any news about Burnsy.'

'Good idea. Say hello from me.'

Inside the lift, the reception on Zeke's phone cut out, so I phoned from mine.

Anders answered the phone with, 'Problem? Zeke OK?'

This was the sort of thing that wound me up about Anders. It was as if he was determined to prove to me how inconsequential I was in his eyes.

'Yes, he's terrific.' *And so am I, thanks for asking*, I thought. 'We're just ringing to see how Arron's doing.'

'Not great.'

'I thought you said he was going to be all right?'

'Physically, yes. But he says as far as surfing goes, he's done.'

'No way!'

'I mean, I hope the lad'll change his mind, but it's not looking likely. He really thought his number was up there. Says he's out.'

Zeke was staring at me, waiting for me to tell him what was going on.

'Put Zeke on.'

'Shall I put you on speaker?'

'Pass him the phone.'

We stepped out of the lift, and I passed Zeke the phone.

73

'No, I haven't,' he said. 'No, nothing. Maybe next week. I don't much care either way. Yeah, I'll let you know if I do. OK, bye.'

He passed it back to me.

'Iris?' Anders said.

'Yeah?'

'Hang tight and look after Zeke.'

And there it was again. Typical Anders. Always trying to protect his most valuable asset.

'He can look after himself just fine,' I said. 'Say hi to Arron if you talk to him and send him our love.'

'Will do.'

I hung up and turned to Zeke. 'I can't believe Burnsy's saying he's given up surfing for good.'

'He nearly died, Iris. He'll come around, but he's in shock.'

'I hope so. Nothing sadder than an ex-surfer,' I said, trotting out the old surf-bum phrase that had been knocking around for decades.

'He'll surf again for sure,' Zeke said, letting go of my hand.

'You don't know that.'

'Yeah, I do.'

'He might not though,' I said.

'If he can't surf, he'll wind up killing himself.'

'Shut up, Zeke.'

'I'm serious.'

'Why would you even say that?'

He held up his forearm to me, and there it was, tattooed in black letters: *Surf or Die*.

'Because I would.'

tuesday

chapter eleven

'No point taking our boards,' Zeke said, coming in from the balcony and pulling shut the sliding door. 'The ocean's asphalt.'

'I hope it picks up for the kids' thing tomorrow.'

'They'll dig it whatever.'

'Zeke,' I said, 'did you hear anything else from Anders?'

'No, I think he's screening my calls.'

'Why would he—'

'I don't know. He's acting weird lately.'

He wasn't the only one.

'Shall we run to the beach?' Zeke said, turning to me. 'Burn off some off those donuts we ate for breakfast?'

My trainers were wet from being left on the balcony, where they got caught in an early-morning tropical shower, so I laced up my old Converse All Stars instead.

Zeke did not seem impressed.

'You'll get shin splints,' he said.

'Says who?'

'Me,' Zeke said. 'Go put on some kicks.'

'Stop worrying. I'll be fine. Let's go.'

Running along the crowded streets of Miami Beach felt amazing. There was a buzz and an energy there that I hadn't felt anywhere else in the world. Zeke seemed to know his way around and took us down a few alley shortcuts, where dumpsters, wooden pallets and cardboard boxes were the most attractive part of the scenery. Halfway down one of these alleys, I stopped for a breather and called Zeke back.

'What's up?'

I reached up and kissed him. 'Thanks for this holiday,' I said. 'I really appreciate it.'

He beamed with happiness at this and it occurred to me that maybe I didn't tell him often enough how I felt. Didn't tell him how much he meant to me. I just sort of assumed he knew. The idea of sitting him down and going through my feelings made me feel queasy – it was the sort of thing my art student sister, Lily, would do, or my dad, and I avoided it. Maybe that was a mistake.

I was self-aware enough to realize that wasn't the whole story. I was embarrassed by the love burning inside me. Afraid of the intense devotion that slid around my throat. What if he used it against me?

I pushed him against the wall of a building and kissed him more fiercely.

*

There was a sound of someone clearing their throat. When we looked up, a young wealthy-looking guy in a sports jacket and chinos was staring at us from about twenty feet away. His sheltie ran over and licked me on the knee.

To my mortification, this man seemed to think I was a hooker, because he shouted to Zeke, 'Hey, man, when you're done, can I have a turn?'

Without missing a beat, Zeke answered, 'No thanks, dude. I'm straight.'

The guy looked confused and then walked off, while I laughed myself into a stitch.

When we reached the beach, Zeke kicked off his trainers and stretched out on our beach blanket.

'You're not going to go sleep again, are you?' I said.

'I didn't sleep so good last night. Couldn't stop the wheels turning.'

'Thinking about Burnsy?'

'Yeah, I really hope he's gonna be OK. Plus, I think I'm like deficient in iron or something. I had crazy restless legs and ended up pacing round our room for two hours straight.'

I'd evidently been completely out for the count, as I'd slept through all of this.

'You should be on multivitamins, Zeke, especially since you're a vegetarian. I'll buy you some.'

We were sitting near the lifeguards' booth, and while Zeke slept I went to talk to them to find out what was happening with the shark situation. The rumour was that earlier in the day the shark flags had been flying, courtesy of a giant hammerhead eating a ray not even a hundred yards out, but the blood had cleared and the shark seemed to have moved on. They didn't seem too bothered.

'So is Newquay in London or Birming*ham*?' the lifeguard was asking me, as I scanned the surface of the water for fins with his binoculars. Then I heard someone call my name.

Chase.

I handed the lifeguard his binoculars and walked quickly down the steps of the booth to help Chase with his belongings – he'd brought a large rucksack, two paddles and two twelve-foot-long SUP boards. He was sweating heavily, having hauled them all the way from the car park.

'Where's Zeke?' he asked, scanning the crowded beach.

I pointed to a pair of legs sticking out from beneath our blue beach umbrella.

'Asleep. Again.'

'Late night?' Chase said, elbowing me lightly in the ribs.

'Not really, although we did watch the first and second *Harry Potter*.'

'Jet lag kicking his ass?'

'We only came from the West Coast.'

'He's probably just exhausted. He's been travelling for

79

pretty much four years straight, you know. Takes it out of a guy. What's that thing he says, about the tank?'

I shrugged.

'You remember: when he flies in for a contest he only has sixty per cent in the tank, even on a good day. Or was it fifty? Whatever. He's running on vapours. He really needed this vacation.'

'Yeah,' I said, 'he did.' But Zeke had never told me any of that. Up until this trip, it had seemed as if he had a never-ending supply of stamina and energy. 'And maybe quitting smoking has done something to his brain,' I said.

'Could be.'

He looked as if his arms were about to fall off so I took one of the ridiculously heavy SUPs and dragged it behind me, ploughing a furrow in the sand. When we got to our umbrella, Chase set his board down and sat on it.

It felt super-awkward to sit there in silence with someone I hardly knew. Then Kelly texted me to tell me about a huge storm hitting Newquay which had thrown up storm waves so massive that the beaches had lost half their sand. I texted her back to say that I hoped everyone was OK and also to point out that in Miami it was thirty-five degrees and sunny. Her reply was a single emoji of one finger.

Chase was also texting away on his phone, but after thirty minutes of this I cracked.

'Zeke,' I said, hoping I wouldn't have to slap him. He opened his eyes instantly.

'I was just having the craziest dream about . . .'

Chase threw a handful of sand at Zeke's feet.

'Buddy!' Zeke said. 'I thought you had to work today!' His eyes locked on the SUPs.

'Perks of working for the old man. So I'm here to rescue you from crushing inactivity.'

'Thank you, sweet, sweet Jesus,' Zeke said, jumping up and tearing off his T-shirt. He threw it down, but I intercepted it and folded it, in an attempt to embrace tidiness.

I had to give it to Chase, he was a great friend, coming to distract Zeke from the surf DTs. He seemed to really care about him. They weren't just friends, they were more like family. It made me think of Kelly. Made me miss her even more.

'Iris, do you mind?' Zeke said, his voice all quivery with excitement.

'*Go.*'

I watched them from the shore. Chase looked like such a land-shark, with his sharp outfits and cool hats, but he was a natural on the water. He had a skinny, strong body, and managed the SUP like it was an extension of his feet. I watched until they paddled out of sight, and when they appeared again, two hours later, Zeke's whole demeanour was different. Instead of sleepy, he looked completely energized.

Chase went off to find a loo, leaving his board

at my side. I ignored it and cracked open a packet of crisps.

'Ha,' Zeke said, stretching out beside me, 'you have quite the eating plan here.'

I'd popped to the nearest 7-Eleven to grab Zeke some vitamins, and had also bought a feast of junk food and laid it out in a mockery of a picnic. I'd done this deliberately, to make a point. The point being: I am eating and I am not going out with you on a bloody stand-up paddleboard, Zeke Francis, no matter how much you nag me.

I'd tried SUPs in Newquay and completely embarrassed myself. I kept dropping the paddle and could barely manage to stay on my feet as every crossways ripple sent me into the water with an immense, mortifying splash. Then, once I was in the water, I couldn't scramble back on the board while clutching a paddle in my hand, so I'd inevitably drop it again. All my coordination deserted me on an SUP and I really didn't want Zeke to see that.

'Wearing your tourist hat, huh?'

'Exactly. I'll get back on the salads tomorrow.'

'Ha ha,' Zeke said. 'I know what you're doing. I've got you all figured out. This is Procrastination 101.'

'No idea what you're talking about, mate.'

'I know you're twitchy about that hammerhead, but you gotta chill. It's just a fish.'

'Yeah, *the hammerhead*,' I said, sensing an opportunity. Zeke assuming I was more afraid of sharks than of making

82

a fool of myself was fine by me. 'I think I'll sit this one out.'

But Zeke was having none of it; he was the sort of adventure junkie who didn't believe that fear, danger, risk of death were reasons not to do something – if anything, those three things were his main criteria for picking a new hobby.

'I saw, like, one spinner shark out there,' he said, 'and even he was just cruising.'

Spinner sharks were known for leaping out of the water close to shore, often right behind the line-up, which was a little bit alarming when you were out there waiting to catch a wave.

'I'm busy here,' I said, popping another Cheeto and following it with a Dorito.

'Tanning? Come have fun. I'll go back to the hotel and get the Shark Shield for your board, if you want, so you'll be totally safe.'

The Shark Shield was supposed to repel sharks, stop them getting closer than five metres. It had been tested on most species and seemed to work, but no one could be completely sure.

'Don't bother,' I said. 'Battery's flat after yesterday. It was flashing red and green this morning, so I put it on charge.'

'We don't need it anyhow. Hey, we just saw a bunch of cobia fish following migrating manta rays. It was so awesome. Come on, you might never have another chance to see that your whole life.'

'I'm fine here, thanks.'

'If you really want a career as a pro-surfer,' Zeke went on, 'you have to get used to sharing the ocean with wildlife. Otherwise you're basically just limiting yourself to Fistral Beach and indoor bathing pools, so let's do this thing. If something awkward goes down, we can jump on our boards and paddle back.'

Awkward would definitely be going down the moment I stood on a stand-up paddleboard. I knew I'd make a tit of myself and everyone on the beach would notice, as I'd make a giant splash every time I fell in, which is exactly what had happened the last time I'd tried SUPing at Fistral.

'Look, how about we both go out on the same board?' I said, finally seeing the obvious solution to my problem. 'You can paddle and I'll sit on the front.'

'Deal,' Zeke said, going for a handshake.

'Just promise me one thing,' I said.

'What?'

'That we won't end up chumming the water with our entrails.'

'Hey, you're with me, aren't you? Nothing bad can happen if you're with me.' His eyes were twinkling and I knew he was laying on the charm, but I let myself be won over.

I sat on the front of the SUP, turquoise water all

around, and Zeke stood behind me and paddled. Once we got past the sandbanks and the ocean got quieter, he started telling me about his childhood with his brothers and Chase in Hawaii, and I told him about adventures I'd had with Kelly and my sister Lily, knocking around on Fistral Beach. Memories that were important to me, but which I'd never shared with him before.

Eventually he sat down, straddling the board too, the paddle tucked under his knees, and we faced each other.

'*I love you so much, Zeke*,' I said, but only in my head. I wanted to say it aloud, but there was that feeling again, stopping me: a vague sense of dread, of tempting fate.

'Thanks for bringing me here,' I said. 'Miami's brilliant.'

'It's even better now you're here,' he said, deadpan.

I cocked my head at him, unsure if he was joking or serious.

'Smooth,' I said, and he laughed.

I shuffled towards him, reached up and kissed him for a long time.

chapter twelve

Later we lay in the sun, talking superficials with Chase, when Zeke said, 'It's so hot. I vote we find a bar.'

'Good idea,' Chase said. 'Warm us up for the party. You up for a spot of early drinking, Iris?'

'Yes, but I'll need to go back to the hotel first.'

'Why?' Zeke said.

'Look at the state of me.'

'We can wash up in the public bathrooms.'

'Uh, really, Zeke?'

'You look great. Splash some water on your face and we can go get drinks now.'

'Zeke! I look horrendous. I'm not going out looking like this. What's the rush?'

'No rush. How long do you need to get ready? Like, twenty minutes?'

'Twenty minutes,' I agreed, nodding, and planning out hair-washing, drying, straightening and make-up that would take an hour and twenty.

'Great, we have to go celebrate.'

'Wait up,' Chase said, reading a text message, 'My trainer, Nishi, wants to take me kangooing.'

All I knew about kangooing was what I'd seen of it on the streets of Miami: people who hopped past the rollerbladers wearing weird springs attached to their feet.

'You're really going to do that, in public?' Zeke said.

'You ain't too cool to kangoo,' Chase said. 'Burns twice as many calories as running and I ate a giant bag of chips this morning. Catch you later.'

Chase and Zeke embraced and then Zeke helped him take the SUPs to his truck.

'So what exactly are we celebrating?' I asked.

'That it's almost your birthday. That we're in Miami. That a bunch of fans queued two hours yesterday just to get your autograph?'

'Three.'

'Three hours?'

'Three fans. The ones in the queue were there for you. Trust me. Anyway, we shouldn't get too wrecked. Look a bit unprofessional, wouldn't it, especially if you ran into any other surf fans.'

A shadow crossed Zeke's face.

'It's a few drinks. Loosen up.'

'I am loose. Is . . . something going on?'

'No.'

'You seem different here. Two days in a row now you've slept in the middle of the day.'

'Gimme a break, Iris. I'm on vacation.'

'OK, take a chill pill. I was just saying.'

But he was already picking up his rucksack. He turned. 'You staying or coming?'

I paused. Things were tense between us, but I couldn't see that changing if I sulked and stayed away from him for the rest of the day. At least if we were together, we'd have a chance to talk things through.

'Coming.'

He was already halfway to the car park and his stride was so long that I had to run to catch him up.

So much for early drinking. By the time I'd finished getting ready it was nearly seven o'clock, but I'd really made an effort. Generally I didn't bother with make-up or hair-straightening – I was in the sea almost every day, so trying to glam up, when it would be instantly ruined by seawater, felt like a total waste of time. But there was something about the glamour of Miami that made me feel self-conscious, or at least more confident with freshly washed hair and decent make-up.

'Chase is coming to pick us up, and we won't have time now to go somewhere before the party,' he said, as I was putting on eyeliner, 'so if you want booze, you'll have to grab it from the minibar.'

'OK.' I wanted to pace myself, so I went for a small

bottle of apple cider, which would take the edge off my nerves but not mess me up. I noticed then that the contents of the fridge were significantly reduced, and there were empty miniature bottles on the floor by Zeke's side of the bed. I hadn't even noticed him drinking.

He'd taken a quick shower two hours before, and spent the rest of our 'getting-ready time' surfing the Internet on his iPad. He wasn't on any of the surf e-zines or Magic Seaweed though. Instead he was on Reddit, obsessing over some crime podcast he'd listened to.

'I'm ready,' I said, waiting for him to notice my super-skimpy pyjama party outfit, which included very short shorts.

'At last,' he sighed, without even looking up at me. Instead he picked up some of my make-up products scattered all over the dressing table and placed them neatly in my toiletries bag.

'Hey, I sort of made an effort. I painted my toenails with glitter varnish for God's sake.'

He looked up then and grinned.

'You look beautiful,' he said, 'from the top of your head, right down to your toes.'

'Yeah, you're *a day late and a dollar short*,' I said, parroting one of his favourite phrases in my best impression of his voice.

'I sound nothing like that,' he said, frowning. 'Can we go now?'

chapter thirteen

Chase gave us all a lift to Coral Gables in his fancy blue sports car; Zeke in the front, and me, Saskia and Gabe squashed into the back. Saskia had gone for some antique black silk nightdress that was backless and floor-length, and Gabe was in Bart Simpson pyjamas and army boots.

When the house came into view, I heard myself say, 'Farking 'ell!'

'So, Chase, you're the eldest brother, you say?' Saskia said, giving me a wink, 'Heir to the family fortune?'

Gabe scoffed and said, 'Millions of people in this world are living on a dollar a day.'

'Hey,' Chase said, 'this party is for charity, remember, so quit being judgemental. My folks worked hard for this house.' He was smiling as he said this, but I had a feeling Gabe had touched a nerve.

'If by working hard, you mean inheriting a bunch of money . . .' Zeke said.

'OK, so maybe luck played a small part,' Chase said, grinning now.

'How many loos does it have?' I asked, still staring at the house, completely in awe that this was home to Chase, who had seemed so normal to me. I remembered how pleased my mum had been when she'd saved enough money to put in a tiny downstairs toilet. No more waiting for Lily to finish washing her hair while we hopped about outside, shouting, 'Hurry up!' and banging on the door.

'If by loos, you mean bathrooms, then it has six,' Chase said.

'That's a lot of toilet roll,' I said, imagining a Morrison's trolley full of it.

Beyond the wrought-iron gates, a long driveway led to a house like some ancient Roman palace, all white walls, pillars and huge vertical windows. Behind it, a golf course rolled out in all directions.

I got out my phone, took a photo of it, and sent it to my mum and Kelly. Kelly replied instantly with 'Well jell!!!' and five kisses. My mum replied with 'Very nice indeed.' And then followed it up with, 'I forgot to say! We won half a pig in the meat raffle! Night night.'

We were early, but the place was already jam-packed with partygoers. Saskia and Gabe went off in search of food, as both claimed to have not eaten carbs in a week.

Expensive sound equipment was racked up to one side of the infinity pool, and the music was thudding so loud it seemed like my skull was vibrating in time with it. But the thing that really stood out, the thing that became instantly clear, was that what Chase termed a 'pyjama party' did not fit my definition of a pyjama party, at all.

True, most of the men were rocking comedy pyjamas with printed superheroes or cartoon characters, or were doing the bare-chested boxers and dressing-gown thing, like Zeke, but the women were kitted out in basques and sheer slips, and many of them had opted for bras and pants. Amber had on emerald lace underwear and huge, real-feather wings, like a Victoria's Secret model, which, it occurred to me afterwards, she probably was. Basically, there were boobs and bums everywhere.

Zeke looked amused by this, but I turned to Chase and said, 'Pyjama party? Really?'

'Yeah, maybe I had that wrong. It kinda looks more like a lingerie party.'

I undid the buttons of my overshirt and knotted the ends over my navel.

'You know you could just take that off, if you're uncomfortable,' Zeke said.

'Yeah, no.'

Chase and Zeke went off to engage the DJ in mysterious chat of some sort, and a curvy older woman in a long nightgown and feather wrap, who it transpired was Chase's mum, came up to me and said, 'Nice shirt.'

'Thanks,' I said, touching the knot over my stomach

and wondering if I should have in fact ditched the shirt, and just gone with the shorts and vest, which would at least go a little way towards blending into the scantily clad crowd. 'Nice boa.'

She shimmied it over her shoulders and said, 'Oh, this old thang? Here, you can borrow it, as you like it so much.'

She handed me her boa of golden feathers and I wound it a few times around my neck, like an actual constrictor, and then immediately loosened it, as the feathers tickled my nose.

'You came with Chase?'

'Yeah.'

'You're his girlfriend?'

'Zeke's.' After six months of travel I was well and truly fed up of having to define myself by whose girlfriend I was, but I didn't want to seem rude.

'Really? I never knew Zeke to have a girlfriend before. Truth is, I always wondered if he was gay, although it turns out that was his brother!' She followed this with a little laugh, that made me feel uncomfortable. 'Oops. I hope I haven't just outted someone!' she said, and laughed again.

'Not at all. I know Wes really well, and his boyfriend Elijah too. They're awesome.'

'What's your name, hon?'

'Iris. Nice to meet you. Thanks for inviting me.'

She smiled at this, and I realized that she hadn't invited

me. Chase had. She hadn't even known I was coming.

'Veronica. Enjoy the party,' she said. 'Oh, did you make your donation to the charity yet?'

'Zeke has the cheque in his wallet.'

'Well, don't forget. That's why we're here. It's not just an excuse to wear pretty nightshirts in public, you know,' she said.

'What is the charity? Chase said it was something to do with depression?'

'Teenxiety. Our target for tonight is thirty thousand dollars. Here's hoping.'

It was a ungracious thought, and I knew it, but once again it occurred to me that maybe this fundraiser wasn't the best way of getting money to the charity, given that the sound equipment, cocktails and buffet probably cost more than that. But who was I to criticize people raising money for charity?

'Go dance. Be merry.'

And talking of dancing, Zeke already was.

It was no secret that Zeke liked to dance. He made out that he didn't, but all it took was one beer and he'd start throwing shapes. Two beers in and he busted out the big moves, but I liked that he didn't give a toss what anyone thought of him and just went for it.

He spotted me hanging around by some empty chairs, danced over and grabbed my hands.

'I just need a bit more Dutch courage first . . .'

'No, you don't. Get over here.'

As we danced to Katy Perry I tried to imagine how it must feel to be Zeke, self-confident and free enough to do the twist in public without his head providing a running critique on how he must look to anyone watching.

Three whiskies in and Zeke got up on stage with the DJ and did a karaoke rendition of 'Sittin' on the Dock of the Bay'.

Listening to him belt it out, I could see that the song actually meant something to him. He even did the whistle part at the end, although he stopped halfway through to laugh and he couldn't recover.

'Nice one, Zeke. I loved that.'

'Yeah, it's kinda my jam.'

'Really? Because, let's be honest, if you're watching the tide roll away, you're generally *in* it.'

He laughed. 'Well, you know, I've always wanted to be the kind of person who could relax more.'

Chase appeared in between us, a hand on each of our backs and said, 'Duet.'

'I don't sing in public,' I said, feeling as if I'd already made quite enough of a spectacle of myself on this trip.

'Yo, I meant Zeke and me.'

'Oh, in that case, knock yourselves out.'

'What song?' Zeke asked.

'I'm thinking we stay retro,' Chase replied.

'"House of the Rising Sun"?' I said.

'Uggh, nope. Way cooler. Guess again.'

Chase's version of 'way cooler' transpired to be the Lovin' Spoonful's 'Summer in the City' and somehow, and I would never ask how, Zeke knew all the words.

They followed this up with Scott McKenzie's 'San Francisco' and Cyndi Lauper's 'Time after Time', which was surprisingly touching, and people clapped along as they gazed into each other's eyes and did a slow waltz around the pool.

Sweaty but happy, Zeke turned to Chase, who was cracking open his second bottle of eight-hundred dollar champagne, and said, 'Can we swim in the pool?'

I butted in. 'Neither of us has a cossie, Zeke.'

'So we'll wear this.'

'All right, if you want everyone's outfits to go completely transparent.'

'Definitely,' Chase said, giving me some comedy creep-eye.

Zeke gave him a light punch on the shoulder and said, 'Don't make me hurt you, bro.'

'Ha, I love that you see that as a possibility.'

'You may punch harder, dude,' Zeke said, 'but I'm faster.' He got his fists up and started ducking and weaving.

'Yeah, at running,' Chase said.

'Hey, you remember the time you busted up my bike

and launched it into the ocean, and Garrett and Wes stripped you naked and threw you in a patch of wood-nettles?'

Chase winced and said, 'They're still on my hit list for that.'

I felt it again – the closeness they had, the history, and I missed Kelly so badly that I considered sitting down with my iPhone and flipping through old ussies of the two of us on Fistral.

'Come on, I wanna show you something,' Chase said, linking arms with me and Zeke.

We walked through a corridor busy with cocktail-drinkers and into the kitchen, where Zeke started inspecting the units. 'What wood is this? Koa?'

'Yeah, Mom had it imported from Hawaii.'

'Nice.'

'The cabinets are handmade. Blue marble floor. I actually helped design this kitchen,' Chase said, looking proud of himself.

'If you ever remodel, call me,' Zeke said. 'My pop always built his cabinets from scratch, with, like, eucalyptus and coconut wood, and I used to love helping with that.'

I had nothing to contribute to a conversation about kitchens, and when 'Thrift Shop' came on the sound system, I said, 'We should totally dance to this.'

'No can do,' Chase said. 'Didn't you see me earlier?

I was tripping over Zeke's feet. I dance like a cinder-block.'

'Really? I thought you'd be a great dancer.'

'And that is what the people call judging a book by its cover.'

'But even your name makes you sound like a good dancer. *Chase*,' I said, doing a weird little wiggle dance that made no sense whatsoever.

'Ah, Chase is actually not my birth name. Zeke knows it, but he's sworn to secrecy.'

'Oh yeah?' I said. 'Bet I get it out of him.'

'No, I made a promise,' Zeke said. 'It's been eleven years and I've never told a soul.'

'Yeah, but you can trust me. I won't blab, will I?'

'Iris, he made a *vow*,' Chase said. 'You can't mess with that.'

I was smiling, but Zeke and Chase both had serious faces on, as if the mere idea of Zeke telling me Chase's birth name was scandalous.

'What? Come on, tell me!' But Zeke just shook his head.

'What can I get you guys to drink?' he asked, sliding off the countertop where he'd been perched.

Chase jumped in first with, 'Surprise me.'

'Really? You're like the pickiest drinker on the planet. How about you, Iris?' he said, turning to me.

'Half a Coke. Thanks.'

'Get her a real drink,' Chase said. Then he turned and sang at me, '*You're in Miami, girl.*'

'Alcohol is not her friend. She already had some tonight and she usually gets drunk off of vapours, then spends the next three hours puking or running to the john.'

'Rude. I'll have a mojito.'

'Whaat?' Zeke said, looking pained. 'Anders was pretty insistent you stay off the liquor. He'll have a coronary if you wind up getting busted for underage drinking.'

'What a tool,' Chase said, picking a piece of olive out of his teeth with the edge of his credit card.

'Zeke,' I said, '*you're* underage and you're drinking! Why is there one rule for you and one rule for me?'

'Because I can have three beers and not fall over.'

'Stop stressing,' I said. '*You only live once.*'

Zeke couldn't really argue with that, since he basically had it tattooed on his back.

'OK, *one* drink. After, you think we should head back to the hotel?'

'You guys aren't leaving yet,' Chase said. 'The night is young.'

I shrugged, like it was nothing to me either way, but I secretly felt a shiver of nerves. When Zeke had suggested this holiday, in a super-fancy hotel, I thought it was to get some uninterrupted, decent alone time together, since Anders usually made us get separate accommodation during our contests, saying something like, 'Let's try to keep up an appearance of decency, shall we?' which I thought was ridiculous, since anyone who knew about professional surfing knew me and Zeke were together. The sort of together where you sometimes wake up together. Since arriving in Miami, apart from those brief moments in the marquee and the alley, we had not exactly connected, and in the hotel room it was as if an invisible force field was running up the centre of the bed. But there was something in Zeke's face that made me think that could be about to change.

As if deliberately dispelling this idea, Zeke touched my arm and said, 'Just promise me you won't throw up. I'm, like, emetophobic or something. Blood I can handle. My baby cousin's dirty diapers I can handle. Pee, no problem. But vomit? Count me out.'

'I promise.'

chapter fourteen

Two hours later, when Zeke and Chase were fully over the high of serenading each other in front of four hundred strangers, and Saskia and Gabe had locked themselves into one of the bathrooms, we were into the chill-out portion of the evening, stretched out on sunloungers under a sky full of stars.

'So, buddy,' Chase said to Zeke, under his breath, 'you get it yet?'

I could have sworn Zeke did that thing where you pretend not to hear something, just to buy yourself more time to answer.

Zeke and I were sharing a sunlounger, and I was nestled into the side of his body.

'What was that?' he said.

'You get it yet?' Chase asked, louder this time.

'Get what?'

'Buddy, come on, you know what I'm talking about here.'

Zeke shrugged.

Zeke never did that. You asked Zeke a question, he answered; no bull, no front.

'Is that a no?' Chase said, confusion in his eyes. He looked from Zeke to me and back again.

'What haven't you got?' I asked.

'Nothing,' Zeke said. 'Nothing important anyways.'

Did Zeke get what exactly? Something secret? Something for me? A birthday present?

'Me and my big mouth,' Chase said, looking sheepish.

'What am I missing here?' I said to Zeke.

'Don't sweat it,' Zeke said. 'For real, it's nothing you need to worry about.'

Zeke and Chase reached across the void between our loungers to fist-bump, their touch gentle, and I felt totally outside. They'd known each other for years and had history that I could never be part of.

'So how do you guys know each other?'

Chase laughed, 'I was Zeke's best friend since kindergarten. Oh, and I was also his dealer, but, you know, not until a few years later.'

chapter fifteen

My face must have registered my disapproval. Zeke looked supremely uncomfortable and Chase said, 'Hey, I'm kidding. He just shared my weed sometimes. But, you know, Zeke's a reformed toker these days, so no cause to stress.'

I looked at Zeke and he was actually blushing, like a kid whose mother had just caught him doing something unspeakable.

'Chase got you into dope?'

'Dope?' Chase said, looking scandalized. 'Hell no. Just pot.'

'Dope *is* pot,' I said, not understanding why Chase would need clarification.

'Dope can also mean heroin here, Iris,' Zeke said gently. 'Can we not talk about this? It was a long time ago.'

Since Zeke was only nineteen, I guessed it wasn't all that long ago.

'I wasn't some Walter White, yo,' Chase said. 'It was

dime bags of pot that I split with my best friend. No one ever died of pot.'

I wasn't sure about that. People said marijuana was a gateway drug, and Zeke had definitely gone through that gateway. In fact, from what I'd heard about his life before he met me, about ten gates had slammed behind Zeke. He'd rehabbed like crazy and by the time I came along he was clean, but I knew from his family that it had been a hard, long fight. And here we were, hanging out with the guy who'd led him down that path.

Zeke put his arm over my shoulder and leaned over to kiss me, properly this time, and once again the worst of my doubts vanished. Funny how that always seemed to happen.

'You guys wanna ride to the Everglades tomorrow morning? I have to go see a man about an alligator.'

'Totally.'

'We probably won't have time,' Zeke said. 'After tonight, Iris has to train for New Smyrna. It can be a tricky wave.'

And that was that: language switched to surf-speak.

'Yeah,' Chase said. 'It has a sketchy little lip that's hard to figure out – even the top seeds who compete there don't always progress to the next round.'

'Hell yeah, it's so inconsistent out there. Some of the waves are closing out, some are running, some of them that you *think* are going to be shockers turn into good ones. The best surfers in the world struggle; you have so many yellow jerseys taking out the reds there, it's crazy.'

But I didn't think it was just a diversion tactic. Zeke sounded genuinely worried about me surfing New Smyrna. He often tried to give me insider knowledge on certain breaks, and sometimes he'd get out old heat sheets and talk me through previous contest drama. He'd look at those numbers and remember it all. It reminded me of *The Matrix*, with the guy monitoring the computer code and seeing redheads, blondes and brunettes, except Zeke did it with heat sheets and waves.

I wasn't actually too worried. The biggest problem, I thought, apart from the many, many sharks, would be wind chop, but I'd surfed plenty of blown-out breaks in Cornwall, so I was sure I'd manage. As the saying went, *Bad surf is the best teacher*, and the thing I'd noticed about the Hawaiian and Australian girls was that they were so used to pristine peeling waves that they panicked at the first sign of poor conditions. Whereas, for me, it was business as usual.

Anyway, the thing I wanted to talk about was the Everglades, which I still really wanted to see. A unique subtropical wetland, home to alligators and turtles, was worth another half-day of slacking, surely.

'Who knows when I'll be in Florida again? It's not far. We could just go down there for a few hours, couldn't we?'

'Maybe, but I don't think it's gonna be possible to swing it with our schedule.'

'OK, OK,' I said. 'You win.'

'So when you paddling the Cortes Bank, brah?' Chase said to Zeke. 'Word on the street is Greg's putting together a crew.'

Greg Long was the most famous of the big-wave surfers and Zeke completely idolized him. The Cortes Bank was a reef a full hundred miles offshore with a fearsome reputation. It was basically a shipping and navigation hazard, because when the bank broke from a storm swell it could kick up waves with faces of a hundred feet.

Surfing that wave was definitely a risk, and because it took twelve hours to get there by boat, if a surfer got into trouble there, that surfer was probably dead. But Zeke was experienced with giant waves, and to him the high of riding that wave would be worth the risk.

'I can't go. I promised Iris.'

I looked at him, frowning. It was true that right after his accident he'd said he'd avoid big waves in the future, but I hadn't really believed he'd keep to that and I hadn't tried to make him promise. Ever since I'd met him, Zeke had been frothing to surf the Cortes Bank, and I didn't expect him to walk away from that opportunity just because of me.

I was figuring out how to put all that into words when Chase said, 'You said no to Greg? Wow. It must be love.'

'Must be,' Zeke said, looking at me with a suddenly serious expression.

'But don't you feel like you're letting Greg down?' Chase asked.

'Are you kidding? Tons of guys will be lining up to fill my spot.' A look passed between them and I could tell they wanted to talk without me there.

'I'm going to the loo,' I said. I'd had a few glasses of white-wine spritzer and a mojito, and my head felt funny.

The house had so many different rooms that I kept getting lost, but eventually someone directed me to a bathroom suite that was bigger than the whole downstairs of my home. It actually had a dressing table, where three girls in camisoles and French knickers were redoing their make-up.

I went through to the toilet, which weirdly turned out to be two toilets side by side, locked the door and resisted the urge to lie back against the cool cistern.

When I came out, two of the girls were bent over a table snorting up some white powder through a rolled-up banknote. I froze.

They looked up at me, their eyes glazed, not seeming the least bit concerned.

'Line?' one of them asked me. She had long yellow hair in a braid down to her bum and what appeared to be purple contact lenses.

'No, thanks.'

She said, 'You don't do drugs? But you're with Zeke, right?'

'She's, like, sixteen years old,' another girl said with a laugh.

It took me a few seconds, but then I recognized her as Amber's friend Inga.

'I'm seventeen in two days,' I said, 'And Zeke doesn't do drugs any more.'

'Maybe not around you,' Inga murmured.

I stared at her hard. 'Not around anyone, actually.'

'Well, that boy used to party real hard,' her friend said. 'Guys like that don't change.'

'Word,' another girl said. And then, 'You know this girl, Inga?'

'Kinda,' she said. 'This is Iris Fox. Yeah, you won't have heard of her. She's trying to make it as a pro-surfer, like Zeke.'

'Zeke has changed since you knew him,' I said, still eyeballing Inga.

'Guess he'd have to since he shacked up with Pollyanna. You ever taken an illegal substance in your life, girl?'

I thought about it. Apart from Daniel smoking weed around me and me possibly inhaling some of his smoke second-hand, I was clean as a whistle. It wasn't like there were many opportunities to get hardcore drugs in Newquay. Not unless you knew the right people, and I didn't. Most of my friends were like me: surf junkies, addicted to the stoke of a great wave.

But then, even though it was stupid, I thought, *Maybe I should*. Zeke had all these experiences that were mysteries to me, and if I had some experiences of my own, perhaps I'd understand him better.

'I guess that's a no.'

'I didn't say that,' I said, when the door swung open and I heard a posh grammar-school voice ring out, 'Iris Fox, what in the name of holy hell do you think you're doing?'

'Nothing.'

'Don't give me that rubbish,' Saskia said. 'You're Zeke's girlfriend; you know how he's struggled with drugs, and you're shoving coke up your nose?'

'I haven't done anything!'

'And even if she did, Zeke would be the last person to judge,' Inga said.

'Oh, I see you've met the super-tramp,' Saskia said, looking at Inga. 'I should give yourself a thorough delousing tonight, Iris. Unless you fancy a case of trailer lice.'

'You think I live in a trailer?'

'Apologies. I meant kennel lice.'

'What is your problem? Why are you always such a little bitch?' Inga asked, rolling her eyes.

'Sas, please don't say anything about this to Zeke,' I said, because suddenly I absolutely did not want him to know. 'It'll only stress him out.'

'Maybe you should have thought of that before you started snorting narcotics with Bimbos United.'

Like a snake striking, Inga lashed out and slapped Saskia hard on the side of her face.

Saskia looked completely furious and for a second I thought she was going to hit Inga back, but instead she said, 'Which does rather prove my point,' and she sailed out of the bathroom like a queen.

I chased after Saskia, but she said, 'I really don't want to speak to you now.'

'Please don't tell Zeke.'

Gabe appeared at our side and said, 'This party blows. They don't even have pizza. What is *this*?' he said, holding up a tiny salmon canapé.

'I agree,' Saskia said. 'Let's go.'

'You're leaving?' Zeke said, and drowned the dregs of a beer.

'No question,' Gabe said. 'Twenty different kinds of cocktails, but no food bigger than a quarter? The insanity must cease.'

'Chase has a driver who'll probably give you a ride,' Zeke said.

'It's fine,' Saskia said in a frosty voice. 'We're perfectly capable of making our own way back.'

'Everything OK, Sas?' Zeke asked.

I waited for her to mention the coke incident, but she just straightened the straps of her nightgown and said, 'Oh, everything's wonderful.'

Before she left, Saskia kissed me on both cheeks, but did it without a word or a smile, which Zeke missed, as he was looking over his shoulder towards the bar, now ten deep in waiting guests.

He turned back to me, positioned his mouth so it was right over my ear and said, 'You wanna come for a walk with me?'

A walk sounded like bliss.

'Do you know where you're going, or are we planning to get lost?'

'Golf course.'

'To do what?' I said, a bit suspicious. On the few occasions we'd slept together outdoors, it had never gone well. On one particular occasion, both of us drunk, we'd been messing about on a beach in South Africa when a young bloke carrying a fishing rod and a bait bucket spotted us from a distance, got out his phone and took a photo.

'Talk.'

'Just that?'

'Yeah.'

'Won't Chase mind if we bail?'

'We're not bailing. We're coming back; we're just taking a walk first.'

And so we walked until we found the green, where we lay back and looked again at the sky, which lasted five minutes at most, before the kissing started, and from there other things. Suddenly Zeke stopped, and we both sat up.

'What's wrong?' I said.

'Nothing.'

'You said you wanted to talk.'

'I was thinking about Arron.' He closed his eyes.

'Yeah, I've been thinking about him too.'

'Chase said I can have a job here, if I want. In his dad's firm.'

I cocked my head, unsure if he was serious. 'In Miami? Doing what?'

'Real estate. He works high-end, makes between fifty and a hundred grand commission on every sale.'

'Are you taking the mick? You want to stop surfing and become an estate agent?'

'I could still surf here, but I know, it's crazy. I was just thinking about it, is all. Obviously I'm not gonna do that.'

'Good! For one thing you'd have to get a haircut and wear a suit every day. Although you could use the haircut.'

'It's more money than I make now. A lot more. And Chase thinks I'd be good at it.'

'You probably would, but you'd hate it, and who in their right mind would give up the best job in the world to make a bit of extra money? Madness.'

'Yeah, you're right. And anyhow, it's likely just Chase being Chase.'

I was sitting cross-legged, and Zeke stretched out and laid his head in my lap.

We stayed like that for twenty minutes, both of us lost in our thoughts, when, finally, a dozen of the other partygoers spilled out on to the greenway.

It was only when I said, 'I think we should go now,' that I realized he was asleep.

'Really, Zeke?' I said, not able to hide the frustration in my voice. 'Again?'

'Too many whiskies,' he said, sitting bolt upright, like he'd been caught out doing something reprehensible. 'But I feel better now.'

'You wanna blow off the party and find a club?' he said, his voice normal again, the mask of *I'm OK* firmly in place.

'Yeah,' I said. I'd had just about enough of the lingerie party.

We walked hand in hand back to the house, and relayed our plan to Chase.

'You can't go clubbing in boxers,' Chase said, 'Not even in Miami.'

'Ya think? Can you lend me a shirt and pants?'

'What about me then?' I said. I unbuttoned my shirt to show Chase what I had on underneath, and he appraised the vest/shorts combo.

'That's tame by Miami standards. Lose the shirt and you're all set. Or I guess my mom might have something you could borrow . . .'

I looked at Chase's mum, who was at least two sizes bigger than me, and said, 'Um, we're not the same size.'

'How about Amber?' Zeke asked. 'She can probably loan you a dress.'

'She's about two sizes smaller than me.'

'She is?'

'Er, yes. I'm usually a ten or twelve, depending on the brand, and she's probably an eight. Or a six.'

'You're a twelve?' Zeke said.

'Yeah. A British twelve. How do you not know that?'

'I'm supposed to go through your clothes and look at the labels?'

'Never mind,' I said. 'Let's go, but you are both banned from taking pictures, got it?'

Zeke went to change into Chase's clothes and came back wearing a very loud shirt and skinny jeans three inches too short. Chase made him wear this outfit with a trilby hat, which was quite the contrast with Zeke's scruffy surfer hair.

'I think I have a cab number,' Zeke said, looking for a card in his wallet.

'No need,' Chase said, nodding his head at the white

stretch limousine parked up closest to the gates. The driver, who'd been on a smoke break, caught Chase's eye and put out his cigarette.

'To Flavour!' Chase said.

chapter sixteen

Leaning over the pool table, my knee hitched up over one side to get the best position, I cracked the cue as hard as I could, blasting the white down the table. It caught the stripe on the left side and sent it spinning into the bottom pocket.

'*Banzai,*' I said, punching the air and grinning at Zeke. He sat down on one of the sofas set around the pool table and leaned back into tapestry cushions, legs stretched out in front of him, readying himself for imminent defeat.

I lined up my next shot and potted another stripe. I didn't think I could get away with punching the air again, so I went with, 'I bloody love pool.'

He hooked his foot over his other knee, and the second he did it, Chase swooped in, laughing, and ran away with his shoe, holding it to his chest like a baby.

'Random,' I said to Zeke, and we watched Chase twirling a size-eleven Vans trainer around the pool table.

'You gotta get some new hobbies, bro,' Zeke said to Chase, sinking his fifth JD and Coke.

'Erm, why *does* he have your shoe?' I said.

'Tradition,' was Chase's only reply.

I went after him to retrieve Zeke's trainer, but Zeke didn't seem bothered. He stood up lopsidedly, sock on the sticky floor, and picked up his own pool cue.

'Hey, I haven't finished,' I said. 'It's still my turn, thank you very much.'

'My bad. Show me how it's done, boss.'

He sat down again, cue between his knees, and I sank another stripe, leaving only one of my balls on the table, along with the black and Zeke's five spots.

Chase deposited Zeke's shoe on the top of the metal lamp hanging over the table and said, very seriously, 'Surrender, Ezekiel. A guy just can't come back from this kind of epic ass-whooping.'

'Sure he can,' Zeke said, grabbing his shoe and looking determined. 'That's literally the story of my pro-surfing career right there. Which bar-room legend taught you how to shoot pool, Iris?'

Daniel. My ex-boyfriend Daniel taught me how to play. In the first autumn, when the weather was hideous, the waves were a mess and the only thing to do was hang around Newquay's excuse for a youth club and kill time until the ocean was surfable again.

But I didn't want to talk about Daniel, especially

117

not to Zeke, given that they absolutely hated each other.

Zeke put on his shoe and stuffed the laces down the side. He never tied his laces, even when he went jogging, for reasons that were unclear to me.

'Kelly's really good at pool,' I said, which wasn't a lie, because my best mate *was* brilliant at pool, but it wasn't exactly a truthful answer either. 'Want me to pot something for you?' I offered. 'Get your balls out of the way of my shot on the black?'

'It's all about the balls, dude,' Chase chipped in. 'And Iris is handing you yours.'

I could see a flicker of annoyance on Zeke's face as Chase teased him about his dodgy pool skills.

Then the cloud passed and he laughed. He tucked some hair behind his ear, and just looking at the curve of his jawline gave me an attack of the butterflies. Cue still in my hand, I went and kissed him, but he withdrew from me after about three seconds.

There it was again: that horrible feeling. Something was wrong. Something about Zeke was different.

No.

I had to stop obsessing about Zeke being different in Miami. Like he said, he was on vacation. Of course he wanted to relax. He'd had a few drinks, but he wasn't hammered. He just wanted to concentrate on our game of pool without being mauled.

I'd obviously inherited the stressing-out-over-nothing gene from my mother. Why couldn't I just let myself enjoy it? The hassle of life back in Newquay was behind me. Homework, housework, drizzle, annoying customers – I didn't need to worry about any of it any more. I was in a foreign country with new friends, new waves and new adventures.

Zeke went off to the bar and queued behind a throng of sorority sisters and football players who were milling around. I didn't take my eyes off him, my mind jumping ahead to our hotel room. The alcohol would take the edge off my nerves, which was just as well, as my body was about as relaxed as a headstone.

Then, as if he sensed I was staring, he looked over his shoulder and blew me a kiss, and I felt my cheeks flush red. He'd quite often do dorky stuff like that, not caring how it looked to other people.

I dropped my gaze back to the pool table and potted my last stripe, but I messed up the white positioning and couldn't get a clear shot on the black. I was snookered.

I walked slowly around the table, bending to look at the balls at eye level, even though I knew it was an impossible shot.

This was the first thing that Daniel had taught me. If you've got no play and people are watching, you have to make out that you've got it in hand, that you know what you're doing. So you front. You take your time and observe; pretend you're just working out the angles. Then, when you mess up, it seems to everyone else like you had a strategy: you were going for some insane trick shot, not flying blind.

I knew this type of bluffing was pathetic, but it was also fast becoming my surfing strategy.

Zeke came back, trying not to spill my pink drink with its tiny little umbrella. He had two beer bottles in his other hand. I walked up to him, wrapped my arms over his shoulders, bending to drink some of my cocktail in the process. It was so strong it made my eyes water.

'Go easy — the bartender put, like, five shots in there.'

'OK, I'll sip it. How much do I owe you?'

'I wasn't letting you pay anyhow, but it turns out happy hour was just about to start. Chicks drink for free. Guys drink half-off.'

'Whaaat? Free drinks?'

What kind of bar was this that could offer free drinks? And why didn't they have places like it in Newquay?

'Yeah, I mean I tipped the guy a few dollars and all — he's making minimum wage.'

'Can I get another one? Actually, maybe another two, since they're free?'

Which I knew was pushing it a bit, especially with my promise not to puke.

'Lady, you are gonna be so drunk after just that one that I'm gonna have to carry you all the way back to the hotel.'

'Think of it as good cardio,' I said.

Zeke held up a brown bottle and handed it to Chase, 'Here. Porkslap. It's a kind of beer.'

Chase held it in two fingers, squinted at the label and handed it back to Zeke.

'You know what?' he said. 'I love you like a brother, man, and I thank you from the bottom of my heart, but consider it yours. I need to get me a latte – I have serious caffeine withdrawal going on here.'

He sidled off to the glitzy coffee bar, where I watched him set the barista to work on some novelty coffee concoction.

Zeke looked down at the pool table, 'Huh, looks like you don't have a makeable shot.'

'Course I do.'

I whacked the white, missed the black by a foot and sat down with my drink.

My teasing obviously brought out the super-competitive side of Zeke, because he potted all five of his spots without breaking a sweat. Had he been hustling me? Or just trying to give me a chance? Both ideas annoyed me.

Then he paused to look at me, like he was asking for my approval to sink the black.

I shrugged, as if I didn't care, but I was rattled, because

the black was only about two inches from the pocket, and even though the white was right up against the top cushion, it was still an easy shot.

'So, what's Chase's real name?' I asked, hoping to put him off his game.

'Hey, I already told you I'm not at liberty to disclose that information.'

I picked at a loose thread on the hem of his shirt. 'I assumed you were kidding. What's the big deal?'

'The big deal is I gave the guy my word.'

'But you were, what, seven?'

Zeke stretched back, looked down the cue and sent the black hammering into the bottom right pocket. He was just going to seal the win with his signature double-shotgun surf claim, when the white bounced off the top cushion and followed the black into the pocket.

My win.

'Ha ha, Mister Always-Wins-at-Everything. *You lose.*'

Zeke slammed his cue back into the rack and took a swig of his Porkslap. I danced about, making an L on my forehead, but after a few seconds I backed off, because even though Zeke was smiling, there was this fierce look in his eyes. He really hated to lose. At anything.

I'd seen that look before, when he competed in surf contests, but I'd never seen him use it on me.

He had another swig of beer and without saying

another word he drifted away towards one of the big screens showing a basketball game.

As I was putting my cue in the rack, a stranger's voice said, 'Damn, she fine,' and I felt someone graze their fingers across the back of my shorts.

chapter seventeen

I flinched and spun around to face two guys in football jackets. The first looked like an even skinnier version of Eminem and his friend was a ball of bad acne and garlic halitosis, which I found out when he breathed down the words, 'Hell yeah, she fine.'

I was far from fine in the English sense of the word, and I wasn't fine in the American sense either. I instantly regretted my choice of outfit. I knew I should've gone back to the hotel and got changed. A flash of leg and some Lycra was evidently all it took to get the attention of these desperados.

Zeke still had his back to me, so he didn't see what was happening. The guy moved closer and held his hand out again, his fingers splayed.

I could feel myself staring at them, still not believing that they were genuinely being this gross. Was it some kind of bad joke?

For a few moments I was speechless, and then, when

a punchline didn't arrive, I got it together and said to the Eminem-alike, 'OK, let me stop you right there. Any part of you that touches me, you're not getting back,' which was Kelly's standard phrase for any creeps who tried to feel her up in crowded pubs or on public transport. I'd never had to use it before, but Kelly said it usually worked.

'Man, that accent. Australian or British?'

'Neither.'

They looked confused.

'Huh. So you're what exactly?'

'Cornish,' I said, feeling sure that these blokes had never even heard of Cornwall, and hoping they'd never get to see it either.

At that moment I saw some girls approach Zeke and say something to him.

One of them, a girl with blood-red heels, long hair and spray-on jeans, got close enough that she was practically standing on his toes.

Inga. I hadn't even known she was there. She must've left the party and changed her outfit before coming out – like I should have done.

Her friend started snapping pictures of them together.

Zeke bowed his head, and I watched as Inga whispered something in his ear.

I was itching to go over to them and find out what was going on, but thanks to the two jocks with the combined charisma of an armpit, I was completely cornered.

The quarterback looked down at my shorts yet again, and said, 'Super-fine outfit, but I like what's in it even better.'

'Look, thanks for the compliment or whatever,' I said, properly creeped out, 'but I'm one-hundred-per-cent not interested in talking to you. Also, I have a boyfriend. *Who is here with me.*'

'Do you see him, Troy? Cos I sure don't!'

They thought this was hilarious, which made me wonder if they were in fact very stoned.

It was massively frustrating, because part of me, a big part of me, wanted to be really aggro and tell them to fuck off, but I just couldn't. It wasn't even that I was worried they'd turn nasty. I just couldn't bring myself to be that rude, even to confirmed dickheads. All of which made me feel even more unhappy with the situation.

Then garlic breath got down in my face so I couldn't even see Zeke's back any more.

'Chill. We ain't gonna hurt you. We're just sayin' hey.'

Back pressed up against the cue rack, I stood there, frozen, as garlic breath put his hand up my top.

Suddenly my brain flashed to Daniel, and how he always said that if you were going to have to fight, it was best to get your punch in first. I inhaled, cracked my knee into garlic breath's scrotum and elbowed Eminem-wannabe hard in the gut. Caught off guard and totally hammered, they groaned.

My path was clear, and just as I was thinking my three tae kwon do lessons had paid off big style, I saw that Inga had her hands in Zeke's hair, and her tongue in his mouth.

chapter eighteen

What. The. Hell?

Zeke – lovely loyal Zeke, whom I'd never even caught checking out anyone else – was kissing another girl? The most annoying one on earth, no less? Right in front of me?

I pushed open the fire-escape door and walked out into the humid air of the Florida night.

Heart beating hard, all I wanted to do was get out of there.

I couldn't believe how fast things had turned bad. I'd just been groped and no one had seen or helped, and my boyfriend, who I was head over heels in love with, was apparently a complete shithead.

My face was on fire with I didn't even know what. It felt like embarrassment or shame, but that was crazy, because why would I feel like that? *I'd* done nothing wrong.

And then I got it: what I felt was humiliation.

It had happened. Exactly what Daniel, the moment he clapped eyes on Zeke, had said would happen. *You know he's gonna end up with a Barbie on his arm.*

Oh God. That made it so much worse, knowing that even an utter moron like Daniel had been right about Zeke. And it wasn't even just him. What had my mum said about Zeke? About "butterflies"?

'*He seems great, Iris. Capable and strong. Like the sort of person who could set down on a runway in some war-torn nation and know exactly how to get to where he needs to go and get all his surfboards there without putting a single ding in one of them. Seen it all, done it all, got all the T-shirts. But sometimes, you know, these world travellers are hollow in the centre. They're looking for something, and even they don't know what it is. But they can't stop searching.*'

She'd had her soft face on – the one she used when she really wanted to get through to me.

'*Do you see what I mean, Iris? You can't count on them. There's nothing holding them anywhere. They have no solid core weighing them down. They're just butterflies flitting through the air. And who can build a life with a butterfly?*'

'Zeke is not a frigging butterfly!' I'd said. 'And anyway, I'd rather be a butterfly than a worm.'

'I think you mean a caterpillar.'

'Whatever!'

My mum tried to talk to me some more, but I was having none of it. Life-building sounded so old and boring anyway; it was the last thing I wanted to talk about right before I left for my big adventure.

I clawed at the skin on my throat, feeling my nails dig into the sunburn.

I hadn't wanted to believe that Zeke was hollow where it counted, or that he was just like any other manwhore pro-surfer with a gaggle of girls ready and waiting on every beach. Zeke was different. He wasn't a liar. He couldn't be. Because if he was, everything we'd been through together was bullshit.

I turned a corner, and at the end of the block I saw two youngish black guys walking towards me. Deep in an argument, they didn't see me. One was waving his hands around, and the other had his head down, his mouth set in a grim line. As they came nearer, I heard the first one saying the same thing over and over: '*This is not working.*'

The other guy rubbed tears out of his eyes and looked up, straight at me.

I nodded, by which I hoped to convey an *I see you're having a bad night, I am too* sort of message.

Then I saw a girl who looked suspiciously like one of Zeke's female friends from the beach, walking arm in arm with two other girls. I kept my gaze on the pavement and made a sharp turn off the street.

wednesday

chapter nineteen

Walking between dumpsters, where a day ago I'd been snogging the face off Zeke, it occurred to me that maybe this sudden change in direction wasn't my cleverest move. A rustle to my left made me jump, and I waited for a knife-wielding maniac to run at me. Instead a stray cat sauntered across my path, gulping some piece of edible garbage.

The alley came out on a busy street and I exhaled. I was, however, totally lost, but I couldn't even be bothered to load up Google Maps, because I didn't want to be found.

If I kept walking, I could stop thinking. But it wasn't so easy. On the crowded night streets of Miami, couples seemed to be everywhere. Laughing as they tumbled out of hipster bars; groping each other's arses as they waited for taxis; gazing into loved ones' eyes as they walked, hand in hand, towards their bloody Lamborghinis.

I'd been such an idiot. You only had to look at Zeke to figure it out.

It all flashed through my head: the poster campaign for a Nike diver's watch that appeared on billboards in Tokyo; the advert for a Burberry coat; the Givenchy aftershave double-page spread – and the last two were both ridiculous as Zeke would never wear tweed or any kind of fragrance. You didn't need those things on a beach, which is where he spent his life.

But he looked the way those brands wanted their male models to look, so he was hired. They didn't care about his surf skills or how much work he put into his fitness and stamina. Or the fact that he gave fifty per cent of his contest winnings to ocean-preservation charities like Sea Shepherd and Surfers for Cetaceans. They just thought he was hot, thought his look could sell stuff for them. And they were right. His campaigns were all successful and so they kept signing him for more. But every time he came back from one of those shoots, had part of him slipped away from me?

Yes. Why hadn't I seen it before? Was I really that deep in denial?

The wild child of the sea I'd fallen for was turning into someone who chatted to make-up artists as they smeared foundation over the scars on his back, who took direction from experts in posing, who knew how overhead lighting could give extra definition to his abs, who went around signing the necks of strange girls just because they asked him to.

So Zeke had been changing for a while. He had. But had he really changed into the kind of creep who'd suck the face off some girl who'd fluttered her eyelashes at him? Right in front of his girlfriend?

My head was banging from the alcohol, and I kept my eyes on my pointless, uncomfortable shoes so I didn't have to see any of the happy people. I walked along endless pavement, until I found my way to one of the entrances to South Beach.

Further up the beach, I could see a couple rolling around, and the still forms of rough sleepers. But the path to the sea in front of me was completely clear.

I took off my shoes and walked barefoot on the sand, which looked silvery grey in the moonlight. It wasn't soft like the sand on Fistral Beach; it felt sharp and crunchy underfoot. I grabbed a handful of it and stuffed it in the inner zipped pocket of my bag. I tried to collect some sand at every beach because I knew my little cousin Cara back in Newquay would like it.

Something about that sand gave me an intense pang of sadness. I missed home, missed Fistral, missed walking with Kelly along hedgerows pink with valerian, past brightly coloured beach huts down to Tolcarne Beach, ice creams dripping on to our trainers. I missed the scent of yarrow and wild garlic floating on the sea breeze. I missed telling Kelly jokes as she practised cartwheels; people looking, Kelly not caring a bit.

If only I had her with me, she'd know what to do. She'd make everything OK. My mum would make me feel better too, even if she *was* secretly thinking, I warned you about bloody butterflies. She'd give me one whole day to wallow, and then tell me off for caring so much about a boy's bad behaviour when I should have been flashing my feminist credentials at him and telling him to sling his hook.

Maybe I should jack it all in, I thought. The surf competitions, being a girlfriend, the big dream. All of it. Just give up. Use the money I had left to buy a ticket on the next plane back to England.

I took my phone out of my bag and saw that it was almost one o'clock. I'd put it on to silent earlier, and my heart flipped as I saw that there were seven missed calls from Zeke and a load of text messages.

My finger hovered, but I knew I wasn't ready to talk to him, so I went into Contacts instead. There was someone whose voice I desperately needed to hear. I pressed Call, but the phone didn't even ring, instead going straight to voicemail.

'This is Kelly. I'm probably out of credit, so call me back later, m'kay.'

'Kel, it's me. I really need to talk.'

It was the early morning in the UK, too early for Kelly

to be up and about, so no wonder her phone was switched off, but I wished so hard that it wasn't. For a second my finger hesitated over Daniel's name.

I pressed Call.

chapter twenty

Two rings. Three. Four.

I moved the phone away from my ear, preparing to hang up.

'Hello?'

He didn't even sound groggy. He sounded alert.

What could I say?

I'd cut him off completely. He was dead to me – that's what I'd told myself for months. Told myself I'd never speak to him again.

Talk or hang up? And then I stepped over the edge of the moment.

'It's me.'

'Iris?'

'Yeah. New number – sorry.'

'How's it going?'

'I shouldn't have phoned. Sorry for disturbing you.'

'You all right?'

'No. I'm really not.'

'What's wrong?'

'Christ, I don't even know where to start.'

'Where are you?'

'Miami. I was at a bar with Zeke and then I left. I'm on the beach.'

'Wait, ain't it like the middle of the night there?'

'Yeah.'

'You safe?'

'I think so. There's people around.'

What was he going to do, even if I wasn't safe? Reach across an ocean and save me? But it felt good that he'd asked.

'So why'd you ditch the Yank?'

I sighed. He couldn't just ask a question; he had to be a git about it.

'I'd better go. Sorry I woke you up.'

'D'ya want me to do something?'

'No. Of course not . . . Like what?'

'I dunno. Come out there.'

'To Florida? Uh, no. Anyway, I'm leaving soon.'

'Well, why did you ring me? Must've had a reason.'

'It's just, what do you think of Zeke?'

I heard him exhale. Why had I said that? Asking my ex-boyfriend for an opinion on my new boyfriend was the definition of stupidity. I'd hardly get an objective response.

'Fake as fuck.'

'Fake?' I winced. I thought he might have gone for

poseur, or pretty boy, or manwhore or something, but not fake. 'Seriously? You think he's, what, putting on some act with me?'

'You and the world. No bloke's like that. All that meditation and yoga and shit, and the way he does that blatantly fake smiling thing all the time. He makes out he's so perfect, but deep down he's just like the rest of us. Plus, I hate his fucking teeth.'

'What's wrong with his teeth?'

'One: he's got too many of 'em; and, two: they glow in the dark.'

'No, they don't.'

'Yeah, they do, and considering the bloke's a smoker, it's not natural. He must get them bleached. That and his hair.'

'He doesn't bleach his hair or his teeth. Why do you have to be so mean all the time?'

'Why do you have to sound so American? You've only been there a few months.'

'I don't sound American.'

'Well, you sure as shit don't sound Cornish. Talk normal.'

'I am.'

'Come home. You belong in Newquay. Not there.'

'I can't just come home, even if I wanted to. Which I don't.'

'Iris, get a fucking grip, woman. You need to—'

'Bye, Daniel.'

After hanging up, I opened Google and tapped in the search term I'd been secretly using, like a drug, since I'd left. *Fistral beach webcam*.

And there it was, my home break at high tide, a glorious dawn on the horizon, perfect clean waves stacking up and a bunch of surfers already in the water.

Someone with a yellow longboard walked right in front of the camera. My friend Caleb had a board like that. Was it him? Maybe.

I watched as two figures kicked a ball around for a dog. The dog chased it down to the water, where wave after wave pushed on to the beach.

At that moment I'd have given anything to be one of the surfers riding those waves. Real waves. Not the tiny green micro-waves of Miami.

I closed down Google and promised myself that would be the last time. Looking never solved anything, and every time I gave into the urge, it got stronger.

If I went home, I knew I'd never leave again. Travelling the world was awesome, but did it make me happier than being with my family and friends in Newquay?

I slumped down on the sand, pushed the heels of my hands into my eye sockets and refused to cry.

OK, I thought, I was on a path and I couldn't get off it until I got to the end, but this was what I'd wanted. This had been my dream.

My phone lit up again as it received a call, but it wasn't from Kelly or Daniel. Zeke was trying to get through.

No. I wouldn't pick up. Screw him.

I stuffed my phone back into my bag and dropped it on the sand.

Moonlight made a soft silver path on the black water, and even though it was night-time and I knew Florida's waters were super-sharky, visited by bulls, hammerheads and even tigers, my stupid drunken brain urged me to get in there. Submerged in water, I could be myself, I could relax.

I waded so far into the water that my yellow shorts turned black.

If only I could swim home.

The sea had a faint tang of oil and decay, but after the heat of the bar it felt wonderful to have cool water swirling around my legs. If some sea beast was eyeing up my calves at that very second, then it was a risk I'd have to take, because no way was I getting out. I dunked my face into the water, picturing black lines of mascara staining my cheeks.

'*Just breathe*,' I told myself. I'd told myself this exact thing so many times over the preceding few months that anyone listening would have thought I was asthmatic.

Something cool moved against my leg and I jumped, but it was only a glass bottle.

I fished it out and saw it was some kind of wine. I

wondered who'd drunk it and then I thought of Chase, with his outrageous clothes and expensive champagne. Had he seen Zeke kissing that girl? Was he surprised? Maybe he knew Zeke was a player. Had he seen what happened to me?

I looked up to the bright silver sky overhead, and tried to do the ujjayi breathing that Zeke's yoga-teacher friend had taught me. Eventually my heart began to slow down and my brain too.

I turned shorewards, and that's when I saw them.

A group of lads were walking down the beach towards me, joking around. I saw one of them bend down and pick up my bag.

My cash and all my bank cards were in it. I couldn't let it get nicked.

I waded back towards shore and, when I was fifty feet away, I made eye contact with one of them.

He looked really startled to see a person coming out of the water. Maybe he'd assumed the bag was lost, or left by someone on a suicide mission.

'Hey there,' he said. He had a grade-two buzz cut, an eyebrow piercing and dark eyes.

'That's mine,' I said, pointing to the bag. My voice came out really weird; sort of posh and bossy, much like Saskia's.

Then my gaze went to the guy's pocket, where something was jutting out.

A gun.

No, it couldn't be a gun.

It was totally a gun.

I held on tightly to the glass bottle in my hand as the baby waves swirled around my ankles.

No, no, no. That was panic talking. It was probably just his wallet or phone.

But loads of people in Florida walked around with guns, or had them in their cars. One in three – that's what my mum had said. She'd warned me to be careful, to stay safe, and this was the exact sort of situation that would crop up in her nightmares: her daughter, alone, at night, face to face with an armed gang.

'Girl, are you insane?' he shouted over the swish of the sea.

'No, I was just hot.'

'You don't look so hot.'

'Thanks,' I said, alert to the insult.

'Cold. You look cold. Maybe you should step out of the ocean and warm up?' I put my arm across my chest, in case my nipples were doing something mortifying, and I tried to decide what to do.

I couldn't stay in the water forever. One way or another, I'd have to get off this beach, even if it did mean fighting a potential gangbanger for my handbag.

As it happened, I walked out of the sea with my head held high and the boy handed me my bag straight away.

'Thank you,' I said, and then added, 'Good evening.' I figured politeness was a good strategy, but I really was starting to sound like I was doing an impression of Keira Knightley. I tried to dodge around them, when the boy I'd been talking to touched my arm gently.

'You OK? It's kinda late for a swim.'

'It's not really that late, considering,' I said, in the lamest retort ever. 'And yes, I'm all right. Sort of. Rubbish day.'

He nodded.

'That your wine?'

'It was floating in the water. I'm not an alky. I just need to find a bin – a trash can.'

'Well, Lady Di, you shouldn't be out here alone,' one of the others said. 'There are some shady dudes out tonight.' They looked at each other and grinned, and I wondered if they meant that they were the shady dudes in question.

'I'll be fine. Thanks for the concern though. That's nice of you.'

'You hear that? We're nice. Ha ha. Y'know, you look like you lost a dollar and found a quarter.'

He had me there. I felt totally and utterly gutted, and was about two seconds from crying. This random guy's concern was not helping on that front.

I shrugged.

'Do you need us to take you somewhere? Play chaperone?'

They seemed decent enough, but they had me surrounded, on a night beach, and my hackles were up. My mum had drilled me, since I was about three, in scenarios that might lead to my violent death. But by wandering off in a strange city on my own, I'd already seriously departed from her script.

'This is going to sound sort of tragic, but my mum would kill me if I went off with a load of strange blokes in the middle of the night. She's been mainlining *CSI*.'

'Your mom might like it better than you walking the streets alone,' one of his friends murmured.

'Cheers, but I should go find my boyfriend. He'll be around here somewhere.'

'He ditched you in the middle of the night? Some boyfriend.'

'Yeah, ex-boyfriend is more like it,' I said, trying to sound tougher than I felt.

But Zeke hadn't ditched me.

'Technically I ditched him. I was provoked though. Massively provoked.'

'He hit you?'

'God, no. It wasn't like that.'

'Stepping out on you?'

'Well, no, I don't think so. But he did kiss another girl in a bar just now.'

'So you ran off?'

This was not the answer I was expecting. He was frowning at me as if *I* was the one in the wrong.

'What was I supposed to do? Stay and watch them get to second base?'

They didn't get it. Zeke had completely betrayed me. He'd kissed her and he hadn't even cared if I saw. Maybe he'd kissed her because I'd beaten him at pool and he couldn't handle being beaten by a girl. The whole idea of that was revolting.

'What if you got it wrong? You should have, like, asked the dude for an explanation. Or homeboy pulled this shit before?'

'I don't think so.'

The boy with the nice eyes took a breath mint out of a pack and offered me one. I shook my head and watched him suck it.

'So you broke up with him, right?'

'Not yet, but I'm going to.'

'His loss.'

That was not true though. If I broke up with Zeke, it would be my loss, because Zeke would always have zillions of girls that wanted to be with him. Whereas I almost never found kindred spirits who got me.

I looked down at the sand.

'You gonna puke?'

'No, why do people keep asking me that?' I said. I had gone past the hot, flushed stage and gone straight over to nauseated and weak. My head was swirly and I had become very, very cold. The vest/tiny-shorts combo was fine in a bar, but not so great when soaking wet and stranded on a beach.

'What's your name?'

'Iris.'

'Irisss?' he said, rolling the word around his mouth.

I nodded.

'Nice to meet you, Iris. I'm Seb. This is Javier, Paul, Ernesto and AJ. So what's your next move?'

'Don't exactly have one.'

'Where you wanna get?'

That was a good question, with no good answer. I totally didn't want to go back to my hotel and face Zeke but I had nowhere else to go.

'Grove Hotel.'

'British chick don't stay in any *no-tell motel*, huh? OK, so we're gonna hit the streets and walk to the Grove Hotel. You can stay out here and take your chances if you want, but if you follow us, you'll get to the Grove safe. How's that work for you?'

My choices were limited. Even if I called Zeke, it'd take him a while to get to me, and in the meantime I'd be alone, trying not to get in the way of anybody serious.

I didn't usually trust people I'd met five minutes before, but there was something about Seb that seemed decent.

146

'Great. Thank you so much,' I said, my teeth chattering. Seb pulled his blue hoodie over his head and passed it to me. His wallet fell on to the sand, and he stuffed it into the back pocket of his jeans, which made them sag even more.

'You sure?' I said. 'Aren't you going to get cold out here?' I looked at the black vest top he had on underneath and couldn't help noticing great arms.

'I'll be absolutely fabulous, darling,' he said in a mock British accent, grinning. Then he said, 'OK, we're gonna go now.'

I put on his hoodie, which smelled of boy sweat and aftershave, and watched the five of them cut across the beach and walk on towards the car park.

I weighed up my options and decided to follow them. I also decided to keep carrying my empty wine bottle, just in case. Not the greatest weapon, but better than nothing.

Seb looked over his shoulder every now and then to make sure I was still with them. After fifteen minutes of walking I recognized an awesome fifties-style diner next to an Italian place with foot-long pizza slices, and then we were at the mini-mall. The guys crossed a side street which led to the hotel's underground parking, and stood outside the main entrance, where the doormen gave them dirty looks.

I ditched the bottle in a bin, caught them up and held out a twenty-dollar bill to Seb.

'For your trouble,' I said. 'Split it with your mates.'

This moment was admittedly quite awkward, but I knew there was a big tipping culture in America and I didn't want to offend anyone.

He laughed and waved my hand away.

'Honestly,' I said. 'Please take it.'

Seb nodded to his friends to go ahead, and they walked down the street out of earshot and waited for him there.

'Keep it. We don't want your money,' he said, and added, 'What's your number?'

'My room number?' I asked, slightly scandalized.

He laughed again and made the phone sign.

Oh. I really *was* drunk.

Without thinking it through properly, and not wanting to be rude, I got one of my business cards out of my purse and handed it to him.

'That's me,' I said. 'My mobile number's on there.'

'*Iris Fox. Face of Billabong UK*,' he read. 'Surfer girl?'

I nodded, but didn't want to elaborate, because whenever I attempted to explain my current Face of Billabong status it wound up sounding braggy or pathetic, or both.

'Hey, you weren't at that signing thing yesterday? My sister made me drop her at the mall so she could get scribbled on by some surfer dude she has the hots for.'

Zeke. Brilliant, just brilliant.

'Yeah. I was there.'

'Cool. Maybe she got your autograph too?'

'How old is she?'

'Fourteen. No, fifteen.'

'Then, no, she didn't.'

'How long you staying?'

'Not long. Leaving after the contest.'

'If you want to talk tomorrow, we can grab a cup of joe?'

He was sweet and I couldn't help smiling.

'My dad runs the best coffee joint in Miami. Free espresso right there.'

'Wow.'

'Wow yourself, Iris: Face of Billabong UK.'

'That was kind of an accident. There was this sabotage thing. Not from me, like . . . by another girl who messed with my board and it all went crazy . . .' And talking of crazy, my stupid babbling was definitely making it sound like I was. 'So, um, tell me more about this coffee place.'

'Garcias, in Little Havana. I'll call you.'

'No, don't worry. I'm sure you have better things to do than show some tourist around.'

'Yeah, not really. I can cut class.'

'You're in college?'

'Miami International University of Art and Design. Graphic and web design, but I'm more into the web stuff.'

'Cool.'

'Yeah, I love it.'

I looked down at the pavement and could think of

precisely nothing to say. I couldn't exactly ask for my business card back, even though I had a feeling I shouldn't have given it to him, so I just nodded and said, 'Thanks for the help. Oh, take your hoodie.'

Except, I couldn't get it off. Some loose threads on the inside had managed to get hooked on to my bra, which had clasps all over it, in order to be fully convertible.

'Here,' Seb said, 'let me help you.'

He had his hand down the back of the hoodie, trying to work the fabric free, when I heard running footsteps behind me.

chapter twenty-one

A figure crossed in front of me, and Seb shot backwards and his head hit the exterior wall of the hotel's restaurant.

Zeke had arrived.

And his face was contorted with fury. He was sweating heavily, telling Seb to beat it before he called the cops.

'Stop it,' I shouted. 'He was helping me!'

When Seb regained his balance, he squared up to Zeke, all flashing eyes and set jaw, and I saw blood trickling down his face from a gash on the side of his head.

'Are you high?' he asked Zeke. 'I was helping her out of my sweatshirt.'

Zeke's anger was replaced by confusion, and then fright, when he turned to Seb and saw the blood. He started to apologize, 'Sorry, man, I——' when Seb punched him in the face.

'Now we're even,' he said.

Seb's friends were watching from a distance, without moving, and without even looking particularly concerned.

Judging by the right hook he'd demonstrated, Seb could obviously handle himself in a fight.

Zeke made no move to retaliate. He checked his nose for blood, and said, 'Feel better?'

'Kinda,' Seb said.

'He showed me the way back to the hotel when I was lost, all right?' I said to Zeke, so furious that I could barely get my words out.

'I guess I got hold of the wrong end of the stick. Nice punch though,' Zeke said, touching his eye, which seemed to have caught some of the blow.

'Yeah, Zeke, you did. He was just helping me out of his hoodie! I was cold in this stupid bloody outfit you and Chase made me wear.'

'Wait,' Seb said, looking Zeke up and down. 'You're Zeke Francis?'

Zeke nodded, looking very uncomfortable.

'You never said your boyfriend was Zeke Francis,' Seb said to me. 'This is the guy my sister's obsessed with. Dude, she has money on you to win the tour before you hit twenty-one.'

'Shit. I feel bad. I'm real sorry,' Zeke said.

'Forget about it.'

'How much?'

'Huh?'

'How much did she bet on me?'

'A hundred bucks.'

152

Zeke got his wallet out of his back pocket and counted out five twenty-dollar notes and handed them to Seb. 'Here, take it. Give her back her money.'

'What? Why?'

'I'm not gonna be world champ before I'm twenty-one. Probably not gonna be world champ ever.'

Seb put up his hand. 'What is it with you people trying to give me your money?'

'You tried to give him money?' Zeke asked.

'For helping me find my way back. I thought you were supposed to tip everyone here!'

There was a pause, the most uncomfortable silence imaginable.

Finally Seb broke it, with, 'Y'all have a nice night,' and walked off shaking his head and muttering, 'I can't believe it. She said he was such a good guy.'

'Thank you,' I called after him, but he only nodded without looking back.

Then I turned to Zeke and said, 'You have some bloody nerve.'

chapter twenty-two

Zeke's eye was already starting to swell up. In a few hours it'd probably close over. Part of me wanted to run to reception and ask for an ice pack, but another part of me wanted to grab a biro and stab him in the other eye.

We stood in front of the lobby with its trailing ferns and massive indoor fountain and squared off.

'Iris, baby, I'm so sorry.'

He tried to hug me, but I was having none of it.

'Don't "baby" me, and don't touch me.'

'Just tell me you're OK?'

'Yeah, I'm super.'

'You sure? You're not hurt?'

I looked at my arms and legs in an exaggerated way, as if I was expecting to see burns or blood.

'Doesn't look like it.'

'Sheesh, Iris. Where the heck have you been? And why are you wet?' He didn't wait for an answer. 'I'm running around all the bars and diners, going out of my mind. I stood in line for like a half-hour to get into that dive club on the corner to look for you, since the assholes on the door wouldn't just let me in, even though I totally told them it was an emergency. Chase made his driver take him around the backstreets, in case you'd gotten lost. I was just coming to check the hotel room one last time, and if you weren't there I was gonna call the cops.'

He had sweat on his forehead and he looked so panicky that a tiny part of me felt bad.

'Well, I didn't know you'd flip out. I didn't even think you'd be looking for me. You seemed pretty busy back there.'

'*Flip out?* You took off – left me high and dry.'

I shook my wrist free of his grip. 'Why, Zeke? Why did I do that?'

'You're asking *me?*'

'Oh, get lost, Zeke. You totally know why.'

I could tell he was on the verge of shouting at me, but I didn't care. I wanted to push him, see him lose his rag.

'Because you say you wanna be treated as a grown-ass woman, but you're a little kid who acts out when things don't go her way?'

That one hurt. I shook my head and made a scoffing sound, too annoyed to answer in actual words.

He looked up at the atrium ceiling high above us, fingers interlinking at the back of his neck as if he'd cricked it. Then his gaze came back down to me, eyes accusing.

'Where did you even go tonight?'

'What's Chase's real name?'

'Are you serious? How are you even still talking about that?'

'I want to know.'

'If Chase wanted you to know, you'd know.'

'Fine. I don't give a toss anyway. South Beach.'

'At night? Have you lost your mind? There are gangs here. Anything could have happened. What were you THINKING?'

'Nothing did happen though, did it? I was fine. Chill out.'

'Don't – This is not pretend, Iris. This is real life. There are real bad guys out there. So how about you grow the hell up already?'

'Oh yeah, cos you're, like, so much more mature than I am, being, what, a whole two years older. Ooooh, Zeke Francis's got it all figured out. What a legend.'

He exhaled and put his hands in his back pockets. When he spoke, he put on his 'reasonable' voice, the one that made it seem like he was perfect and I was a lunatic. 'Come on, Iris, I'm not trying to be a jerk. I just don't want you to ever pull a stunt like that again. Jeez, I thought you were smarter than this.'

Who was Zeke to tell me I was stupid? His greatest achievement was what exactly? Pissing around at the edge of the ocean on a surfboard?

'I know what I'm doing. I don't need you to protect me. I'm not your responsibility.'

'Yeah, you are. I made a promise to your mom.'

'What? No, you didn't.'

'Sure I did! Your friends and family are in Newquay. Without me, you have no one. And you're sixteen!'

Ouch. A dig at me for not having made any of my own friends yet?

'I'm practically seventeen, actually, and I can handle myself. You're not my knight in shining armour. I managed just fine before I met the mythical Zeke bloody Francis.'

His face lifted into this incredulous, fake smile and then it was gone, replaced by pure anger.

'What the hell is with you tonight? You're acting nuts.'

'No, I'm not.'

'Yeah, you are. One-hundred-per-cent loony-tunes wackadoodle.'

I opened my mouth to deny it, and throw a drink in his face for good measure, when it occurred to me that maybe he had a point. I took a breath and said the words that should have come out of my mouth the moment we ran into one another: 'I saw you getting off with that girl. Amber's friend. INGA.'

'She kissed me. I wasn't kissing her. Like the time you made out with your psycho ex-boyfriend.' He made the jerk-off motion with his hand, which I'd never seen him do before. 'Y'know, on that frickin' rust-bucket fishing boat?'

'Oh, so you're still hanging on to that one, eh?'

Zeke always made out that he was so Zen about everything, but when it came down to it, he could obviously hold on to a grudge with the best of them.

'Hanging on to it? Nope. Remembering it from time to time, yeah. But I get it: sometimes stuff just happens.'

'So you're actually saying you didn't kiss her back?'

'OK, for one thing, I've known Amber and Inga for years. And, two, the kiss was for a picture.'

'Oh, well, that's all right then.'

'It's not as if I was making out with her. I kissed her two seconds for a picture. You think I'd kiss another girl for real?'

'Of course it was real. I saw it. You kissed her, Zeke.'

'For one breath. What – am I pushing her across the room the second she touches me?'

'Cool. The next time I get talking to a lad, I'll snog him and we'll see how you like it.'

'Iris, *come on,* it was a second before I stepped away. It meant nothing. And PS, even if I did make out with some other chick, you don't get to put yourself in danger just to spite me, OK? That shit is not gonna happen ever again.'

'So I should just smile and pretend everything's all right, even when my boyfriend's getting off with another girl?'

'No. That's not what I'm even saying.'

'Yes, you are.'

'That's a flat-out lie and you know it. Just rethink the scorched-earth policy. You don't have to burn everything down the second I mess up.'

A group of people had left their glasses of red and white wine on the shiny coffee table next to me. They'd hardly been touched. I picked up a red, and my fingers twitched to throw it in his face, twitched so hard I almost did it, but instead I raised the glass in front of his eyes, said, '*Cheers, brah,*' and downed it in one. It tasted horrid, like some chip shop's cheap vinegar. I slammed down the empty glass and with my eyes dared him to say a single thing about it. Then, before I could back down, change my mind, I picked up a glass of the white wine and downed every last drop of that too. I did this with another two glasses before I was done.

I belched and shoved my hand over my mouth because I sensed the belch was a prelude to a stream of winey vomit. I waited a moment, and when the danger was over said, 'You can't control me, so don't even try,' which was admittedly a dramatic thing to say, but I'd been listening to Greg Holden's 'The Lost Boy' a lot, which had a chorus that banged on about not being commanded and controlled. To make it less weird, I added, 'You're not the boss of me.'

'I don't want to be.'

'Right, so I can do whatever I want.'

'Not if you wanna be my girl,' he said. 'I can't deal with that BS. You scared me to death out there. I thought you were getting trafficked out of the country on some cargo ship.'

I rolled my eyes. 'Your imagination needs to calm right down.'

'How was I supposed to know you were fine? You totally ditched me. Wait,' he said, remembering something, 'I need to call Chase and tell him I found you.'

Zeke got out his phone. *'Bro . . . Yeah . . . At the hotel . . . South Beach . . . Uh-huh . . . Right? That's what I said . . . Because of Inga . . . Yeah, I'll tell her you said hey. Catch you later.'*

He sank down on one of the lobby sofas and put his head in his hands. I moved to stand in front of him. He sighed, and when he looked up his eyes looked old and tired.

What the hell, I thought. I'm gonna go for it. Come out with the thing that had been bugging me for months. Why shouldn't I tell him the truth?

'I'm fed up with girls throwing themselves at you. You just let them. You should tell them to get lost. You shouldn't even be talking to them.'

Zeke looked genuinely shocked. 'I shouldn't talk to any girl but you? You sound like a twelve-year-old.'

'And you sound like a dickhead.'

'I'm gonna talk to people, and since half the people in the world are girls, I'm gonna talk to girls.'

'Even when they're blatantly trying to pull you?'

'Girls can talk to me without wanting to get with me. I mean, I'm flattered that you think I'm this babe-magnet, but it's really not like that.'

'At least fifty per cent of your friends are female. What bloke has that many female friends?'

'Fifty per cent of human beings are female. Yeah, I have plenty of chick friends. I like hanging out with girls. They're fun and cool. So what? It doesn't mean anything. Sometimes people are just being friendly, you know?'

'Over-friendly if they're giving you their number, or sticking their tongue in your mouth.'

'Hot damn, Iris, what am I supposed to do? Step away each time a girl asks me how my day is?'

'Yeah, maybe. You're allowed to walk away if you don't want to speak to someone. I would – why can't you?'

He was looking more and more shocked by the second.

'Because it's freakin' *rude*.'

I looked over to the two women standing at the reception desk. One of them was reading a paperback, completely uninterested in us, and the other one was doing her best to appear so.

I held up my mobile phone in his face and loaded up Twitter. 'Look,' I said. 'Just look.'

When I searched for him, @Surfgeekzeke, it was one long string of tweets from girls. Some of them had even tweeted photographs they'd taken with Zeke, and the composition of those photos usually went like this: the girl would be holding Zeke's surfboard, he'd be standing next to her with his hand on her lower back and they'd both be smiling into the camera, or he'd be smiling into the camera and she'd be gazing up at him. The captions were always along the lines of 'Awesome to meet the amazing @Surfgeekzeke. You're soooo hot and talented!!! DM me, baby . . .'

'When did this even happen?' I said, looking at the latest one, taken on South Beach and featuring a girl with a button nose, absolutely no hips and a ridiculously inflated cleavage. 'Where was I?'

'Iris, they're fans. How am I supposed not to talk to fans? Without those guys I don't have a career.'

'Firstly, they are not guys, and secondly, they are not fans. Surf fans know about surfing. Those right there?' I said, jabbing my thumb at the screen. 'Groupies.'

Zeke looked aghast.

'You know that just by looking at them? Damn, girl, teach me your mind-reading skills. Be real handy in the line-up. Besides, guys say stuff about *you* all the time.'

'No, they don't. Not like this.'

'Uh, how about last week when that picture of you in a bathing suit went up on the Billabong Facebook page?'

'I didn't even know it did – I haven't been on Facebook much lately. What did they say?'

'Let me think: "If there's grass on the field, play ball",

and like a million worse versions of that. Oh, and one douchebag just posted a picture of lotion.'

'Why would he—'

'For jerking off!'

'Ew. Rank.'

'I know!'

'Well, what happened to not caring about stuff that people say on the Internet? *It's nothing to the universe*, remember . . .'

'You wanted to talk about this!'

'This was supposed to be a relaxing break between contests,' I said, sighing, as if he was completely responsible for this blazing row.

'So why are you spoiling it?'

And that's when I remembered, and felt so ashamed I wanted to stick my head in an oven. I had just given my number to a boy. A boy who seemed interested in me.

There I was, slagging off girls who flirted with Zeke, and I had given my Billabong business card to Seb, a complete stranger. Why? Just because I was angry with Zeke? Was I really that pathetic?

I was a hypocrite.

My head throbbed and I sat down on the sofa next to Zeke. I could feel my stupid eyes welling up with tears and I wiped them away.

Zeke was quiet, and then said, 'Let me find you a Kleenex.'

He walked off and I heard murmured voices as he approached the reception desk staff.

The wine had been strong and the room was starting to spin. Black circles around the edges of my vision closed in and suddenly I was lurching sideways and falling into upholstery.

The last thing I registered before I passed out was Zeke saying, '*Oh, brother,*' then getting a grip under my arms and lifting me.

chapter twenty-three

When I woke up even my eyelids felt depressed, and I couldn't seem to bring myself to open them, because once I did, I'd have to face up to what had happened.

I was still wearing my vest and damp shorts, Zeke had his arms around me and I could tell he was fast asleep, his chest rising and falling against my back. Morning was a long way off and my head was still hot and thumping from too much alcohol.

Not moving a muscle in case I woke him, I lay there, turning it all over.

Why had I immediately thought the worst?

Why had I been so completely melodramatic?

What was wrong with me?

I swore I could hear my own heartbeat in my ears — *ba-boom, ba-boom, ba-boom.* Even worse, my mind kept offering me all these flashes of Zeke with Inga, of those gross jocks feeling me up, of me handing over my business card to Seb, of Zeke looking frantic with worry and overwhelmed with relief when I told him I was all right.

Please sleep, I begged my own brain.

Suddenly I felt my phone vibrating under my pillow.

Kelly.

I weighed up my options, pressed Answer, whispered, 'Hang on,' and extracted myself from Zeke and snuck on to the breezeway outside.

'Can you talk? Or you out on the lash with Ken?'

'Kel, don't call him that – you know I hate it.'

'Come on, he does look a bit like the Surfer Ken doll, you've gotta admit it. So, anyway, how's the trip going?'

'Not great. Being away from you sucks. I miss you so much.'

'Are you hammered? You sound hammered.'

'I had a massive row with Zeke tonight.'

'Oh no. What'd he do?'

I didn't want to tell Kelly about Zeke and Inga, as even if he did have an explanation, I knew Kelly would think it was well dodgy and I didn't want her to think badly of my boyfriend, no matter how annoyed I was with him.

'It's just hard out here. Harder than I thought. Sometimes it feels so claustrophobic being with Zeke all the time. Maybe we've overdosed on each other.'

'Well, it's bound to be tricky. You've gone from being strangers to basically living together in no time at all.'

She was right. Reality had set in, and no amount of

picking our way across palm-edged beaches for dawn surfs on deserted coral reefs could change the fact that I now saw him at his worst; he saw me at mine.

'How are things going with Garrett?' I asked, deliberately changing the subject. Kelly had been so excited for me to travel the world, surf its best breaks, and play out some epic romance with Zeke. I didn't have the heart to tell her the truth; that it had all gone to ratshit.

'Don't ask,' she replied, her voice sounding tense.

'Why not?'

The idea of Kelly and Garrett having problems actually made me feel a bit better. At least it wasn't just me and Zeke who were struggling. I felt seriously bad for this thought when Kelly took a deep breath and said, 'Garrett's poorly.'

My heart sank.

'What do you mean? Like, seriously?'

'Yeah.'

'Shit.'

'I know.'

'Oh God, Kel. I'm so sorry. Do you wanna talk about it?'

'Not really.'

'He should tell Zeke though. Zeke has a right to know if something's wrong with his brother.'

'Nothing's wrong.'

'Well, you just said there was.'

'God, judgey much? Poorly is a legitimate lifestyle choice.'

'Being *ill* is a lifestyle choice?'

We were both silent and suddenly Kelly laughed.

'I said POLY not POORLY.'

'Oh. Well, what the hell is *poly* supposed to mean?'

'God, Iris. Haven't you ever read a sex blog?'

'Um, no.' As if I could spend time reading sex blogs with millions of events in my diary and Zeke constantly three feet away.

'Poly is short for polyamorous.'

I searched the memory banks and came up empty.

'Not a clue.'

'It's the opposite of monogamous.'

'So, wait a minute,' I said, trying to get my inebriated brain around what she was telling me. 'Garrett just goes around cheating on his girlfriends. Cheating on you?'

'No, because it's not cheating. Everyone is honest from the start, so there's no lying.'

'And you're cool with that?'

'Yeah. I think I am. I mean, monogamy is so full-on and controlly. When you love someone, you want the maximum possible happiness for them, don't you? You want them to make the most of every great opportunity that comes their way, and maybe a great opportunity is a person.'

This all seemed very unlike Kelly.

'You love Garrett?'

'Christ, no. What am I – stupid?'

I imagined Kelly head-over-heels in love with Zeke's brother. Something told me that would not end well for her, that the power dynamic had to be tipped towards Kelly for the relationship to have any chance at all. Kelly's natural tendency to play it as cool as possible, something that had jinxed her other relationships, would probably be a good thing with Garrett.

'But I suppose I could love him, one day.' She said this as if it had only just occurred to her. 'If he plays his cards right.'

'I don't get it. This poly thing just sounds like a good excuse for someone to treat their girlfriend like shit.'

'Or boyfriend. I'm trying it out too.'

'Sleeping around?'

'No, neither of us actually are, yet. But if we meet the right people, we will.'

'Aren't you worried it's gonna get weird?'

'Life with Garrett is already weird. So, is that the end of the interrogation?'

'Sorry, Kel. As long as you're cool with it, that's all I care about.'

Kelly's revelation made me feel even more childish for going nuts at Zeke for a photo kiss. She seemed to be in some properly grown-up relationship based on trust and honesty rather than jealousy.

'Iris, I have to go now, but don't worry about the row

with Zeke. You're gonna have times where you hate each other's guts. That's all part of it. Like my mum says, "If you don't want to leave him or murder him at least once a day, it's not a real relationship."'

'Thanks, Kel,' I said, laughing and wishing for the millionth time that she could be on tour with me.

I padded silently into the room and lay back down next to Zeke.

He turned and kissed me on the forehead, and his alcohol breath could've stripped paint.

'Kelly says hi,' I said, as gently as I could.

'You miss her.'

I groaned. 'So much.'

'It gets less, with time.'

'Do you miss anyone?'

Silence.

'Zeke?'

'Sorry. I was thinking. Yeah, I miss a lot of folks.'

'What were you thinking? That you don't want to be with me any more, probably.'

He shook his head. 'I do wanna be with you, but . . . this is still new for me. Spending so much time with a girl. I guess we both have to get used to it.'

'I wouldn't blame you if you did want to bail. But . . . I really care about you. More than I've ever cared about anyone.'

'Even that Daniel guy?'

'Yeah, course. I can't believe you'd even ask me that. I hate him. When I think about him hurting you like that, I want to rip his head off.' And I hated myself for phoning him.

'Hey, it wasn't all one way – I got in a couple licks.'

The sight of Zeke and Daniel fighting was one of my all-time worst memories. If I let myself think about it, which I didn't often, I remembered the vibration of the punches and kicks, the sound of expelled breath. Wet jeans and pooling blood. So much blood.

'Iris, I'm sorry. I shouldn't have yelled at you tonight. I was worried, but that's no excuse and I feel lousy about it. You forgive me?'

'No, it was me – I behaved like a complete idiot. I don't know what I was thinking. I obviously *wasn't* thinking.'

'It's just one of those situations that a guy hopes will never happen.'

'Being kissed by a pretty girl is so awful?'

'Being kissed by a girl when you have a girlfriend is. Especially when you feel like I do about you.'

I stayed there, my head against his chest, our breathing settling into a joint rhythm.

'I can't believe I went off like that.'

'I would probably have freaked out if I saw another guy kissing you. It's bad enough imagining you with Daniel. I hate the idea of him putting a hand on you. I mean, I'm cool with it in theory, because I'm not a nutjob, but if I let myself imagine it? Man, that shit *hurts.*'

'So imagine how I feel then. Because I don't even know how many girls you've slept with. You never told me your number. Maybe you should. You know, just get it out there? So we're both on the same page.'

'I get that, but the thing is, I don't actually know how to answer that question. After a certain point I lost track.'

I let that sink in. 'So it's more than a hundred?'

'I guess, but I was high for a lot of the time, so it's mostly a big blur. I can barely remember faces, let alone names.'

'Terrific. When did you stop counting?'

'Pretty early on. But I wasn't going home with chicks every night. Maybe one out of three nights.'

'That's still ten girls a month. Bloody hell, Zeke.'

He put his hand over his eyes and ran it over his forehead, sweeping loose strands of hair from his face. 'Yeah.'

'And this went on for how long?'

'Maybe two years.'

He'd slept with over two hundred girls. I tried to picture them standing in one long row and me walking past them all. How long would that take? What would they have told me about Zeke if I'd asked them?

'Please don't tell my mom,' he said. 'That is not the way she raised me.'

'I won't say anything,' I said, thinking that Sephy probably wouldn't be as shocked as Zeke thought. She seemed open-minded about everything. Still, talking to Zeke's mother about his sexual history was not on my to-do list. I'd pretty much rather grate off my own tongue than have that conversation.

'Does Garrett know?' I asked.

If Garrett knew, then Kelly would know.

'Most of the time he wasn't around. He did a year of college before he flunked out to go on this road trip across the mainland. He had a personal challenge thing going on. He was travelling alone, and the idea was to swim in every river he came to.'

'That's so Garrett.'

'I know, right? But after a few months he got some ear infection that kept him out of the water, so the mission changed from swimming in every river to drinking in every bar. That went on until he got into a motorcycle accident, broke his foot and took the next flight to Oahu. You know, I think if Garrett hadn't been away so long, I wouldn't have gone so far down Route Meth, because if he'd seen what I was getting into, he'd have beaten me about the head and hauled my ass back home.' He looked away, remembering things he would never be able to fully share with me.

'What was I saying? What did you ask?' he said, looking up.

'About the girls. If Garrett knows.'

'He probably has an idea.'

'What about Wes?'

'Wes doesn't ask me about stuff like that. He minds his business. And you gotta remember, the drugs were a big part of it. Everything was a blur, out of control. I wasn't exactly writing a daily journal.'

'So no one knows except me?'

'Right. I wouldn't just go tossing out that kind of information, even to my brothers.'

I could understand that. It wasn't as if I'd ever opted to have a deep and meaningful conversation with my sister. Lily was the last person I'd confide in.

The next question I had to ask was beyond awkward, and there was no polite way of phrasing it.

'Could you have got any of those girls pregnant?'

Zeke recoiled a little at this. I didn't see how he could be surprised though. It was surely something he had to have considered.

'Not that I know. I was . . . careful.'

Careful. The idea brought images into my mind that I could have done without.

'Always?'

'I think so. Mostly.'

'But you're not sure cos you were high so often?'

'Right. I think I'm in the clear, because if I were that gone, I wouldn't be able to, um, you know, but I can't be one hundred per cent.'

'But in theory it's possible that there could be a bunch of little Zekes running around out there?'

'I sure hope not, and, you know, I think I'd have heard by now if there were.'

Not necessarily, I thought, and definitely not if Anders had anything to do with it.

'Man, I'm sorry, Iris. I regret it, like, so much. I wish I didn't have to put all this BS on you and I wish I could go back and do things better.'

I knew that feeling so well. Wanting to go back and reverse all the terrible decisions I'd made, but there came a point where you just had to swallow shit and hope to keep it down.

'You were going through stuff. And anyway, you were doing what loads of people would have done in your circumstances. I mean, I'm not stoked to think of so many girls getting it on with my boyfriend, but we were both different people back then.'

'I'm glad you know, even though I'm sad too. Is that the way you feel?'

'I'm glad you were honest with me. Don't freak out when I tell you I'm getting an STI test, but I'm not doing it to make a point. I just need to know.'

'I get it. I'll come get one with you, even though those things are like *terrible* for guys.'

'They're no picnic for girls either, by the way.'

'Iris?' he said.

'Yeah,' I said, looking up into his face.

'Don't ever do that again. Don't leave me like that.'

I felt such a rush of heat then, like my body was coming round from pins and needles. I'd loved Daniel, but that wasn't anything like this. Zeke and I were travelling together, having new experiences together, doing everything together, with no family or friends as a safety net. All we had was each other.

'I won't,' I said.

Zeke kissed me, and though I was still raw with sadness and embarrassment, I felt like we'd turned a corner. I'd allowed him to see the very worst of me: the petty, angry, jealous sores I usually kept hidden because they were so ugly, and he hadn't walked away. We'd been through the fire and we hadn't given up on each other, which had to mean something.

He curled around me, his skin damp with night sweat.

'You think we can start fresh in the morning?' he said.

chapter twenty-four

When I came around again, the French windows were open and I could feel the morning breeze on my face. The sun was low in the sky and Zeke was cross-legged on the end of the bed, playing with his iPad.

He was showered and dressed, and looked perfectly fine. Whereas I had horrendous morning breath and the body odour of an alcoholic street-sleeper.

'Urrr,' I said.

'I just threw on some coffee. You want some?'

I shook my head. 'Maybe later.'

'Feel better?'

'A bit.' Which was to say: not at all.

My phone started ringing and Daniel's name flashed onscreen. I pressed Ignore and added him to my phone's block list.

'Who called?'

'I don't know. Spammers, probably.'

'You think you can eat breakfast?'

I felt my stomach lurch. Even though I was quite hungry, the idea of food was horrendous. A bite of toast and I'd puke. A glass of water and I'd puke. In fact, I thought, jumping out of bed, right now I'm gonna puke.

I ran to the bathroom and managed to get the majority of it in the loo, but sick spatter decorated the floor tiles and the toilet seat too. My knees were weak and my eyes watered. I stared at the redness of the vomit, thought it was blood and then remembered the wine. I was attempting to use some toilet roll to clear up the worst of the mess when my chest heaved again.

I didn't hear Zeke come into the room, and even though it was mortifying for him to see me like this, I was glad I wasn't alone. He rubbed my back and told me to get it all out so I'd feel better, and when I was finally through with emptying my stomach, he led me towards the shower, helped me out of my clothes and ran me a stream of cool water, which was just what I needed.

When I stepped out of the shower, twenty minutes later, I saw that Zeke had cleaned up my disgusting mess, which must have been torture for him, puke-phobic as he was.

I brushed my teeth, towel-dried my hair and then went into the bedroom, which was empty. I opened the doors to the balcony and saw that Zeke had set the table with a glass of water and some graham crackers.

'What time is it?' I said.

'Nine twenty. Can you eat crackers?' he said, concern in his eyes.

I nodded, and he got up to pull out a chair for me. He hadn't said a critical word, hadn't blamed me for getting so drunk; he just cared that I was all right.

I drank my water and ate my crackers, which were actually more like digestive biscuits. I didn't want to think about the night before, our first major argument, but I punished myself with other thoughts. Like flirting with Seb. Like calling Daniel.

'Oh crap,' Zeke said, as his iPad started pinging out its alert tone. 'We better get down to the port. We have that photo shoot for Ursula.'

When we arrived down at the docks – huge cargo ships everywhere, stacked high with brightly coloured shipping containers – Ursula ran at us, kissed us both on both cheeks and said, 'What is this black eye I'm seeing, Zeke? MAKE-UP!'

'Yeah, I hit my face on my surfboard,' he said, lying his arse off but at least looking sheepish about it.

Ursula shook her head and started giving us instructions in a hyper voice, while jogging on the spot. She was wearing a bra top and hotpants and she had her hair in loose bunches. She'd decided against a motorcycle spread and was instead going to include Zeke in some health-and-fitness feature – how to get a six-pack in three days or some such rubbish. And as well as the spread, she wanted a short video to put on their website. She'd brought two photographers with her, a camerawoman, several assistants and a dozen extras. Worse, she insisted I be in the picture too, and wouldn't take no for an answer.

I didn't mind keeping fit and did a few hours' exercise most days: yoga; a nice jog along the beach; some open-water swimming; a bit of coasteering when the swells weren't too crazy, and surfing every minute I could. Stuff that felt fun. Stuff where you didn't really notice you were training.

This was not that.

This was constant, muscle-shredding repetitions in the blazing morning sun, surrounded by fitness-obsessed strangers in Lycra. And worse, this was in front of cameras, so I couldn't even slack off. I'd been expecting a bit of light posing.

'Zeke,' I said, gasping for breath, 'water.'

'Sit this one out. We'll get drinks after.'

I tried to crack on for a bit longer but it was agony. It wasn't just that my muscles were tired. I felt as if I had torn my abdominals, done damage that would take a week or more to heal. And the fact that I had a brutal hangover made it all so much worse.

Five reps into the third set of stomach crunches, I got up and walked to the main road.

Zeke was right behind me.

'I'm so sorry about this – I should've said no.'

'You're fine. I've just had enough.'

'So you're going? Like, halfway through?'

'Yeah. I didn't even want to be in this picture anyway.'

'Wait up – I'll come with you.'

We turned back and everyone was staring at us, waiting for us to come back to the set.

'Ursula's arranged all this for you, and she wants you to stay. You should stay.'

'I'm not ditching you.'

'No, I'm ditching you. I have Google Maps on my phone. I'll be fine. Go do press-ups and look pretty. I'll find myself a cafe and chill out.'

And that was exactly what I did. For the next two hours. And it was exactly what I needed.

When I finally texted Zeke to tell him where I was, I felt better; and when he arrived, he looked better too.

The waitress brought our drinks over and I sat there sipping a tea, which was basically lukewarm water in a china cup, served with a fresh teabag on the side of the saucer. I dunked it in but it barely changed the colour of the water, and there wasn't even any milk. Then she brought me my biscuits, which turned out to be savoury scones, which immediately sucked all the moisture out of my mouth.

Zeke popped to the loo to wash away the make-up they'd plastered all over his face in an attempt to cover up

181

some spots and his black eye, and when he came back he sat across from me and jabbed at his phone.

I was tempted to ask him what he was doing, but I thought I'd take a leaf out of Kelly's book and play it cool. Eventually he said, 'I just sent you a link to Dropbox. Check it out.'

I loaded up Dropbox on my phone, and frowned.

'What is this?'

'Hypnosurfing.'

'My aunt Zoe did hypno*birthing*.'

'This is for surfers.'

'Pregnant surfers?'

'All surfers.'

'And you want me to listen to it?'

'It can't hurt.'

'*Hypnosurfing? Are you serious?*'

'Why not? I mean, you said you've been stressed here.'

'Because we've been arguing. And because there's hardly any swell. If I was surfing proper waves, I'd be fine.'

'OK, it was just an idea.'

Suddenly Zeke's face registered shock, he jumped up out of his chair and I heard a familiar female voice say, '*Surprise.*'

chapter twenty-five

She was wearing a hippyish orange dress, her dark hair lost under a printed scarf, and she was cooling herself with a Japanese fan. She looked utterly beautiful.

'Hey, kids! What's cookin'?'

'Mom!' Zeke said, jumping up and launching himself at her, 'You made it!'

'You knew she was coming?!' I asked, surprised that Zeke had managed to keep this brilliant secret to himself.

'Of course I knew she was coming! We arranged it last week. I just called her from the john.'

'Is Dave here too?' I asked.

'He wanted to come, but he's working sixty-hour weeks right now. A couple of the other paramedics left without much notice so his hands are tied. He sends you both so much love.'

'How long can you stay?'

'Half a day only, unfortunately. It's just a layover on

my way back to England. So, Zeke, I wasn't going to ask you this, because I'm not sure I need to hear the answer, but why do you have a black eye?'

'I earned it.'

'Fighting? Child of mine, I thought you outgrew fighting with G.I. Joes and squirt guns.'

I could think of at least one other fight Zeke had been involved in, and three other occasions when he'd seemed on the brink of getting involved.

'You know, you're nineteen. You need to take a breath before you swing. And if you do swing, you need to move.' She reached up, cuffed Zeke lightly around the head and he grinned. 'When are you going to go visit Newquay? Garrett and Wes miss you.'

'They can come see me.'

'I guess everyone's just wondering if there's a reason you guys haven't gone and visited yet.'

'We've been so busy,' I said.

'Anders?'

'Yeah. He just keeps booking stuff for us.'

Sephy looked at Zeke, 'And you're not asking him to do that?'

This seemed like a weird question to me. Why would he want Anders to keep us so busy with engagements that we hardly ever had any free time? Zeke was massively into his career, no question, but some downtime would mean we could freesurf, and so many of the events Anders lined

184

up for us were land-based: PR stuff, meet-and-greets, awards ceremonies, interviews with surf journalists and bloggers; stuff that actually took us out of the water. This had definitely surprised me; I'd had no idea that being a pro-surfer would involve, for instance, so much time spent on the Internet, developing Facebook, Instagram, Twitter and YouTube profiles.

What confused me, though, was why this stuff didn't seem to bother Zeke. At times it was almost as if he was glad to have a break from the water, which didn't at all tally with what I knew of his mad surfing addiction.

'It's contractual BS we can't get out of,' Zeke said.

'Honey, it's not forever. Keep your eyes on the prize – one of these days you'll be freesurfing full-time. You'll have enough security to go surf wherever you want, whenever you want.'

'One day,' Zeke said, looking glum.

'So guess what – I swung by our place in Oahu and put it on the market.'

'To lease, right?'

Sephy frowned. 'To sell.'

'You're gonna let go of our family place?'

'It seemed wrong to keep it. People need homes there. It shouldn't lie empty. And Newquay is home now.'

'Wow,' Zeke said. 'I can't believe you did that, without even talking to us about it.'

'Honey, this should not come as a surprise. I haven't

been there in months. You haven't been there in almost a year. A family could be living in that house. There was mould. And termites. It's not right. But forget about that. Look what got delivered for you.'

She passed him a gold envelope.

'What is it?' I asked. But Zeke already seemed to know.

'Can you believe it, baby? You finally got picked!'

Sephy was hugging her son and saying something so quietly that I couldn't make it out.

'Mom, I know,' Zeke said, 'but it's not that easy. I can't just . . . I mean, I promised.'

'Can't what? Surf Mavericks? You can totally do that,' she said. 'You did it before, you can do it again, right? The only difference is that you'll be competing with other guys this time.'

'Wait,' I said. 'You've made the Invitational?'

'Who even cares? It's just another surf contest.'

The Mavericks Invitational was a huge deal in surfing. It was a specialized wave contest for an elite group of big-wave surfers. Super-elite. Only the very best were invited. That Zeke would be included at the age of nineteen was an honour and a show of faith.

'Was this what you've been waiting for? What Chase and Anders were asking you about?'

Zeke nodded. 'I didn't want to mention it to you until I knew for sure.'

'This is it,' Sephy said. 'This is the big league, baby.'

'Bloody hell, Zeke. Congratulations,' I said.

He looked at me and said, 'Thanks.' Nothing else. Just thanks.

'I hope it happens soon,' Sephy said. 'I'm gonna be so nervous until it's over and done with. I know you'll be just fine, but that is such a heavy wave.'

'When do you think it'll be?' I asked Zeke.

'Not sure. Whenever the next big storm swell rolls in. As soon as the charts look good, they'll give me a call, I guess. Who knows what I'll be doing though. I might not even be able to make it.'

'Zeke,' I said, 'whatever you're doing, you'll drop it to surf Mavs.'

'It's not the only thing in the world, Iris. There are other opportunities out there.'

Better than the Mavericks Invitational? I didn't think so.

'If you say so.'

'Geez, what's with the attitude, Iris?'

He was suddenly so defensive, and I realized I'd touched a nerve that I hadn't even known had been exposed.

'This is just such a massive honour,' I said. 'Everyone will be there. If you win, you'll be set for life.'

'So no pressure, right? Hey, you know what? I don't want to talk about this any more,' he said. 'Mom, are you hungry? They have terrific entrées on the menu.'

'Iris,' Sephy said, looking confused, 'you mind if I talk to Zeke a second?'

'Not at all,' I said, getting up. 'I could do with some fresh air anyway. I'll be back in an hour.'

'You don't need to leave,' Zeke said. 'I'm sorry I was touchy. I'm not feeling so good today. Too much whiskey last night. I don't want you to go.'

'Zeke, you haven't seen your mum in ages. Catch up.'

'But where are you heading out to?'

I held up my wallet. 'We have a swanky event tomorrow. Don't you think it's about time I bought a dress?'

A tiny spitball had formed in the corner of his mouth and he rubbed it away with the back of his hand.

'You wanna take my AmEx?'

'Not necessary. I have my own money, thank you. See you later.'

chapter twenty-six

Precisely thirty minutes later, I was in the extravagant fitting room of a ridiculously expensive boutique, four dresses hanging up beside me, when I received a call from Sephy.

'Something's not right with Zeke.'

So it wasn't just me who thought so.

'Where is he? Did he leave?'

'Bathroom. We need to talk.'

'OK. When?'

'I'm gonna tell Zeke you called me to say you need my help choosing your dress. Where are you?'

'A shop called Tallulah. You probably walked past it on the way to the cafe. The mannequins in the window are green.'

'I remember it. Stay there.'

'What about Zeke?'

'He says he's tired and needs to take a nap. He's going back to your hotel.'

'Another nap? He's sleeping a lot on this trip.'

'I have to go – he's coming back.'

When Sephy arrived at the shop, she looked really worried.

'Is something happening between you two? Zeke says everything is fine, but I don't buy it.'

The assistant handed me another three dresses. 'Do you want to come into the fitting room?' I said to Sephy. 'I'm the only customer, so we can talk in there.'

She sat in a heavy armchair set to one side, and I pulled on a blue halter-neck number that was about a foot too long.

'So what's really happening with you guys?' she asked me, looking concerned. 'Did you have a fight?'

'We did, but we made up, and he was acting weird before that anyway. I don't think it's that. Zeke seems different in Miami,' I said. 'Distant. Does he have history here or something?'

'I don't think so. Leastways, not the kind that could make him unhappy. He used to come and visit Chase here a lot, after Chase's parents moved their real-estate business from Oahu. I never heard of anything bad happening to Zeke here – he always loved Miami.'

'Oh,' I said, my heart sinking even further.

Sephy reached out for my hand and held it tight.

'Zeke makes his own choices. I wondered if you might know something that would help me make sense of this change in him, but you are not responsible for Zeke's behaviour, Iris, you hear me? Whatever happens, whatever he does, you are not to blame.'

'He hasn't really done anything bad,' I said, starting to feel defensive, and Sephy raised her eyebrows.

Cynicism. Had she seen these signs in Zeke before? Was he about to go off the rails?

She bit her lip and said, 'You wanna hear something kinda heavy?'

I didn't, particularly, as I was already feeling worried and down, but maybe I needed to know. 'All right.'

'Zeke wrote me an email the week after he met you. He said he'd found someone, this local surfer girl, and he didn't know what to do, because he had to leave, but he really, really wanted to stay. And one of the things he said about you, I'll never forget. He said you have the eyes of a shut-in. I thought that was a strange thing to say about a person you just met.'

'A shut-in? You mean, like a hermit? Someone who won't leave the house?'

'Yeah.'

Great. Apparently I had mad-person eyes.

'He said your eyes looked alarmed by the world, until the moment you were in the ocean. In the ocean you were calm, and he thought that was because in the ocean you felt home. Zeke's that way too. And I knew then that he was right. He'd found someone who could be with him.'

'Did he say anything to you just a minute ago, about what's been going down with us? . . . Actually, don't worry. I don't want you to get caught in the middle.'

'Honey, Zeke loves you. But something's eating him and he won't open up about it to me. At all. You have to try.'

'I have, but I can't make him talk if he doesn't want to.'

She must've heard the upset in my voice, because she said, 'You're right. It's just hard for me to remember that he's not little any more. I still want to sweep in there and rescue him.'

I nodded, because I could see how much love Sephy had for Zeke and vice versa. But if she couldn't get him to admit what was bothering him, what chance did I have?

Sephy broke the worry chain that was starting up in my head by saying, 'So, there's actually another reason I wanted to talk to you: Iris Fox, will you be my maid of honour?'

chapter twenty-seven

'Wait, you're getting married? To Dave?'

She nodded. 'Second time around maybe it'll stick,' she laughed. 'So, will you?'

'Course I will, yeah. I'd be honoured. Does Zeke know?'

'I just told him back at the restaurant.'

'I bet he was so stoked!'

'He was. I don't think he believed it at first. We both swore we'd never risk those vows again.'

'When is it going to be?'

'A little while yet. There are people we want to be there. Two of them are climbing mountains, one is on a sailboat somewhere in the Pacific and a few we've lost track of altogether. To give us time to round everybody up, we're going for early June. So, what do you say?'

'I'd love to,' I said, hugging her. 'And congratulations.'

'There's something else.' She paused. 'What is that

funny phrase the English use for *hapai*? Oh yeah: "up the duff". I am, I mean.'

'Oh my God! You're pregnant? Wow, that's wonderful. Congratulations! Two lots of congratulations!'

I hugged her again, more gently this time.

'That's not why we're getting married though. Just in case you were thinking that,' she said.

'Of course not.' Sephy and Dave would never get married because they thought society expected it. Sephy couldn't give a rat's ass about those kinds of expectations; it was one of the many things I admired about her.

'I bet Zeke's thrilled to bits.'

'He sure is, and a little shocked. He didn't say too much, so I think he's still processing it, you know? So, these plans you have for this afternoon . . .'

'Yeah, we have to teach some disadvantaged kids how to surf.'

'Sounds terrific. Can I come along?'

'Absolutely. You could take a group out too, if you feel up to it. It's not just pros.'

She beamed. 'I'd love that.'

The charity surf lesson with some of Miami's underprivileged kids was yet another event Anders had slid into our schedules, but this was one we were looking forward to. It was billed as an Inspire event, and although I'd played it cool when Zeke told me about it, I'd been secretly frothing to teach some kids to surf. The littlest ones were four – not much older than my cousin Cara, who I missed like crazy.

We collected Zeke from the hotel, where he emerged looking bleary-eyed, and when we got to the beach the other instructors were there already. One of them, a certain girl with red hair, was sitting with ten small children around her, explaining the theory of surfing. I watched her pop up on her board, and they clapped. She had them eating out of her hand. Then she tied up her hair into a high pony, and looked directly at me. Saskia.

I waved at her, and was really relieved when she waved back. I hoped it meant she'd forgiven me for the bathroom incident at Chase's party.

Another of the instructors I recognized was Beth, who competed on the Billabong tour with me. As soon as she came over, I felt the nerves kick in.

Beth was an insanely talented charger, who grew up surfing Maroubra – one of the coolest, toughest beach breaks in Australia. She had a military haircut, a full sleeve of tattoos and a junior kick-boxing title. Most of the girls in the contest prepared for heats with meditation and yoga, others pulled ballet moves and one girl loosened up her hips by solo ballroom dancing up and down the waterline. The cameras loved that. Beth, however, stuck in earphones, pulled her hood down around her face and spent every spare minute before the buzzer jumping rope or shadow-boxing. If I could've picked anyone on the tour to be friends with, it would have been her.

'Hi, Ivy,' she said, grinning.

'It's, actually, um, Iris.'

'That's what I said.'

'I, err, thought you said Ivy.'

'You wanna stick your hearing aids in then!'

She knew my name. We'd competed at the same events, gone to the same after-parties, we'd even made a short promo film for Billabong together. I sighed. This was all part of it. It had started already, in readiness for Saturday. The psychological warfare.

The advice Anders gave me right before my first tour contest was: 'Do not allow yourself to become the omega animal.'

'What does that even mean?'

'The omega animal has the lowest status. It's the animal that binds the rest of the pack together. The scapegoat. The rest of them get their kicks from picking on it. Eventually, when its weakness becomes a hindrance, they kill it and find a new omega animal.'

'And you think that'll be me? Thanks a bunch!'

'Depends how you play it. The omega animal has an important role, don't get me wrong, and there has to be one, but nobody wants to be it, Iris. The other girls will want it to be you, just so it's not them. Do you understand?'

It had sounded a lot like school, I thought, but the

reality of contest surfing was worse, because the money up for grabs, and the pressure to impress in front of a bunch of cameras, made everyone even more desperate. And at the end of a long day there was no going back home to your family and your best mates.

I rooted through my bag for some surf wax. I was looking forward to trying out a new board our shaper had sent. He'd experimented with a new template, just a few subtle changes to the width and volume, but I knew it could really impact my performance.

Beth saw my fruitless searching and started pulling her own stash of surf wax out of her bag and arranging the little white discs into a flower shape on the sand.

'Can I borrow a tiny bit of your wax?' I said.

'Don't have any spare,' she said, piling up her stash into a tower.

'You've got enough there to wax an aircraft carrier.'

'Sorry, mate.'

I gritted my teeth and said nothing. I didn't want to pick a fight with Beth. For one thing, the girl could take me down, and not just in the line-up.

But it was so tedious to have to go through this drama. One day a girl would act like your best friend and you'd have a proper laugh together, the next she wouldn't even acknowledge your existence. Or she'd go from freezing you out for a week to being all charm ten minutes before your heat. Some of them would attempt to sing Top-40 hits in the line-up, awful tuneless numbers by Beyoncé or Katy Perry, always in the wrong key. And when they exhausted their song repertoire, they'd whistle.

It was like they were always trying to find out what your weakness was, what would most rattle your cage. Zeke warned me that you had to have a spine of titanium not to be bothered by the mind games, or if you couldn't manage that, the only thing to do was keep to yourself as much as possible, which was pretty lonely. Zeke didn't get sucked in. He didn't talk to anyone in the water. Not for big contests anyway. If the guys tried to talk to him during heats, all they'd get is blue steel. His eyes would be to the horizon, waiting for set waves. The judges called Zeke a super-freak, because he was so calm in the water, so exceptional under pressure, but he'd forced himself to be that way, made blanking someone feel normal.

But this wasn't even a competition; it was a charity event and it was supposed to be friendly.

Each of the adult surfers took out a child for thirty minutes, and Sephy covered for one of the local instructors who was a no-show. By five o'clock we'd taught at least eighty kids how to stand on a small crumbling wave, which felt absolutely amazing – even Beth was thawing.

To end the day, the organizers put together a fun heat, where all the coaches duked it out in one winner-takes-all mini-contest, with a bag of fresh cronuts as the prize.

It was a mixed heat and I was up against Beth, Saskia,

Sephy and a girl called Kate, plus Zeke, and three other male pros local to Florida. Zeke outclassed them completely and I knew he was the guy to beat.

But, when we were out there, it was like Zeke had lost all of his grace. It was embarrassing. His timing was off and he was choosing all the wrong waves.

Sephy locked eyes with me over an approaching ripple, and I saw Saskia further out, watching Zeke like a hawk.

One of the local guys won and held aloft his bag of cronuts like it was a solid gold trophy. We all clapped and I tried to process what had just happened. If it had been a real contest, I'd have beaten Zeke. I'd surfed better than him. Miles better.

I'd have been scrapping for third place, and he'd have come in sixth at best.

'Are you feeling all right?' I said to him as we walked up the beach.

'I'm fine.'

But he wasn't, and I knew it. I knew he wasn't fine, and I did nothing.

chapter twenty-eight

I went and made small talk with Sephy, and when I came back Zeke was staring down at his favourite shortboard, which he'd somehow managed to ding on the lifeguard booth – a rookie mistake.

The event commentators, a couple of guys who'd volunteered to help out and keep the kids motivated by shouting encouragement over the loudspeaker, were having a field day: *'Wait, wait, wait . . . would you look at this! Seems like Zeke Francis has dinged his surfboard! How'd ya manage that, Zekey-boy? Checking out the girl in the red bikini?'*

They started laughing, and I saw Zeke flush scarlet, along with the girl in the red bikini.

'Ignore them,' I said, but rather than do that, he decided that a good course of action would be to take his board and start smashing it up against the side of the lifeguard booth. Its beautiful clean lines gone forever, it was junk, a fortune of cutting-edge surf tech reduced to worthless rubbish.

It happened so quickly, and I was so aghast, that the only words I could get out were, 'Stop it, Zeke!'

The commentators continued, even louder than before, *'Whoa, he's having a meltdown! Took out some serious aggression on his surfboard just then. Who'd have thought it, Mike? All that yoga obviously not paying off for the kid.'*

'That's not good. No one wants to see that from a world-champion contender. Boo!'

Zeke's face was still burning up, whether from embarrassment or anger it was hard to say.

'Fuck it,' he said. 'Total waste of time coming here and trying to teach anyone to surf in these conditions. What a shit show.'

'He's used to winning,' they went on, getting into their stride, *'but he made mistakes today, had a shocker.'*

'Having a bit of a powwow with his girlfriend, newbie Iris Fox, from a thumpy little beach break in the United Kingdom, here today on Billabong dollars. Let's hope she can talk some sense into him!'

'Christ, just cool it, OK?' I said. When I'd first met Zeke, I couldn't believe how chilled out he seemed; the Aloha spirit practically seeped out of his pores, but I guessed that was all in the past, because the Zeke in front of me, Miami Zeke, had just gone mental.

'What the hell is going on?' I said.

He put his hands over his eyes and murmured, 'I just can't even . . .'

I wiped the sweat from my upper lip and fanned my neck with my ponytail. Florida in the afternoon sun was a furnace and the beach shimmered in the heat haze. On another day I'd have found the scene beautiful, but with everything that was happening, the heat was overwhelming and made my brain feel like it was melting into my throat.

'Zeke?' Sephy said, joining us. 'Honey, what's going on?'

He wouldn't look at either of us. He turned towards the sun-sparked ocean. Suddenly a fourth person was with us.

A spiky-haired grom of about ten was staring up at Zeke and asking, 'What up, yo? You keeping the buckled board?'

Zeke looked at the boy and said, 'Why? Wanna sell it online?'

'Free money.' The boy touched the surfboard, appraising it like some sixty-year-old pawnbroker. 'Double concave for control, extra beef for paddle power, four-fin quad set-up. You trashed it real good, but I'll take it.'

'There's no fixing that, child,' Sephy said. 'It's gonna be surfing landfill.'

'This board? Famous owner, yo. Might fetch a few hundred dollars on eBay if the crazy dude signs it. So I can have it, yeah? Yeah?'

Zeke rubbed the blond stubble on his chin and then

said, 'Kid, it's yours. You have a sharpie?'

The boy didn't have a marker pen but did produce a spray can out of his school bag. Zeke shook up the can and sprayed his name over the broken nose of the board.

'Thanks,' the boy said, and grabbed the tatty board before running back to his friends.

Zeke pulled off his shredded blue rash vest, and his bare chest looked awful, with a deep graze from the final wipeout, which must've smashed him against an underwater rock. He hadn't even complained. Little rivulets of blood snaked down his abs and stained the white drawstring of his board shorts.

'Oh lord,' Sephy said. 'Let me get something for that.'

She went in search of antiseptic cream while I took a clean T-shirt from my beach bag and dabbed the cut, hoping I could at least get the sand out of it, but Zeke flinched and turned away.

'Leave it,' he said.

'You're bleeding. We need to get you cleaned up.'

'A little blood is the least of my worries, Iris,' he said, shielding his eyes from the sun with his hand. When he moved his hand away, I half expected to see him crying, even though he'd never done that in front of me before, not even when his nan died. His eyes though were dry.

I looked around me. The narrow beach was packed with people who had come for the charity event, and at that moment it seemed as if half of them were staring at us.

A hundred yards away, a cameraman was walking our way, his lens trained on Zeke.

'Come on. We have to get out of here,' I said. 'Or this is going to end up in the surf mags.'

'Here.' Sephy was at our side again, dabbing antiseptic on to Zeke's cut. I opened my mouth to ask him something else, but he pursed his lips. Message: *Zip it.*

The commentators piped up with, '*Drama aside, it's been an awesome day and we'd like to thank the surfers who gave their time today for this great cause. Zeke Francis, if you need the number of a therapist, come see us and we'll fix you up.*'

Saskia, who'd been very obviously keeping away from me, waved Sephy over to help teach a bunch of the older kids some yoga moves. 'They'd like to learn how to do a headstand!' she shouted.

'This is what happens when people hear you once had a yoga studio,' Sephy said, 'even if it was fifteen years ago.'

As soon as she left, I grabbed Zeke's hand, which was sweating just as much as mine, but he wriggled free of my grip, raked his hands through his hair and said, 'Everything is so messed up.'

The cameraman got closer, and some other journos turned in our direction.

'Seriously, Zeke, we need to go,' I said.

Then he was right on top of us, shouting questions at Zeke, the other guys right behind.

'Bad day, Zeke?'

'No comment,' Zeke said.

'Back on the juice?'

'What? No.'

'You were on it though, right? Just last year?'

'Get lost. I don't want to talk to you people.'

'Golden boy off his head on . . . crystal meth, was it?'

'Leave him alone,' I spat. 'He said he has no comment, so bugger off.'

But the questions kept coming.

Zeke's back was rigid, his fists clenched, and I dreaded him lashing out at the guy – an assault-and-battery charge was all he needed.

'Please, Zeke, let's go,' I said, and then turned to the reporters, 'Happy now? We're off.'

We went over to Saskia and Sephy, and Zeke said, 'Mom, we have to bail. You need us to drop you at the airport? The organizers arranged us a car service.'

'No, I'm gonna help Saskia a little longer, so I'll find my own way. But I'll call you when I land at Heathrow. I love you, baby. You too, Iris.'

Heads down, hands not touching, we left the beach, questions and camera flashes hitting our backs.

chapter twenty-nine

In our hotel room, Zeke switched on the enormous TV and flaked out on the bed. I sat beside him and tried to feign interest as he flicked through the news channels.

All the way back in the car, I'd tried to get him to talk, and even though he'd made it very clear he didn't want to, I felt like I had to give it one last shot.

'So, you really have no idea why they were asking you those questions?' I said.

He gritted his teeth and said, 'Leave it. I told you already.'

'It's in the past though, yeah, the drugs?'

'How can you even ask me that? You're with me every damn day. What, am I shooting up every time you go to the bathroom?'

'No, it's just . . . I don't know what you're thinking any more.'

He shook his head and flicked the channel to CNN.

The more I tried to break through to him, the more

he pulled away. Eventually, when words had failed us, and both of us were exhausted with the effort of trying, we turned to our bodies.

Afterwards, in the stillness, sweat-cooled sheets beneath me, I realized that it had passed midnight. It was technically my birthday. I thought of home, the year before, on the day of my sixteenth birthday. Everything was so different then. Being with Zeke and winning the surf competition had changed my life so much I didn't even recognize it.

We fell asleep entwined in each other and I slept soundly, with no nightmares of a lifeless Zeke pinned down in black water.

thursday

chapter thirty

In the morning I threw back the covers and noticed blood dotted around the bedding.

My period. My implant meant they were totally irregular, but I could have really done without a period two days before surfing New Smyrna, which had the unfortunate title of 'Shark Bite Capital of the World', with more recorded attacks than any other beach on the planet.

When I stood up, I saw blood smeared on the armchair, a finger-sized splodge of blood on the pillow and a few drops on the floor.

Zeke had never once asked me about my periods since an excruciatingly awkward conversation, which included, 'The blob? What the heck does that even mean? Oh . . .' and me burning with embarrassment.

Ever since then, I had maintained silence on the subject, the sudden appearance of tampons on the toilet cistern being the sole communication to Zeke that I was in fact shedding innards.

I couldn't see that tacit silence continuing, now that I'd bled all over hotel property.

I moved the duvet to cover the mess in the bed and went to the bathroom, cupping my nether regions with as much dignity as possible.

The door was locked, and I could hear the shower running.

Zeke never locked the door when he was showering, and it occurred to me that I'd probably bled on him.

I felt a splodge of something on my cupped hand, and I rummaged through my bags.

No tampons, no sanitary towels, and the toilet roll and hotel tissues were both in the bathroom with Zeke. I briefly considered using an old vest as a sanitary towel, but it seemed a bit gross. Desperate, I searched through the wastepaper basket, past the litter of Coke cans, Hershey bars and condom wrappers and found a used serviette.

Twenty minutes passed, with me clamped around that scrunched-up tissue, until finally Zeke emerged.

'Happy birthday! Why are you on the floor? You OK?' he said, coming out of the bathroom, a towel around his waist, his hair hanging wet on his shoulders.

'Not really,' I said, pushing past him. 'You took long enough.'

'Hey, what's up? Are you sick or something?'

I locked the door behind me, just as he had done, and

tried to calm myself down as I sat on the toilet and had the heaviest period of my life.

Ten minutes later, I still sat there, turning the toilet bowl crimson, when Zeke knocked on the door, and shouted, 'I'm stepping out for a minute. You need anything?'

'Yeah. Wait for me. I'll be two seconds.'

I made myself a makeshift sanitary towel from a bundle of bog roll, flushed the crime scene, washed my hands and opened the door.

Zeke stood at the window, looking to the blue line of the sea. He wasn't usually one for gazing at seascapes, unless he was sizing up the surf, trying to work out how the tides, sandbanks and rips were working.

We'd once had an actual row about going for lunch in a room with a sea view. I wanted to go to the Headland Hotel, which had a gorgeous view of Fistral and Towan Head, but he kept suggesting inland places. Eventually he admitted he couldn't stand to look at the ocean, because one glimpse and he'd need to go surfing that second, and if he couldn't do that, he'd be in agony.

I waited for him to allude to menstruation, and when he didn't, I nodded at the sea and said, 'Charts make it even flatter today. What is it you call it – tarmac?'

'Asphalt.'

'It's doing my head right in. You must be gagging for some decent waves.'

'It's kinda nice to have some time off.'

Nice to have some time off?

'Who are you, and where is my boyfriend?' I said, trying to lighten the atmosphere.

'It's been a real long year.'

'We're only in April.'

Zeke moved away from the window and began searching for something in his rucksack. When he couldn't find it, he looked in mine. I'd never seen him do that before. One thing I'd learned about travelling with my boyfriend is that there seemed to be weird unspoken rules about touching each other's belongings. So much of our privacy had gone, but our baggage was ours alone.

'What are you after?'

'Razor. I need to shave. Look at you. You have beard-burn.'

I touched my chin, felt the soreness and got up to check it in the mirror. My chin and upper lip were pink and chafed.

'Don't worry. It'll calm down in a bit.'

'Fricking stubble. I hate that I hurt you.'

'It's fine. Honestly.'

Suddenly Zeke laughed. 'Um, you wanna talk about this?' he said, holding up the teddy he'd found in my bag.

'I don't know how that got in there,' I said, trying to look unconcerned that Zeke had found something so deeply personal and mortifying.

'You don't need to feel bad about it,' he said. 'We've all been there.'

I shoved it back in and moved a jumper to cover it. I could feel my cheeks burning up.

'I didn't bring it. It must have got in there by mistake.'

'Don't sweat it. It's no big deal.'

'My mum probably put it in there, for a joke.'

Zeke fished it out of my rucksack again.

'Uh-huh. Your mom. Does it have a name?'

I coughed. Tried to buy myself some time, but my mind was coming up with nothing. 'Maybe, maybe not.'

'It so has a name. Let me guess. Er, Maverick? No? Fistral? Something watery for sure.'

He was holding it between his thumb and forefinger, like it was toxic. I had to admit it looked quite gross and battered, but still. I snatched it away from him and held it behind my back.

'Come on, tell me already.'

'No way am I telling you that.'

'It's Teddy, right?'

The jig was up.

I walked my tiny stuffed bear over to the bed and placed him on my pillow.

'Teddy says get stuffed.'

Zeke started laughing so hard that his knees went weak and he fell back on to an armchair, eyes streaming. At last I started laughing too.

chapter thirty-one

'So I really have to run out now,' Zeke said, opening the glass doors to the balcony.

'All right.' I waited for him to tell me where he was going, but he said nothing.

'I won't be long.'

'Are you going to see Chase?'

'No, he has to work. He's helping his dad with the sale of some sky-loft condos. We probably won't see him until your contest.'

'Did your mum ring yet?'

'Yeah, her flight was on time and she made the train from Paddington. She says hi. So, I'm gonna go grab us some breakfast. You have any requests?'

'Anything that looks good. I honestly don't mind. If you're going past CVS, can you get me some, um . . . Actually I'll come with you.'

'I can pick up whatever you need.'

'No, it's fine. I need . . . girl stuff.'

'Like tampons or something?'

'Honestly, don't worry.'

'Well, I can buy that. I mean, it's clear they're not for me, so—'

'Zeke, I can buy my own tampons. I'll come with you. When are you leaving?'

'Now. Don't sweat it. I'll get your tampons. Here,' he said, turning the TV on again, 'chill.'

And with that, he practically ran out of the room, only pausing to grab his wallet from a side table.

When Zeke got back, he was grinning from ear to ear. The walk and fresh air had obviously done him good.

'Damn, I love this place.'

'What happened?'

'Miami happened.'

He handed me a carrier bag that contained three boxes of tampons in 'Lite', 'Regular' and 'Super' and four packs of sanitary towels, two with wings, and two without.

'Wow, err, thanks,' I said. 'That should keep me going for a while. Probably until Christmas.'

'I didn't know how many you needed. Don't girls bleed a lot?'

'Not quite that much.'

'It's not like I had sisters growing up. I just guessed.'

'Well, thank you. Weren't you embarrassed buying all of that?'

'No. I just told the chick on the register I manage a strip club.'

'Zeke!'

'I'm kidding. I said nothing. She said nothing. It was fine.'

'Did you do what you needed to do?'

'Yeah.'

'And you didn't run into any aggro reporters?' This was a weak joke, admittedly, and he didn't even acknowledge it.

'I might need to run out again later. I forgot to buy a razor.'

'You were literally just in CVS.'

'I got distracted by absorbencies and flow charts.'

Zeke's iPad started playing the familiar Skype ringtone.

'It's for you,' he said.

When I accepted the call, I saw my mum's face, huge, right in near the webcam.

'HELLO, MIAMI!'

'Hi, Mum.'

Before I could say anything else, the sound from the iPad speakers started to distort, due to various unseen people belting out:

'*HAPPY BIRTHDAY TO YOU – SQUASHED TOMATOES AND STEW,*

BREAD AND BUTTER IN THE GUTTER – HAPPY BIRTHDAY TO YOU.'

Zeke looked over at me, one eyebrow raised.

'Don't ask,' I said.

My mum moved her head out of the way, and I saw her hand come down to pick up the webcam, which panned around the room.

Squeezed into my living room were Aunt Zoe, Cara, Uncle Keith, Wes, Elijah, Garrett, Kelly, Zeke's stepdad Dave, my mum's elderly aunt and uncles, plus a few of my neighbours. And standing right at the back of them all, in a room he hadn't been allowed into for a decade, was my dad.

He had even less hair on his head than the last time I saw him, but had grown an alarming moustache to make up for it.

He gave me a little wave and I waved back at him, and was then hit by a wave of homesickness.

My mum's face filled the screen again.

'Aunt Zoe has something she wants to tell you.'

Aunt Zoe's face replaced my mum's, and she was beaming with excitement.

'Guess what?'

'Hi, Aunt Zoe!'

'Guess who has another cousin on the way?'

'Oh my God! You're expecting too?'

My mum's face shot into view again. 'What do you mean, "too"?'

'Calm down, Mum – I wasn't talking about me.'

'Phew. As you were.'

Aunt Zoe came back into view.

'Congratulations! You must be so excited!'

'I am! I'm only ten weeks, but I couldn't keep it a secret any longer. So who else is pregnant?'

'I don't know if I'm allowed to say . . .'

I heard Zeke's stepdad in the background cough and say, 'Sephy is!'

The camera panned around them again, and I could see them all firing questions at Dave, except Garrett and Wes, who had evidently already had the news.

'Two babies coming into the family,' my mum said. 'How wonderful. Iris, don't go making it three, and I'm talking to you too, Zeke.'

'Mum. Please.'

'Now we have that lovely bit of business out of the way, here's your real present.'

She picked up the webcam again and took it to the living-room window.

On the drive was a yellow camper van.

'It's yours,' she said.

'Oh my God, really? I have my own van!'

I heard my dad's voice say, 'Yeah, and it's not a shitheap either.'

'Wow, I love it. Thank you all so much. Woohoo!'

'Your dad's been working on it all year,' my mum said, with a slight grimace. 'Now, when are you going to come home and learn how to drive it?'

I looked at Zeke, who said, 'Your British contest?'

'Mum, it's the Billabong contest final at Fistral on the twenty-third of June.'

'That's the earliest you can come? Two months?' The disappointment was obvious in her voice.

I heard my great-uncle say, 'If the maid's short of money, I'll pay for a plane ticket. Her chap can pay for himself. I hear he ain't short of a bob or two.'

'It's not the money, Uncle Keith. It's finding the time. This is the first break we've had in months, and even here we've had to do a little work.'

'Don't she sound American now?' he said, and I cringed. The accent thing was really starting to get to me. I sounded the same as always.

'It's her agent's doing,' my mum said. 'He's always on her case. Won't let her have a minute's peace that one. If it's not contests or training, it's publicity stunts. Had her jumping from a helicopter into the sea last month. Holding her surfboard! Could've taken her eye out.'

'That was one time for a web series. And we jumped from about two metres. What was *that*?'

A blur of fur had raced past the webcam.

'Oh, that's just Leighton. He's all right.'

'What is it?'

'A cat. Honestly, Iris.'

'I couldn't see. When did you get a cat?'

'Let me see, maybe a month ago. He was found

wandering on Fistral, living on crab legs and the garbage from the takeaway. Thin as a rake, poor thing, but quite the little character.'

'You never once mentioned *getting a cat*.'

'I'm sure I must have.'

'You didn't.'

Zeke tapped me on the arm. 'Mum, can Zeke just talk to his family a minute?'

'Hi, Zeke!' said a dozen voices.

Wes, Garrett and Dave shuffled to the front of the group and crouched down.

'Hey, son,' Dave said. 'How's it going?'

'Good. Hi, bros.'

'Nice shiner,' Wes said, looking concerned.

'Yeah. Iris threw a cellphone at me.'

The ease with which he delivered this blatant lie shocked me. And that he had blamed me shocked me even more.

'Erm, what?' I said, but he shook his head at me.

'It was an accident. I asked her to pass me my iPhone and I was expecting underarm, but she throws like a Yankees pitcher.'

'Zeke,' I hissed.

He held up his phone to me, where he'd tapped out a message.

Don't wanna mention fight.

'Garrett,' Zeke said, 'can you call me back later? I need to talk to you about the apartment.'

'No problem.'

He passed the iPad over to me, and my mum appeared back on the screen.

'So what are you guys doing now?' I said.

'I booked us all into the Headland Hotel for a birthday meal in your honour. We can Skype you again when we're there, if you like. I'm sure one of these chaps has Skype on his phone.'

'It's all right,' I said. 'But take lots of pictures for me though.'

'Will do.'

My heart ached so hard. I was missing my own birthday dinner.

Even if Zeke had a birthday surprise in store for me, how could it be better than being back in Newquay with my family and friends?

chapter thirty-two

'I should have got you a trip home,' Zeke said.

'No, it's fine,' I said, wiping away tears.

'We only had a few days. I didn't think it was long enough. Flying all the way home and back. By the time we got there and unpacked, it wouldn't have been worth it. I thought that would be worse than not going home at all. But I'm starting to think I was wrong.'

'Don't feel bad. I didn't know they'd do some big thing without me.'

'They miss you. Maybe they thought if you see how much, you'll go home sooner.'

'God, I really wish I had a teleporter right now.'

'So go visit after your contest.'

'Will you come too?'

'I can't. You know I can't. I have responsibilities.'

'Screw responsibilities.'

'Not so easy.'

Nothing in Zeke's life, I was coming to understand, was easy.

'Zeke, it's my family.'

'Hey, I have a gift for you. I was planning on giving it to you tonight, but here, take it now.'

He handed me a small turquoise cardboard box, tied up in a white ribbon, with the words 'Tiffany & Co.' on the lid. I opened it up to reveal a smaller black velvet box. Rings came in those kinds of boxes, I thought, and panicked.

I hesitated.

'Aren't you gonna open it?' he said.

I opened the box, and inside were two beautiful diamond solitaire earrings.

'Bloody hell, Zeke,' I said. 'They must have cost a fortune.'

'Not really. You could wear them tonight, if you wanted.'

I was so relieved it wasn't an engagement ring. Daniel had asked me to marry him and that had ended hideously. But I also felt guilty for feeling relieved that he'd bought me earrings. To make it worse, I couldn't even wear them.

'Oh, I don't think I can.'

'Wait, you have pierced ears, right?'

'They sort of closed over a while ago. I need to get them redone.'

'Shoot, I knew I should've gone for the bracelet.'

'They're beautiful though. I love them. Thank you so much, Zeke.'

He seemed so disappointed in his choice, and I felt so guilty for my overwhelming dread at the mere thought of a ring, that I went into the bathroom, took a deep breath and re-pierced my ears myself, using the backs of the earrings. It actually didn't hurt as much as I'd expected, but my earlobes were indisputably bright red.

'Look,' I said. 'They went in after all.'

'Awesome. What do you wanna do this afternoon?'

'I don't know. Do you have anything planned?'

'Not really. Maybe watch the tube and chill before the party?'

So much for special birthday plans.

Zeke got back on the bed with the remote control.

'We have to leave for the launch at nine, so can you make sure you're ready on time? I don't think we can be late to this.'

'No problem.'

I could feel the stress building up in my veins, so I thought I'd hit the hotel gym and try to burn some of it out.

'We could go and work out first, if you want,' I said.

'I'm still hurting from yesterday,' he said, settling on a true-crime documentary.

'Fine. I'll go on my own.' Happy birthday to me.

*

I killed a couple of hours in the gym, and when I got back to the room, feeling much calmer and thinking more clearly, Zeke had docked his iPod and Sia's 'Breathe Me' was throbbing so loud the floor seemed to be vibrating.

'Trying to annoy the people in the room next door?' I asked, turning down the music.

He hadn't even noticed I'd come in. The blinds were closed and he was slumped on the bed with his head in his hands.

'What's going on?'

'I don't wanna go tonight.'

'What? You're the one that told me we *had* to go.'

'I changed my mind.'

'What the fuck, Zeke?'

'Stop with the cursing.'

'*You* swear loads. So we're just not going?'

He was scratching at a mole on his wrist so viciously that I was worried he was going to make it bleed, or go cancerous. I moved his hand away from it, but two seconds later he went back to scratching it.

'What's wrong?' I said.

'I don't want to be around people right now.'

'We're here, so we might as well go,' I said. 'Anders reckons you could pick up a few new sponsors. He'll go mad if we don't turn up. What's going on, Zeke? Is it because of your mum being pregnant?'

'What, no. I'm super-excited about that. Jesus fuck, Iris.'

'Well then, what's wrong?'

'Nothing.'

'Yeah, right.'

He stood up and started pacing around the room. 'Give me a break, will you? I'm getting real tired of all these accusations.'

'I've accused you of nothing. I've just asked you what's going on.'

'I have to be some place.'

'Fine. Go. Again.'

'I'll be back for the party. Don't stress out.'

I took off my gym vest and yoga trousers, showered, put on a sundress and went across the street to some beauty-parlour place that was kitted out with naff tropical swamp furnishings, to make it look like the Everglades. I managed to get an appointment to get my hair and make-up done, thank God, because waiting for Zeke was driving me demented. I had to get out of that bloody room.

The girl who did my hair was called Cynthia and she talked a lot about the benefits of certain products she wanted to flog me for my sun-damaged hair. I bought them all, just so she'd stop talking about them.

Zeke was losing it. Whatever he said, I could see he was unravelling.

I told myself I needed to put it out of my mind, at least until the media launch and my surf contest were over.

I couldn't handle another argument. My mum used to tell me that when the argument days were more frequent than the fun days, it was time to get out.

I checked the time. 8.33 p.m. and Zeke still wasn't back. Swallowing my pride, I called him on his cellphone.

He didn't answer, so I sat at my dressing table, painted my fingernails silver, and at 8.57 p.m., he came through the door, but it wasn't him at all.

I stared at him, open-mouthed, and couldn't find a single word to say.

'How's it look?' he smiled.

Terrible, I wanted to say. Completely and utterly terrible.

'Yeah, I buzzed it off. My head feels so cool now. Like, I could actually feel the breeze on my scalp just then.' He rubbed his hand over the back of his head, clearly appreciating the suede-like texture. He bent his knees and bowed down so I could feel it too. The hair was so short I could actually see the reef scars on his scalp.

'*You* did that? On purpose?'

'Looks pretty badass, huh?'

I was faced with a choice: be honest and tell him I hated it, which would mean hurting his feelings, or lie and tell him I liked it.

'It looks . . . so different,' I said, with the same tone of voice my mum used on me the time I dyed my hair purple.

'You think I look like Garrett, huh?'

Zeke's brother had super-short hair, but that hadn't even occurred to me. *Make it grow back right now!* was the only thought rattling around my head.

'It's just going to take some getting used to.'

'Hey, I thought you wanted this.'

'No – when did I say that?'

'You told me to get a haircut! Like, eight different times!'

'I didn't mean *all* of it. A trim.'

He looked in the mirror behind me and I could see the doubt pass over his face. A look of, *Maybe this isn't so awesome after all*. And then, *Shit, it's gonna take forever to grow back*.

'It's nice,' I said, buckling under the pressure to lie. 'You know, I actually quite like it, now I'm getting used to it. It makes you look way . . . tidier. Anyway, I'd better change into my dress.'

My ridiculously expensive designer dress, and high heels that cost twice as much again. The dress was backless, silver, with tiny jewels encrusted on the skirt. The shoes were a lighter shade of silver and had a four-inch stiletto heel. The sales assistant had said that the more you paid for shoes, the better they felt, because it was all to do with the quality of the leather. I didn't agree. These were Manolo Blahniks, and when I put them on I had all the grace of a three-legged pig. Zeke came out of the bathroom and stopped in his tracks.

'Wow,' he said and whistled, which made me feel even more terrible for reacting so negatively to his hair.

'What?' I said, instinctively putting my hand to my hair, which the hairdresser had blow-dried straight and slicked into a ballerina bun. 'I look weird, don't I?' I said, feeling incredibly self-conscious.

'No. You look great,' he said. 'Like one-hundred-per-cent smoking hot.'

He had every reason to echo my words back at me: tell me I looked 'tidier', or that it would take some getting used to, but instead he'd been completely lovely. The dart of guilt sticking in my heart would take a while to shift.

I had never owned such an expensive outfit in my life. But when I looked in the mirror, I couldn't really spot myself behind the make-up and glitz.

Zeke changed into a rented tuxedo. He had a definite Bond vibe going on.

I looked at the clock and said, 'We're gonna be late if we don't leave right now.'

'Let's go.'

'I'm not overdressed? Because it seems like a lot of effort for a surf party. I could put on one of my Billabong beach dresses, look more the surfer-girl part?'

'I'm guessing you don't know a heap about the Fontainebleau.'

chapter thirty-three

We'd just got into the car that Chase had lent Zeke, when Kelly called me again.

'Iris,' she said, 'can you talk? Is Zeke there?'

'Yeah, and yeah.'

'Call me back when he's not with you, will you?'

'Why?'

'Just because, OK?'

Garrett, I thought. He'd have done something irritating – probably being poly with half of Newquay – and Kelly didn't want Zeke within earshot while she slagged off his brother.

'OK, but it'll be a few minutes. Driving.'

'Fine. Just don't forget.'

The sunroof was down and as we drove my hair was starting to come loose from the bun. I looked in the glovebox, found a baseball cap for the Miami Marlins and stuck it on backwards in an attempt to make Zeke laugh, which he did.

'You feel like a driver's lesson? Since you have a car now and all.'

'A van, and no, thanks.'

'Why not? When I was your age I'd had my permit for a year.'

'Yeah, you're American. I only qualified for my provisional licence today.'

'Incorrect.'

'I think I know when my own birthday is.'

'I'm Hawaiian. I surf for Hawaii, not the US. I thought you'd be excited to learn.'

'I will learn. I just don't want my first driving lesson to be from my boyfriend, on a foreign road where I don't even understand the road signs. In his mate's car. Especially when that car is a Porsche.'

'I wouldn't have asked you if I didn't think you could handle it.'

'Zeke,' I said, exasperated, 'no, thank you.'

'OK. Forget I mentioned it.'

Zeke was a crazy driver at the best of times, but he was even worse in America, so he fitted right in on the roads of Florida, where drivers undertook us at the same time as others overtook us. It was mayhem, but Zeke seemed fine with it. He clocked my pale face and said, 'Feeling slammed from the gym? I have some Advil if you need it.'

'Nah, a bit of period pain, but . . .'

'Yeah?'

Normally, I'd have defaulted to my usual strategy of covering up feelings that were difficult to talk about, but something about being on the road, side by side rather than face to face, made it easier to be honest with him.

'I wanna be straight with you, all right? So, when you said that about me throwing a mobile phone at you, that was not cool.'

Zeke took his eyes off the road to look at me for a second.

'How come?'

'If you were gonna lie, you should've asked me first.'

'I know, but it was just one little lie.'

'Not the point. You seemed really convincing, by the way. I'd never have known you were talking bollocks.' I let that hang for a moment, to make sure he knew what I was getting at.

Zeke turned to me again and gave me a weak grin. 'I'm sorry. You forgive me?'

'Why didn't you run it past me first?'

'I guess I was worried you'd say no and then I'd have been left telling them I'd been brawling with a stranger.'

'Me saying no is not a reason.'

'Sure it is.' He gave me a cheeky grin, but it didn't work.

'Zeke, you can't just not ask me things in case I say no. That's not how it works. I get a choice.'

'I know. I'm sorry. I'm not good at this. I was never in a relationship before. Not like this. I usually bailed the first day it wasn't fun.'

'What's that supposed to mean? Thanks very much.'

'No. I'm just saying I never, like, committed before. This is new for me. You have to train me, cos I was on my own for a long time.'

'We've been together half a year.'

'And for the eighteen and a half years before that, I only had to worry about me. So tell me when I'm being a dick. Keep telling me.'

I thought about this.

'No problem.'

'So, uh,' he went on, looking sheepish, 'what should I do, when you do stuff?'

'Me?'

'Yeah. Like the jealousy thing you have about other girls. What am I supposed to do about that?'

'Don't remind me,' I groaned.

'It's not your fault. I'd have been pissed too, about the Inga thing, if the situation was the other way. But I'm gonna still be friends with girls. You cool with that?'

'Yes. And I'm gonna be mates with lads.' A needle of guilt pricked at my conscience. 'By the way, I, uh, gave Seb my business card.'

'The guy who punched me?'

'The guy you *pushed*. He's actually called me a few

times today. At least, I think it's him. I don't recognize the number, so I haven't answered.'

'If he calls again, I'll pick up and set him straight,' Zeke said, pretending to look serious. 'I mean, he gets a pass on the punch, because I had that coming, but he doesn't get to harass my girl.'

My girl.

I'd told myself I liked him calling me that, but I realized then that a tiny part of me had always rebelled, wanted to point out that I wasn't anybody's girl, no matter how hot that anybody happened to be, no matter how high his rank in the list of the world's best wave riders.

He took a hand from the steering wheel and touched my wrist. 'Ignore the calls and he'll soon figure out you're not interested.'

'All right.'

'Iris, since we're talking about stuff that we've been thinking about . . .'

'Yeah?'

He started scratching at something on the side of his face. A zit under the surface of the skin maybe, or a mossie bite. Scratching seemed to be becoming a thing with him.

'What, Zeke?'

His whole body looked tense and I braced myself, waiting for him to say whatever major thing he had to get off his chest.

Suddenly his shoulders relaxed and he said, 'Condoms.

Do we still need those? I mean, it's not like anyone's sleeping around, so . . .'

I gave him a hard stare, trying to work out if he was serious.

'Yeah, we need them.'

'After we get checked out, and get the all-clear, we can ditch them, yeah? Since you're on birth control and all.'

'The implant is ninety-nine-per-cent effective.'

'Uh-huh, so we don't need to worry, right?'

'Yes, we absolutely do need to worry. There's a one-per-cent chance it won't be effective.'

I spent loads of time worrying about getting pregnant; I could get lost in pregnancy worry spirals that lasted hours. Even a slight chance of getting knocked up felt terrifying.

'Google says maybe one women in a thousand gets pregnant on the implant. You'll be fine.'

'What's so bad about condoms?'

'Err, nothing . . .'

'Zeke, this is mental. I cannot risk getting pregnant. I was actually wondering if we should be using the ultra-safe condoms. The really thick ones with extra spermicide.'

Zeke looked deeply sceptical about this, and it occurred to me that this conversation had probably not gone the way he'd hoped.

'Whatever makes you comfortable,' he said with a sigh.

'Cool,' I said, already planning to scour the next pharmacy. There wasn't much I could control, but this I could.

'I love you, Iris,' he said, taking his eyes off the road again to look at me. One of his intense looks that made my heart beat faster.

The lights turned green and Zeke put his foot down.

chapter thirty-four

When we arrived at the media launch, I discovered that the Fontainebleau Hotel was a vast waterfront structure lit up like the *Titanic*.

The noise of the party – the music, the voices – could be heard from two blocks away.

We got out of the car and Zeke gave the keys to a young man in livery, who drove it off somewhere to park it.

'I just have to call Kelly back,' I said to Zeke. Our names were ticked off the guest list by a softly spoken young woman in a black lace minidress and we walked along the red carpet and down the stairs into the glittering lobby, whose enormous chandelier I felt sure must have been designed by a man with issues. The lobby was crammed with people and every one of them was dressed impeccably; the heels of their shoes tapping out privilege on sparkling quartz floors.

'OK. I'm gonna go join Anders. Come find us when you're done.'

I went outside, past a woman wearing a metal cage skirt, which was also a champagne fountain, and came face to face with Saskia, who was looking incredible in a tiny gold dress that made her legs seem endless.

'Hi,' I said.

'I'm really not in the mood for this, Iris,' she replied, giving me one of her cool stares.

'I didn't do any drugs.'

'But you were going to, weren't you? If I hadn't walked in. You know, when I withdrew from the Billabong competition so you could take my place, I believed I was doing the right thing. The decent thing. And I thought this opportunity would make you and Zeke happy.'

'It did! I appreciate it so much, Sas. I really do.'

'I simply don't believe that, Iris.'

'Look, maybe we can talk properly tonight?'

'When I'm ready to talk, I'll phone you. Until then, I'd appreciate it if you left me alone.'

'Well, you have to interview me after my contest heats on Saturday.'

'Marvellous. I'll certainly look forward to that. Have a nice night.'

Her tone sounded a lot like the one you'd expect from someone telling a former friend to 'have a nice life'.

'Sas, I'm sorry!' But she had already walked away.

I took off my shoes and sat down on the edge of the hotel's pool, dangling my feet into the warm water.

Nobody else was doing this, but I didn't much care. If there is a pool, I am going to stick my feet in it at the very least, no question.

Kelly picked up the phone.

'Sorry. Was getting the washing off the line. I totally forgot about it, and had to go out in the dark, because it rains every bloody night.'

I thought of her little back garden and for a second I was standing in it, the washing basket between us. I thought of the double hammock, where we'd wasted so many afternoons, staring up at the fairy lights in the cherry tree as we put the world to rights, or threw pebbles over the head of the little gold Buddha that the elderly woman next door called unlucky for no reason we could fathom. Water fights we'd had in that garden, picnics, dance-offs.

'Hey, guess what? I'm at a party and Cameron Diaz and Chris Hemsworth are here somewhere.'

'Cool! Get photos. So, are you alone now?' she asked me, her voice nervous.

'Yes. What's going on, Kel? How come you're still awake? Has Garrett done something?'

'Garrett? No. Well, nothing worth mentioning. You know what he's like. Bit of a moron at the best of times.' I found myself nodding at this. Garrett was the sort of person who always appeared to be mildly inebriated, even when he was stone-cold sober. 'I, um, I talked to Daniel.'

'Daniel?' I heard the tone of my voice shoot up. Kelly

despised Daniel for cheating on me with my friend Cass, and she would never talk to him unless she absolutely had to.

'Yeah. I know, shocking, right? But he's trying to get a message to you. He says he can't get through on your phone – it won't even ring.'

Because I'd added his number to my phone's block list.

'Plus, he says you've deleted him from Facebook and aren't answering emails.'

All of my emails from Daniel were diverted to a folder called 'Do Not Read This Shit', and I never, ever looked in there, not even when I was hammered. Not even when I was miserable and wanted to wind myself into more misery.

I didn't dare tell Kelly I'd called him from South Beach.

'What kind of message?'

'It's about Zeke.'

'Ha. Should've known. Well, I don't really give a toss what Daniel says about Zeke. He's probably just making stuff up to cause trouble.'

'No, it's not like that. He says someone's written an article about Zeke that's gonna break soon.'

Oh God, I thought. This is why. This is why those journalists were acting that way on the beach. Zeke was on their hit list.

'So what?' I said. 'Zeke has loads of articles

written about him.' This was true. In the time since I'd been seeing Zeke, his press coverage had rocketed. He wasn't quite on the same level as the likes of John John Florence and Sebastian Zietz, but he was getting there.

'Not like this one. This one's not complimentary. Have you heard of a reporter called Mitch Jacobs?'

'I don't think so.'

Could he have been the guy on the beach? Had he said his name? I didn't remember. Whatever was happening, I didn't want Kelly to be involved. She had enough going on in her own life, what with all her coursework and exams, without taking on my problems.

'Kel, don't stress about it. Haters gonna hate. No big deal.'

'I dunno. I think it could be serious. Daniel said people in the surf forums are already talking about it and the piece hasn't even dropped yet.'

'So some journo writes a bitchy article. Who cares?'

I desperately wanted Kelly to stop talking about this.

'The article's called "Methsurfing".'

'Oh, crap.'

Zeke had a history with meth. It was hidden history, so the journalist must have got to someone close to Zeke. Offered them money to talk.

'I don't know for sure that it's about Zeke because apparently the names are changed. But the story's about a young pro-surfer from Hawaii called – get this – "Zach Fletcher".'

Zeke Francis to Zach Fletcher wasn't much of a leap.

'Daniel's sure about this?'

'He seems pretty sure, yeah.'

'Kel . . .'

'Daniel Penhaligon is an arsehole, don't get me wrong, but I can tell when he's full of shit,' Kelly said.

'Lovely image, mate. Thanks for that.'

'What are you gonna do, Iris?'

'Dunno. I don't want to mess with Zeke's head. I've been doing enough of that lately as it is. He has to do well tonight, and in his next contest.'

So much of surfing was psychological. A surfer's head game was probably the most important element of their performance. Distractions almost always meant defeat.

And Zeke's surfing was already all over the place. At contests he was either placing in the top two and standing on the podium, or burning out in the first round, due to some stupid error. The commentators were starting to call him a streaky surfer, saying sometimes he was really on and sometimes he was really off; speculating that it came down to how he was feeling emotionally. The name Streaky Zeke was starting to be a thing.

His place on the following year's tour was pretty secure, as he was fifteenth on the board, but many more mistakes and he'd be in the danger zone.

'So you're just going to say nothing?'

'It could be some other surfer. I don't wanna get Zeke all freaked out for no good reason. Maybe Daniel's got it wrong.'

Kelly cleared her throat. 'Do you think you should ring him?'

'Daniel?'

'Yeah.'

I couldn't tell Kelly I'd already called him. I didn't even want to remember it myself.

'I don't think I can. Not after the way we left things—'

'Oh, bugger,' Kelly said, sounding panicky and cutting me off. 'Bloody Garrett's chucking stones at my window. That boy's got some cracking timing. I've gotta go, mate. Good luck with your heats.'

'Don't tell Garrett, will you, Kel?' I said, but she'd already hung up.

When I looked up, Anders was looking down at me.

'Citizen Fox,' he said. 'Why do you look like the Hulk just drop-kicked your hamster?'

chapter thirty-five

'Good to see you too, Anders.'

Standing next to him was an attractive woman in her thirties, wearing a sequinned playsuit and leather gladiator sandals that snaked up around perfectly white ankles. Her nose had a sprinkling of freckles and her mousy hair hung in a fashionably messy bob.

Even Anders looked smart; for once he wasn't dressed like a teenager. The T-shirt he'd been wearing the last time I saw him had depicted a male surfer surrounded by topless girls, with the slogan: *If it swells, ride it,* which surely took the prize for Most Irritating T-Shirt 2015.

I wondered if he'd heard any of my conversation with Kelly.

'Nice work in Santa Cruz. You're starting to relax. Something to write home about – at last.'

'Yeah, it took me a while to get over the stage fright. Hi,' I said, looking at the woman and waiting to be introduced. She held out her hand to me.

'Nice to meet you,' she said. She had an Australian accent.

'Selina here is a documentary filmmaker,' Anders said, winking, for reasons I didn't yet understand. 'She made the eco-surf movie about the dolphin drives. Selina, this is Iris. She's from Cornwall.'

I'd seen the film. It was good, if harrowing. It won awards on the indie circuit, a fact I knew because years ago I'd liked its Facebook page and my news feed still got the updates.

'I loved that film,' I said.

'Oh. Thank you very much.' She looked really embarrassed and I wondered how with those four words I'd somehow managed to say the wrong thing.

'I really did,' I said, in case my voice had made it sound as if I was being sarcastic.

She smiled. 'It's always so weird to meet people who have seen it. And that was always the aim – don't get me wrong – to have the movie out there, but now it is out there in the big wide world, it has its own life. Sometimes I forget it's even mine, or worry that I'll never again be able to make something successful. Classic case of Impostor Syndrome, I guess.'

'Impostor Syndrome?' Anders frowned.

Even though I'd never heard that term before, I could guess what it meant, because I felt it too. Every single day.

'Nothing you'd ever suffer from, Anders . . .' Her

eyebrows flicked up for a second and I could tell she disliked his arrogance. 'So, where's Zeke?'

'He's around somewhere, looking for you, Anders. And getting a drink probably.'

'Selina and Zeke go way back,' Anders said.

Was he trying to suggest that Selina and Zeke had been in a relationship? She was obviously really talented and she seemed nice, but she was at least twice his age.

Zeke appeared, his arm wrapping around my shoulders.

'Good GOD, Zeke!' Anders said. 'What the fuck have you done to your hair?'

'Yeah, I thought it was time for a change.'

Anders was staring as if Zeke had arrived at the party with something unspeakable smeared across his forehead.

'You've just reduced your future net worth by thirty per cent,' Anders said, pursing his lips. 'I hope you realize that.'

'It's just hair, Anders. It'll grow. Hey, I'm so glad you guys met,' Zeke said, smiling at Selina. 'Selina is one of my favourite people in the world. Did you see her film, Iris? It *changed the world*. Selina, this is my girlfriend, Iris.'

It was awkward, because Anders had already sort of introduced us, but not quite, in that he hadn't told Selina what I did for a living, so I heard myself saying, 'I'm a pro-surfer too.' Words that always made me feel stupidly self-conscious.

'You know, Iris, I'm planning a documentary based around the pro-surf teen scene. Maybe you could do some surfing for us, if you're interested.'

'Really? Wow, I'd be honoured.'

'And you're coming to the Faroe Islands next spring? We'd love to have you with us. Zeke's committed to two weeks.'

I didn't think I could handle seeing a load of pilot whales get stabbed to death and not being able to help in any way. I'd have nightmares about it for the rest of my life, and I was already having enough nightmares.

'I'll try.'

'Iris has been to loads of our meetings – she's totally coming.'

'It's important,' Selina said, 'to be there, to observe and document.'

Selina left and Zeke said, 'Hold on, Selina. I'll walk with you. *Gotta take a leak*,' he murmured in my direction, making a split second of eye contact. 'Back in a sec.'

Anders and I stood there awkwardly. I thought about the phone call with Kelly and wondered whether I should let him know what she'd told me. Anders treated me like a little kid at the best of times, so I knew he might not take what I had to say seriously, but if something was going on, he was probably the best person to find out the details and do whatever needed to be done to get it under control.

I watched a pelican fly a track across the hotel

grounds, and said, 'Um, I might need to talk to you about something.'

'Do *not* tell me you're pregnant,' he said, eyes to the sky. 'Just do not.'

'Jesus, Anders. Course not. I wish people would stop thinking that.'

'What then?'

'I've heard that there might be an article coming out. About Zeke.'

'I should hope so too, the number of press releases I've sent out this past month.'

'No, I mean some sort of drugs-investigation article.'

'Where are you getting this?'

'Someone back home . . .'

'The shit-for-brains no-neck who stabbed Zeke?'

As descriptions went, it was fairly accurate, but it still irritated me to hear Anders say it.

'Daniel, yes.'

'What could that little turd possibly know about anything?'

'He saw a rumour on a forum.'

Anders paused, running the odds. 'Right. Did it ever occur to you that your delightful ex-boyfriend might be trying to stir up trouble? Spreading rumours to knock Zeke off his game right before this media launch, where he could very well gain tens of thousands of dollars in new sponsorship?'

That had occurred to me; of course it had.

'Maybe, but I don't think that's what's happening.'

'I must say I'm surprised you're even in touch with that waste of space.'

Anders seemed to have developed a serious loathing for Daniel and something about his insults made my skin prickle. It was one thing for Zeke to have a go at Daniel, because that was justified, given their history, but I really didn't appreciate Anders doing it.

'I'm not in touch with him. Kelly saw him, and she reckons he's for real.'

'And Kelly is?'

'Brown hair, big smile. She was at the Headland Hotel party. You spoke to her, remember?'

Anders shrugged, then stared at me hard, trying to work out if any of this was worth taking seriously.

'I'll make some enquiries. In the meantime, say nothing – and I mean nothing – about this to Zeke. You hear me, Iris?'

'Yeah, I hear you.'

'Because I just have one point to make here: Zeke is not in good shape. Whatever's happening between you two, it's messing with his head.'

Whatever problems Zeke and me had were private. Since when had Zeke been talking to Anders about our relationship?

Before I could find a way to ask, Anders continued,

'I'm worried Zeke might be . . . leaving firm ground.'

'So you think he *is* taking drugs?'

'That's not what I said, and I don't want those words put in my mouth. But, since you're the best placed, I need you to watch him. Treat him like a toddler, by which I mean do not, under any circumstances, allow him to wander off. Can you do that?'

'Yeah, course. I wasn't intending to ditch him, Anders. He is my boyfriend.'

'You have to be one-hundred-per-cent on the ball this evening, you hear? Because I know that boy, and something is not right with him. I need him on his A-game.'

'Zeke's always on his A-game.'

Anders stared at me, trying to work out if I was taking the mick. I wasn't though. When it came to his work obligations, Zeke always tried his best. I'd never seen him deliberately let anyone down. But maybe, I thought, Anders had other experiences.

chapter thirty-six

I found Zeke chatting to a group of guys from the tour, and knocking back the free champagne.

'Did you see Saskia yet?' I asked.

'No, but I ran into Gabe at the bar and he said she's here someplace. You hear Christina Aguilera is singing tonight?'

I felt my eyes widen. Christina was one of my secret music crushes and her songs had featured heavily in my iPod playlists the summer I met Zeke.

'What? Are you having me on?' I said, trying to stop myself from woohooing and breaking out into a happy dance.

'Of course not. I just ran into one of her backing singers that I sorta know.'

'Who's that then?'

'Oh. Um, I think her name is Jenna. Or Jennifer. Something like that. She said Christina is tonight's surprise guest.'

So this was apparently my world now. Parties with Cameron Diaz and Christina Aguilera?

Zeke squeezed my hand and said, 'Come on, let's see if we can track her down. She'll be round here someplace.'

'Jenna?'

'Come to think of it, I'm pretty sure she's called Gina. But I meant Christina.'

As we left the lobby area and walked towards the ballroom, I almost bumped boobs with a girl who stepped out right in front of me. She had a short blonde pixie cut, baby blue eyes and what had to have been false eyelashes. She was wearing a metallic blue minidress, lacquered stilettos and she looked like some Sixties fashion model about to pose for *Playboy*. She cut across us and, right in front of me, like I wasn't even there, she batted her eyelashes at Zeke, put a piece of paper into his hand and said in an ultra-sultry voice, 'Zeke Francis. You're so hot. Here's my number. If you're ever lonely, call me, baby.'

It was awful. Like some bloody Carly Rae Jepsen song.

'Whoa,' was all I could say.

Once again a girl was brazenly hitting on Zeke, with me right there. I looked at him, and his mouth was open, like he wanted to say something but he had no idea what.

'Loving the hair,' she said. 'Told you you'd look hotter without the mop.'

'Well, maybe you'd look hotter if you kept your opinions to yourself,' I said.

'Uhhh, okaaaaay,' she said, in a very strong Southern drawl. Then she flashed Zeke a phony smile and walked off, swaying her hips as she went.

When Zeke looked back to me, his face was flushed and he seemed upset.

'Nice,' I said to him.

'And here it comes.'

'God, sucks to be you, right?' I laughed, but it came out in this weird, shrill way that sounded totally fake and angry.

'You're mad at me? Again? How am I responsible for what just happened?'

'Well, you weren't exactly fending her off, were you? You took her number.'

'I can't be dropping trash in the middle of the Fontainebleau. But I'm sure as hell not gonna call that chick.'

'Sounds like you called her already. She *told you* your hair would look better short, remember?'

'Iris, I swear I never in my whole life saw her before.'

'Sure?' I said, 'because she might have had different-coloured hair or something when you slept with her, and anyway you were probably stoned and can't even remember.'

Zeke stood there, looking as if he was facing a firing squad.

'I'm pretty sure I never met her before just now,' he said, with no conviction at all.

I was furious. At the girl. At Zeke. Mostly at myself.

Why couldn't I let this stuff wash over me, like Kelly would have? My relationship with Zeke was turning into a hideous game of whack-a-mole. As soon as we'd dealt with one problem, another reared its head.

Zeke still held the scrap of paper between his long fingers.

My eyes burned into him, and without even glancing at the number he balled up the paper in his fist and put it in his trouser pocket.

'Please don't be pissed. Let's just move on, forget about this,' he said.

'I'm not pissed. I was just thinking that Garrett was right about the pro-hoes.'

Back in Newquay Zeke's brother had warned me about the girls who followed the surf tour, offering themselves up freely to the pro-surfers. Pro-hoes, Garrett had called them, which at the time I had thought was harsh.

'That's kind of mean, Iris. So much for the feminist sisterhood.'

I blinked. 'Was that not a bona-fide pro-ho right there? I mean, she just pretty much offered you sex. While you were walking with your girlfriend.'

Hearing myself, I knew Zeke was right: I sounded horrendously mean, which just made me angrier.

'Maybe she didn't know you were my girlfriend.'

'Oh, please. She knew. And how can you even defend

that? That was . . . brazen. Or did you like it? Give you an ego boost, did it?'

'Sure, I mean, I'm flattered, but I'd rather some random girl didn't tick off my girlfriend.'

'You're flattered? Why? Because you think she's so pretty?'

'Iris, this whole conversation is stupid.'

'Well, don't get all sensitive about it.'

'*Me* get sensitive? You've been crazily sensitive all week. I just can't seem to get through to you any more. I'm busting my ass trying to do the right thing, but it's like you don't trust me at all.'

We'd moved outside and taken the private path to the beach, where we stood face to face. A light rain started to fall, but I wouldn't have moved even in a hurricane.

'You don't get it,' I said. 'I have no one here. You said so yourself.'

'You have me,' he said.

'And you're the problem more often than the solution.'

A group of Zeke's fellow team riders came down on to the beach to smoke, and they stood huddled in a group, shooting amused glances in our direction.

'I can't stand it, Zeke. It never stops.'

Zeke sneezed. Then he sneezed three more times.

'Bless you. You getting ill?'

'Hay fever. I don't get sick,' he replied.

'You just get numbers.'

'So, yeah, sometimes girls give me their number, but that happens to all pro-surfers. I throw them right in the trash. Not like some surfers, who laugh behind the girls' backs and give the numbers to homeless guys and drifters.'

'Or the ones that call the numbers? That's not you, right?'

'Iris. Come on. I don't call the numbers. We're with each other almost every minute. How am I running off to see other girls?'

'Don't put yourself out on my account. Go. Run off with ALL the girls.'

'I don't want that. But am I gonna keep talking to people, keep making friends? Sure I am.'

'Why do you even care about making friends everywhere?'

'Are you serious?'

'Yeah.'

'Because it's the best thing about travelling – soaking up new cultures, making connections with new people. That's what it's all about, and it blows my mind that you would even ask me that question, because I would think you oughta know the answer already.'

But that was how it was for him, not me. I didn't feel like that. I had friends, and they were all waiting for me in Newquay.

The reality was that I was an introvert and Zeke was

an extrovert and I'd known that from the start. So why did I keep fighting our differences, trying to make us the same?

Rather than staying open and working on figuring myself out, I was letting my jealousy speak for me.

'How many numbers do you get? On an average contest day?'

'I don't know. It's not like I hang on to them and keep them in a big pile on my bed, which I go count every night.'

One of the other team riders started laughing, and our argument continued in fierce whispers.

'A *big* pile? How big is big?'

'Are you ever gonna quit this conversation?'

'Yeah, it's unlikely.'

Zeke sneezed again.

'You're getting a cold,' I said.

'I'm not getting a damn cold.'

He was so stubborn that even if he had the world's most virulent flu, he'd power through rather than admit it.

'So, how many?'

'I don't know, maybe a hundred when I make it to the final. Depends on how big the crowd is that day.'

'A *hundred* girls that you don't even know walk up to you and give you their telephone number? In one day?'

'Crazy, right?'

'It's horrible!'

'It's like I already told you – I don't call any of them.

257

I have a girlfriend and I would never disrespect you like that.'

'These other guys,' I said, waving my hands around to indicate the lads in the middle of the tobacco cloud, 'call those girls? They call complete strangers? For sex?'

'I mean, probably. The ones they think are cute.'

'Have you ever called one of those numbers?'

'Please tell me you're not gonna go all Vanessa on me,' Zeke said, smiling weakly, as if he was about to make a bad joke.

'What? Who's Vanessa? I have literally no idea what you're talking about.'

'A girl I dated when I was thirteen. She bought me an elastic wristband and made me snap it every time I thought about another girl. Her strategy was actually pretty effective.'

'I know you changed the subject, by the way. Just in case you think I didn't catch that. You still haven't answered my question. Have you ever called one of those beach girls?'

I turned to look at him, but he was looking at his phone, his forehead creased in a frown that showed every fine line of sun damage.

'What?' I said.

'Give me a second.' He put up one hand and tapped at his phone with the other.

'Well, don't let me interrupt your texting.'

'It's Wes.'

'I asked you a question, Zeke.'

'You know, this conversation is really not going anywhere good.'

'You have. Oh my God. You've called total strangers for . . . for a *booty call*.'

'I'm not an animal. I took them to dinner first.'

'When you said you had one-nighters, I thought you meant girls you met in bars or clubs or something. Not saddo randoms who walked up to you on some beach and gave you a piece of paper with their number on it. Drug-resistant gonorrhoea is out there. My mum used to go on about it all the time.'

'I don't have drug-resistant gonorrhoea, Iris. I'm not an idiot. I never went bareback.'

'Bareback? What is that supposed to – urggh! Gross.'

One of the guys in the huddle jogged over to us, grinning. He held his hand up to Zeke for a high five, and said, 'Up top!' but Zeke shook his head no.

'Well, congratulations, Zeke Francis. You are living every teenage boy's wet dream,' I said.

'Not lately,' he replied, and his voice wasn't a whisper any more. We were basically entertaining the whole beach with our argument.

'Charming. That's really nice of you to say.'

'I didn't mean it like that. You know I didn't. I just meant I'm not some manwhore any more, and I haven't been that way in a long time.'

'Just own it.'

'OK, I'm owning it. Newsflash: sometimes I act like a self-entitled shithead.'

'That's not news to anyone.'

He sighed. 'Is this because you're on your period?'

This got a really loud laugh from the smokers.

'Don't even go there,' I hissed at him. 'Just don't even go there.'

I stormed off back into the party, found a powder room and spent the next twenty minutes in hot, aching silence.

friday

chapter thirty-seven

When I finally emerged, Anders appeared, a bottle of champagne in his hand and an expression like he had a mouthful of stinging nettles. Waves of hostility radiated from him, and I wanted to turn and walk as fast as I could in the other direction, but unfortunately he'd seen me.

'He in there?'

'Zeke?'

'Yes, obviously Zeke.'

'In the ladies' powder room? Er, no.'

'Well, where the hell is he?'

'I don't know.'

'Bloody brilliant.' Anders paced around me, waving the bottle in the air and pouting. 'What did I tell you? You had one thing to do. One thing.'

'I'm not his keeper, Anders. He can do whatever he wants.'

'Keep an eye on him. That's all you had to do. That's why you're here.'

'That's all I had to do? That's why I'm here? What about all my training and my own surf contests? Am I just here to look after Zeke?'

'Zeke is important. This is business, Iris. Business in which a great deal of money is at stake. Zeke needs to be kept on the straight and narrow.'

I took a deep breath. I had something to ask him; something that I'd avoided asking for months.

'Is that why I won the Billabong showdown? So I could be Zeke's babysitter?'

I could see the disdain sweep across his face. He didn't like me. He hid it, tried to be civil, but deep down Anders thought I was bad news.

'Don't be so ridiculous. Are you suggesting I forced Saskia to step down? Paid her off?'

In for a penny, in for a pound.

'Did you?'

'No, and I resent the implication. I don't like the way you're conducting yourself, Iris. You're on the first step of the ladder. You have a long way to go, and judging by your efforts so far, you might never get there.'

'Cheers.'

'You are just one of my surfers, Iris. Just one, and when it comes down to it, you're replaceable.'

'Not really, since I don't have an identical twin.'

'Aren't you funny? I think we both know that Zeke is the star in your relationship. If you are anything at all, it is the support act and, quite frankly, if I was picking the support act, I wouldn't have picked you.'

'Tell me something I don't know. You haven't liked me from the first night you met me.'

'You mean the night your boyfriend stabbed one of the most promising young surfers in the world?'

That was one of the worst nights of my life, a fact that Anders didn't give a shit about.

'Ex-boyfriend. And Zeke being a star doesn't make me his support act. I'm surfing for me, no one else.'

'How well are you doing in this little Billabong competition, Iris? Zeke is competing in the *World Qualifying Series*. Do you understand the difference between his position and yours?'

'Zeke is older and more experienced. He's been surfing since he could stand. You expect me to be a better surfer than Zeke already?'

'Well, sweetness, I expected you to be higher in the rankings than fourth.'

'OK, it's not great, but I haven't been surfing for all that long, so I'm actually pretty pleased with that. And while we're on the subject of things we expected, I expected you to be able to talk to me as a surfer in my own right, without going on about Zeke all the time.'

'You know what, Iris? I'm getting sick of your attitude. If you're not happy with my representation, maybe you should look elsewhere.'

'Maybe Zeke should too.'

Anders flashed his teeth at me in a smile that had zero warmth. 'Are you threatening me?'

'No, but I don't like the way you've been talking to me, and I don't think Zeke would like it much either.'

I took a second to appreciate this new tougher side of me that I'd developed since touring. I learned pretty quickly that people would take the piss if you let them, and I wasn't going to stand for it any more. Anders was the worst culprit for taking a mile if you gave him a millimetre.

'I see. You're going to run off and "tattle" to Zeke, are you? Tell him how upset you are because of the big bad surf agent. Marking my card, are you? I'm quaking in my boots.'

I looked down at his shiny leather shoes that probably cost even more than my Manolos. Anders would never quake in anything. There was nothing he couldn't handle or fix. He'd always get his own way, in the end. But I wasn't going to let him talk down to me, even if it did mean him going nuclear.

'Just you try it,' he seethed. 'Tell Zeke to fire me and see what happens. There is no way on God's green earth that Zeke Francis is ever letting me go.'

'Yeah, we'll see.'

He walked right up to me, closer than was comfortable, and said, 'BOG OFF,' before flouncing back into the ballroom.

I was angry, but I had to laugh. He was such a drama queen. I honestly didn't know how Zeke had put up with him for all these years. Yeah, the scheming and the workaholic tendencies were probably good qualities to have in an agent, but the rest of it, including the condescension and huffiness, made him seem like he was more trouble than he was worth.

I ran it all through my head, convincing myself that I'd been in the right, and that I hadn't said a word out of turn. I managed that for not even two minutes.

With my anger evaporating and remorse already setting in, I went to look again for Saskia. I hated that she was mad at me, and it was beginning to feel as if I was burning all my bridges, when I didn't have that many to begin with.

I was scouring the crowded ballroom for her when someone touched my elbow.

'Face of Billabong UK. Greetings!'

Wearing a tropical-print evening dress slashed to the navel, and with her hair cut into a 1920s bob, was the very last person I expected to see.

chapter thirty-eight

'Lily?' I said, rushing to hug my sister. 'Oh my God, how are you here? I thought you were travelling through Greece?'

'Zeke paid for me to fly out here as a birthday surprise for you. He wanted Mum and Kelly to come too, but Mum couldn't get the time off during term-time, and Kelly's got exams. Happy birthday, little sis!'

At which point, I burst into tears.

'Oh dear, what's wrong?' she said, putting her arm around my waist.

'Everything.'

'I thought something must be up. Zeke said he'd meet me outside, but he never showed.'

'It was probably when we were arguing on the beach. I don't even know where he is – I think he left.'

'Come and tell me all about it,' she said. 'And don't cry, because you're messing up your nice make-up.'

She ushered me into the toilets again, sat me down on

a blue velvet armchair in the shape of a giant stiletto shoe and handed me tissues.

'So what's happening – what's he done?'

'It just keeps going wrong. I don't even know why. It was like we had this amazing summer together but that's in the past and we can't get there again.'

'Don't be so melodramatic. Every relationship has bad phases. You probably just have to wait it out.'

Lily was giving me the pitying look. The one that usually appeared on her face when she remembered how young I was, and how clueless.

'Every time things are going well, one of us messes it up. We can't make it work.'

'But he's trying though, isn't he? Paying for me to come out here was sweet, and I'm seeing some impressive gems in your ears. It would have cost him thousands if Kelly and Mum had come out too.'

The thought that my mum and Kelly might have been with me too, if not for real life getting in the way, was painful.

'We're just not getting on. It's so much harder than I thought.'

'Do you think . . . ?'

'What?'

'Maybe it's neither of you. I mean, some people just aren't meant to be together.'

Me and Zeke were meant to be together though. The

idea that we weren't was awful. We'd already been through so much. How could we walk away from that?

Just the *idea* of no longer being with Zeke was devastating. I'd see him everywhere on the surf-tour circuit. He could get a new girlfriend in about three seconds flat, and I'd go back to being alone.

'I can't talk about this,' I said, choking down sadness.

'I'm sorry. Take no notice of me. You sound like you need to have a proper conversation with Zeke. Let's find him. He's bound to be around here somewhere. He wouldn't just leave without telling you.'

But the truth was that I didn't know what Zeke would do. I thought I knew him, but the longer we spent together, the more I realized that there were parts of his history and his personality that he guarded.

Lily smoothed my hair, handed me some lip balm and said, 'Pull yourself together, sis, and we'll go find him.'

A few paces down the hall we bumped into a young guy who looked like some Italian model in a sharp suit and tie. I didn't even recognize him until he said, 'Hey, girl, nice dress.'

'Seb? Jesus, is everyone here?'

'Most of Miami, yeah,' he said, looking at Lily. 'But my aunt works for the PR firm running the red carpet tonight, so she added us to the guest list.'

'Hello,' Lily said, shaking his hand, 'I'm Lily — otherwise known as "the sister".'

'I see that. Same eyes. I'm actually here with my sister too. She wanted to meet some of the pro-surfers. I'm helping her get a few autographs. Here,' he said, passing me a small notebook and a fancy fountain pen, 'I'll take yours too.'

'Oh, you charmer,' Lily said, smiling.

For a second I considered signing my name, but thought better of it, handed it back to him, and said, 'Yeah, funny.'

'What? You're gonna blow up and be super-famous one of these days. I saw some videos of you surfing on YouTube. That vertical snap in the lip? Yew! You got game, girl.'

'You reckon? I still can't get the hang of airs.'

'You will. Scrawl there.'

Lily moved next to me to peer down at the notebook, and said, 'Who else do you have in here?'

'Jordy Smith,' I read out. 'Kelly Slater. Wow, you got Slater? We haven't even seen him yet. Nice. Joel Parkinson. Owen Wright. Adriano de Souza. Matt Wilkinson. Carissa Moore. Stephanie Gilmore. Coco Ho. Evan Geiselman. Gabriel Medina.' The list went on and on. The best surfers on the scene.

'You really want me to sign this too?'

'Iris,' Lily said, 'just sign the bloody book.'

'OK then,' I said, and did my best signature, with an extra-long flourish on the F.

'Come find my sister? She'd be so stoked to meet you.'

'We have to go and look for Zeke,' I said, and Seb stuck his tongue in his cheek, probably stopping himself from making some smart-arse remark.

'He's really sorry about the other night,' I said. 'Total misunderstanding, and I gave him hell.'

Lily gave me a look, obviously curious about what had happened.

'Forget about it. See you around,' Seb said.

'Seb is Zeke's friend?' Lily asked, and I shook my head.

'Mine.'

'Oh.'

'What does that mean?'

'Nothing. Nothing!'

Lily and I walked around the hotel, but Zeke was nowhere to be seen, so we ended up standing at the bar while Lily talked about the Venezuelan guy she'd met on the flight over, and I stared at the drinks on the top shelf of the bar.

'Fancy a dance?' Lily said, nodding towards Seb, who was twirling a young girl I presumed to be his sister around the dance floor.

I didn't particularly want to dance, but it was better than agonized loitering at the bar, wondering if and when Zeke would show.

A few dances in, I was opposite Seb, when I saw some of the tour surfers approaching us. Behind them was Zeke.

Zeke clocked me dancing near Seb, and I saw the hurt

flicker in his eyes. One of his friends, Danny, whispered something in Zeke's ear. Zeke shook his head and pointed to another guy I only knew by sight. He wasn't a surfer; he was a hanger-on who followed the tour. He was allegedly the boyfriend of one of the female coaches, but I didn't believe it. He was something to her, but not her boyfriend. Dealer was my best guess.

Lily spotted Zeke, waved at him, and leaned in to me, shouting in my ear, 'Gosh, doesn't Zeke look different without all that hair? Took me a moment to even realize it was him. You know, I think I prefer it. He almost looks like a grown-up!'

'I'll be back in a mo,' I said to Seb and Lily. They nodded, and I walked back to the bar, where Zeke was waiting.

'That dude's here,' he said, steel in his voice.

'Who are you on about?'

'The jackass who had his hand down your shirt,' Zeke said.

'I told you it wasn't like that.'

'You arranged to meet him here?'

'Of course not. He's here with his sister. I bumped into him in the corridor.'

'And I see you ran into your own sister.' Zeke nodded at Lily, who was blowing us kisses from the dance floor.

'Thanks for bringing her here, Zeke,' I said. 'I really appreciate it.'

'Yeah, happy birthday.'

'I think I'm going to get a cab back now,' I said, as Lily appeared, grabbed one of Zeke's hands, one of mine, and held them in hers, as if she was trying to marry us off in some religious ceremony.

'Loving the new hairdo, Zeke! Right, now sort it out, you two,' she said, all bright and breezy, like it was just some game.

'We're fine,' Zeke said. But we so weren't.

I looked up, and walking across the stage in glittering heels, not even twenty feet from me, was Christina Aguilera. The place erupted in applause, Christina started singing 'Beautiful' and I let go of Zeke's hand.

chapter thirty-nine

I thought back to my first contest of the tour, held in Hossegor, France. The week before the contest the beach breaks had been going off, courtesy of a huge Atlantic swell. When we arrived, it was lake-like.

Lay-day after lay-day, and finally the conditions were deemed good enough for the women's heats. Not the men's, of course, because they wouldn't paddle out for one-foot junky slop.

Sucky waves? Send out the girls.

I wasn't ready for my heat. Yeah, I'd done physical training, but mentally I was a joke.

For months afterwards I couldn't bear to think about how badly I surfed that day. On my first day surfing with a foamie I surfed better.

The waves were short and so hard to read that I didn't know what they were going to do until I got to my feet, which was disastrous. I was flailing around like a kook, and with every mistake I panicked even more.

I knew the cameras were on me, and I could only imagine the freeze-frames of my wipeouts that were appearing on the webcast for the whole world to laugh at.

I walked out of the water, absolutely crushed. My score wasn't even in double figures. Wasn't even close.

I looked around to find Zeke, but the only person who acknowledged me was a girl with a microphone, who was walking towards me for the mandatory post-heat interview, which would be broadcast live over the webcast. Even the cameraman behind her looked embarrassed for me. I tried to get myself together before they got to me, because the only thing worse than my performance in the water would be crying on the webcast. That would get me the sort of reputation I absolutely did not want: a bimbo who resorted to waterworks when things didn't go her way.

'This is Kaleigh Bryant with Iris Fox. Iris, *babe*, that looked rough. What went wrong?'

She had a strong South African accent and it took me a moment to tune into her words.

'I don't know. I just couldn't bring it.'

I could tell she was waiting for me to add to this stellar response, but I had nothing.

'What was the strategy out there today?' she asked.

I thought about how to answer this and came up blank. At that moment, if she'd have asked me my middle name, I'd have struggled.

'Was there a strategy?'

'Yeah, course.' *Please don't ask me what it was.*

'And can you tell us what that was?'

'To do my best. You know. To, er, win.'

'Sure, sure, and what was running through your head? What things were you doing to make that happen?'

What was running through my head was that I'd apparently lost all my surf skills in one afternoon.

'Just trying to catch the best waves I could.'

I already knew I'd be bad at interviews, but I hadn't realized how bad.

'You *rarely excel* in these beach-break waves, probably because of the nature of your home break, Fistral in England, but what happened today?'

'I rarely excel in them?' I repeated, offended. 'Little beach-break waves I can usually read pretty well, because Fistral actually has quite small surf in the summer, so I'm totally used to it,' I said.

She frowned at me, and then I realized that I had misunderstood her South African accent. *Really excel*, she had said; not 'rarely excel'.

I tried to cover it with something else to take the focus off my error, but could only muster, 'Beth was just better than me. Picked better waves, surfed them better.'

As tactical analysis went, it was about as interesting as a handful of gravel. I could almost hear her groan.

'OK, that's all from us down here on the beach. Iris Fox, bad luck out there today, but at least it wasn't a knockout round. We're sure you'll do better in your next heat.'

They cut back to the commentators in the box.

Kaleigh looked at me and shook her head.

'You could have given me something there,' she said, as if I'd been deliberately holding out on her. 'You know, I think that was the worst post-heat interview I ever did. You must try harder. That kind of effort won't win you any fans.'

'Sorry,' I said, and meant it. I'd made her look like a rubbish interviewer when the fault was all mine. 'I'm not with it. Weird day.'

'Iris, the whole world is having a weird day. Woman up.'

'I'll try.'

She rolled her eyes and walked off, mumbling something about amateurs.

Zeke had come running over then, tried to congratulate me on the one half-decent wave I'd picked off, and I said, 'Don't bother. I was useless.'

He looked shocked and said, 'No, you weren't. I've had way worse heats than that.'

'Yeah, when you were five,' I said. 'I shouldn't have come here. I'm just going to embarrass you.'

'Don't talk that way, Iris.'

'It's true.'

'No, it isn't. You can win this! I know you can.'

276

He'd always believed in me, always thought the best of me, always trusted me.

Sitting on a kerb in Florida, I wondered if I'd ever really trusted him.

chapter forty

I sat, my legs bridging the gutter, waiting to hail a cab, but the roads were quiet, and when I finally did see a taxi and wave for it, I realized its light was off and it was already carrying passengers. The driver looked at me with pity. Defeated, I sat down again, wishing I'd thought to bring a coat.

Tropical fabric appeared in front of me.

Lily had followed me out.

'Ditching me?'

'I thought you'd want to stay and watch Christina.'

'Not my kind of music, sis, and anyway, she only did three songs. You missed your shout-out.'

I frowned at Lily, waiting for her to elaborate.

'Someone got Christina to dedicate a song to a girl called Iris, which I presume is you, dearest sister. She wished you a very happy seventeenth birthday, by the way.'

Zeke. He must have got his backing singer friend to sort it out. My boyfriend had got Christina Aguilera to dedicate a song to me, and I'd missed it. Worst girl-friend ever.

'Which song? Don't tell me: "Keeps Gettin' Better",' I said, cringing at the irony.

'Incorrect. Guess again.'

'Just tell me which one, Lil.'

'It's obvious, isn't it? "Fighter".'

'Oh God,' I said, squeezing my eyes shut and wishing I was anywhere else in the world. 'What did Zeke do?'

'He didn't hear the song – he left just after you did.'

'Was he really pissed off?' I rubbed my eyes and tried not to imagine the expression on his face.

'Put it this way: I've seen him look happier. Why didn't you stay? I thought you liked that sort of music.'

It would be hard to explain this to Lily. The truth was I couldn't stand to hear Christina sing 'Beautiful'. Those lyrics burned.

'I just . . . couldn't listen to it. Not tonight. Lily, leave me here. Honestly, go and enjoy the party.'

'Enjoy watching a bunch of gold-painted girls in thongs and nipple covers do an interpretive dance of a wave? I came here to spend some time with my sister. We can get a taxi back together.'

She sat down next to me and we were absolutely silent for at least five minutes, while I tried to process the idea of Christina Aguilera knowing my name and singing a song for me and me totally ruining the moment by running off and spoiling another nice thing my boyfriend had tried to do for me. The only reason I was even on the tour was because of Zeke. The thought struck, with great pain, that maybe it would have been better for Zeke and me if we'd never crossed paths. I'd tried to be something I wasn't, and that had made us both miserable.

Finally Lily broke the silence with, 'Do you like it, Iris? Being a pro-surfer.'

Lily had always possessed the ability to put her finger on my weakest spots. She saw through the armour that fooled other people.

I nodded. 'Yeah, but it's so hard, Lil.' It was so much harder than I'd ever expected it to be. I'd imagined the tour as a surf junkie's paradise; I hadn't understood how difficult the pressure, fear and exhaustion would be.

'It's no little thing, Iris. Winning that competition. Of course it's hard. Working as a professional surfer, competing on a world stage. Yeah, maybe you're not at the top of the points board, but what you've achieved is incredible and it's sad you don't see it.'

'Is it incredible? Because I feel like I'm failing. Failing at professional surfing. Failing at being a girlfriend. Failing all my friends and family at home who want me to do well.'

Lily shook her head, exasperated, as if I was missing something very important. 'Don't you remember Dad's favourite Beckett quote? Something about trying and "failing better".'

'Failing better is still *failing*, Lil. I'll probably crash and burn, and finish this tour in last place. No sponsor will want to touch me. I'll go home and back to working in the shop.'

'Working retail isn't the worst thing in the world. But you're not through yet, and even if it does all go wrong and you do finish in last place, you're still one of the best young female surfers Billabong could find.'

'Or maybe I was just in the right place at the right time. I don't think I have what it takes to be good at this. I don't have the stuff. I'm not dedicated enough.'

'So get dedicated,' she said. 'Really try, Iris. Give it everything you have.'

If only it was as simple as that.

She stood up, and pulled me up too. 'Let's get out of here,' she said.

'What about Zeke?'

'Leave him to cool off. He's big enough and pretty enough to find his own way back to your hotel.'

'How will we get back?' I said. 'Every cab's already taken.'

'Give me five minutes.'

Lily disappeared inside the hotel and, when she reappeared, she had Seb and his sister in tow.

Seb jangled his car keys and said, 'I hear you ladies need a ride?'

chapter forty-one

Seb dropped off his sister at their parents' apartment in Brickell, which was a relief, as she hadn't said a single word except 'hi'. She was so shy, she was starting to make me feel nervous, and squashed together in the front of Seb's truck, I could feel that she was actually trembling.

'Nice to meet you!' I called after her, as she clambered out of the truck, but she murmured something I couldn't make out and dashed towards the entrance to a grand apartment block.

'I was hoping you'd live in a house with an alligator lounging by the pool,' Lily said to Seb, disappointed. 'I can't go home from Florida without seeing an alligator. It's practically my life's dream.'

'You never seen the Everglades?' Seb said.

'Never.'

'We could go now. It's nearly four already, and it's not far. We'll be there for sun-up.'

'Definitely,' Lily said. 'That sounds like just what my sister needs.'

'Yeah, but the contest.'

'The contest is Saturday. We'll be back by early afternoon.'

'Zeke will wonder where I am.' I thought about texting him, just in case he was looking for me, or waiting for me to come and find him.

'Screw that guy,' Seb said, gritting his teeth.

'You don't like Zeke?' Lily asked.

'The dude who pushed me into a wall so I had to punch him in the face? Sure, great guy.'

'He was having a really bad night,' I said, although it hadn't been that great for me either, and I hadn't assaulted anyone.

'Just tell him you're going with your sister to the Everglades and you'll see him later.'

Because Zeke would be so cool with that. But then, Zeke had always encouraged me to embrace opportunities, and he'd probably be glad to have a few hours of peace and quiet.

I took out my phone, started a message to Zeke and tapped the words 'I'm with Lily. Need some space. Talk tomorrow.'

But it didn't feel right. 'I really shouldn't go off on a night road trip without telling him. Maybe you should drop us back at Lily's hotel?'

'Iris, if you lived in a prison your whole life and could only pick one thing to see, it'd be an Everglades sunrise.'

How could I turn that down?

'Could we take a ride on one of those airboats with the giant fans on the back that are so noisy you have to wear ear defenders? Actually,' I said, looking through my wallet, 'I have a business card here for mates' rates.'

'So then we have to go,' Lily said, squeezing my hand.

I wasn't entirely sure that I understood what was happening. It felt like I was about to experience one of those once-in-a-lifetime adventures that old people tell you you'll always regret turning down. And it wasn't like I was cheating on Zeke. I just wanted to see the sights.

'We'll spend the morning there, and I can have you back in South Beach by two. Seriously, like your sister says, you can't come to Florida without seeing an alligator.'

I really, really wanted to see the Everglades.

chapter forty-two

Seb's Ford pick-up truck was ancient, but he'd given it a paint job and decent alloys, which made it look kind of awesome. I told him as much and he said, 'What kind of car do you have back in England, Iris?'

'A van,' Lily said, 'and before that, she had a very nice skateboard with some very nice stickers on it.'

'Yeah, the van was a birthday present. I'll have to book in for driving lessons when I'm home.'

Seb looked taken aback at this.

'You don't have your driver's permit? You're sixteen, right?'

'Yeah, but you can't get your provisional in the UK until you're seventeen, and I just turned seventeen today . . . err, yesterday.'

'Oh, man, it's your birthday? Why didn't you say? Happy birthday!'

'Uh, why did you think I was sixteen?'

'That's what it said on the Billabong website.'

Seb had checked me out? I absorbed this information and tried not to read too much into it. Everyone googled everyone.

'Surfers need to drive, Iris. You can't not drive. That's straight-up crazy.'

'So people keep telling me.'

Seb took a moment to think about something and then said, 'Do you wanna drive my truck? I could teach you how.'

'You have to do that,' Lily said. 'No question.'

'Seriously? You'd let me, a total stranger, drive your truck?'

'Yeah. I can't think of a reason why not. It's not like you've been drinking, right?'

I could think of a lot of reasons why not, the same reasons that had led me to say no to Zeke's offer of the same, reasons like the fact that it was probably illegal to teach some foreign girl to drive.

'No, I haven't been drinking. I stay off alcohol for at least twenty-four hours before a contest.' A personal rule of Zeke's that I'd picked up. 'But, I mean, what if I crash it?'

'You won't.' He braked as some enormous lorry pulled out of a junction directly in front of us.

'Jackass,' he yelled, and pulled a face.

'Maybe I'll skip that driving lesson,' I said, envisaging our fiery deaths.

'The Everglades road is real quiet. We'll do it there.'

'I can't believe we're actually going to the Everglades,' Lily said, cracking her knuckles and blowing on them.

'Is it creepy down there?' I asked, thinking about a TV drama I'd once seen, where aliens were hiding in the Everglades mangrove swamps.

'Man, it's another world. It's basically a million acres of flooded jungle – what's not to like? You know, they eat bullfrogs down there. They're kinda a delicacy.'

'Oh,' Lily said. 'That seems . . . unnecessary.'

'It's a cultural thing. Guys go out at night. Frogging. And they just spear those suckers behind the eyes. Then they skin them, cover them in batter and fry them up. You see them on menus everywhere down in those parts.'

'What do they taste like?' Lily asked. 'Don't tell me: chicken.'

'Like heaven on earth. And it's not just frogs: there's wild pigs, panthers, black bears, turtles, rattlesnakes and these crazy cottonmouth snakes that'll kill you in under an hour.'

He gave me a wink and that's when I realized: he reminded me of someone. Daniel. Except with none of the psycho.

'Um,' Lily said, 'perhaps we should go to the Florida Keys instead. Find Flipper.'

'Naw, you're gonna dig it so hard. There's a million alligators. Find them in every ditch, swamp and backyard.

The big lazy road gators? My pop calls those welfare alligators.'

'*Welfare* alligators?'

'Yeah, like on state benefits. Cos they just hang around all day doing nothin'.'

I bristled a bit. There'd been a time, not long after my dad had left, when my family had relied on benefits to keep a roof over our heads. I didn't remember any sitting around doing nothing. We were always doing something, and it was never anything fun like watching TV or playing computer games. Cleaning people's houses for cash was generally the order of the day, and the people who owned the houses were often arsey about paying us, which just made the whole thing even more unpleasant.

Seb stopped at traffic lights and, with an enormous roar, a freight train crossed the road behind us. I hadn't even seen a sign for a train crossing.

'Exciting,' Lily said, watching the train roll into the distance.

'How can you even drive here?' I said, feeling my heart banging in my chest.

'It's not so bad. Beats some of the places I've travelled.'

'You've been abroad? I read that, like, only five per cent of Americans have passports.'

Seb didn't seem to know how to take this remark. 'More like forty. I backpacked through Europe after high school.'

'Wait, how old are you?'

'Twenty-one.'

I looked at Lily, who didn't seem bothered by this information. He was way older than I'd thought. I'd assumed he was around eighteen.

'So what do you think of Florida?'

I looked around. At night, with the roads empty and lit by artificial light, it looked like the places had been planned out in a potato stamp, which had just been printed and printed to infinity. Red Lobster. McDonald's. KFC. Ruby Tuesday, Wendy's. Subway. Burger King. Mall. Red Lobster. McDonald's. KFC. Ruby Tuesday. Wendy's . . .

'It's pretty,' I said, and Lily made a slight coughing sound.

The fast-food outlet pattern went on for miles and miles until we reached the edges of suburbia, where the sleazy strip clubs started appearing. I didn't mention them and neither did Lily or Seb.

Eventually the roads started to look more rural, and in another hour or so we were deep in Everglades territory. He pulled over at the side of the road and said, 'Switch places?'

'Really? Now?'

'Be bold, Iris. You can drive this thing,' Lily said. 'It's easy. Believe in yourself.'

I sat in the driver's side, Seb rode in the middle, with Lily shotgun, and we belted up.

'This is going to be weird, especially since you guys drive on the wrong side of the road.'

'Hey, it's you Brits that drive on the wrong side of the road. Most of the world drives on the right,' Seb pointed out, 'and anyway, the basics are the same, so you'll pick it up easy.'

It still seemed dodgy to me.

'I don't want to wrap it around a tree, Seb.'

Seb laughed. 'You have me as a teacher. I'm right here with you. You'll be great.'

'Iris,' Lily said, 'get a move on, before we're carjacked.'

I put my hands on the steering wheel, and Seb said, 'OK, so easy off the brake and gently touch the gas.'

At least it was an automatic, so I didn't have to worry about stalling.

I did what he said, then pulled out into the road, completely forgetting to signal.

'You need to look a little further up the road so you can steer better.'

'Yes, Iris, you've been looking about two feet ahead of the bonnet and your steering is shit,' Lily said helpfully.

I stopped at a red light and Seb said, 'Right turn. Don't forget the blinker.'

When the lights changed to green, I put my foot down and was suddenly in the next lane across. I hadn't realized how powerful the engine was. I steered back into the first lane, and looked at Seb, waiting for him to tell me off, but he didn't seem at all fazed, as if me potentially causing a fatal road-traffic accident was nothing to worry about.

I drove for about five minutes without seeing another car, and then some guy in an old Ford appeared in my rear-view and started honking his horn. I was doing fifty and the road signs said fifty-five.

'Jeepers creepers!' Lily said, obviously finding it all very amusing.

'What's his problem?' I said.

'Guess the dude wants you to go faster.'

'He can go around me if he's in such a hurry.'

Seb waved the other driver on. As the guy overtook me, he honked again and gave us the finger.

'Such a gentleman,' Lily said drily.

I looked at the speedometer and saw that our own speed had dropped to about forty, without me even noticing.

We drove past signs advertising alligator tours and one even had a photo of a severed alligator head on it, which was, according to Seb, a classic tourist souvenir.

'Maybe you could give the engine just a little more of a whirl?' Seb said.

I put my foot down and watched the speedometer move past fifty and then sixty. I looked at Seb and he was alert, ready to intervene if he needed to.

Lily's face was turned to the window and I wondered if she was drifting off to sleep. I didn't feel the least bit tired. My body was flooded with endorphins and adrenalin.

Then, we hit the pothole. Not just any pothole. This crater was about six-feet square.

'Easy!' Seb shouted, grabbing the wheel.

The car bounced, and I eased off the accelerator, but it wasn't enough, because walking calmly across the road was a tiny alligator.

I swerved, too hard and too fast, the truck's sensitive steering taking us right off the road before Seb could react to counter my mistake.

Somehow the truck didn't roll, but we bumped our way between trees down towards the edge of a swamp.

'Shit,' Lily said, bracing herself with her legs, and gripping the handle above the door.

'Hold on,' Seb yelled. He'd grabbed the wheel and was doing his best to steer around the trees. I was useless, just gone, paralysed with fear. Zeke's face kept flashing into my brain. Our last words were said in anger. And how could he possibly be expected to understand why I was with my sister and another guy hundreds of miles away?

He'd hate me, but I'd be dead so he'd feel bad for hating his dead girlfriend and he'd drink or meth his way into an early grave.

We clipped a tree and I swore in pain.

The truck was slowing to a halt, and before the wheels had even stopped turning Lily and Seb had jumped out and

Lily was trying to yank me out of my window, since the door was completely jammed.

It was so, so dark. The moon had been bright, but under the tree canopy I could hardly see my knees.

'Help me out here, Seb,' she shouted, and he hip-checked her out the way and took over.

I wanted to answer but I couldn't stop shaking. I could feel the truck sinking into the mush of the wetlands, but I just sat there clutching the steering wheel, totally unable to move. My feet turned cold and I saw water in the footwell. The truck was listing; the passenger side sinking faster.

'Iris, shift your bloody arse,' Lily was saying to me.

'Come on, girl,' Seb said. 'Move.'

I tried to undo my seat belt, but my hands were shaking so hard that I couldn't manage it. Seb leaned over me, flicked on the truck's internal light and unclipped the seat belt himself. Then he got hold of me by the armpits and pulled me through the window.

I tried to get my head together and assess the situation. The truck's headlights were shining two bright beams into the swamp, and I scanned the water for any movement that might be an alligator. Or one of those snakes. The swamp wasn't quiet. The noise of crickets, frogs and the rustle of vegetation unnerved me. This was not a dead place; it was teeming with unseen life.

We sat on the ground a little way from the truck and watched it sink halfway into the mire, where it finally settled, but at least it wasn't fully submerged. It would be tricky to winch it out of there, with the soft ground and the steep bank, and I had no doubt it wouldn't be cheap. I'd probably caused at least a grand's worth of damage. I looked at Seb's wrist, which he was touching gingerly. Maybe he'd sprained it, yanking me out.

'Nice one, sis,' Lily said, sighing and looking up through a small gap in the trees at the stars. 'How are we going to get back? Hitch? Or can you call someone, Seb?'

'I really don't want to call my folks. My dad is gonna go crazy, and it'll be even worse if I have to haul him out of bed.'

'What about your friends?' I said.

'Yeah, they're not gonna drive hours to see us in the middle of the night. I'll call roadside assistance.'

He had no service. None of our phones did.

'It'll be better once we're up on the road. I'll try again then.'

He waded to the truck and retrieved a toolbox, some clothes and his spare tyre from the back.

'My dad fixed up that truck for me,' he said. 'Took the guy two years. Either of you want my jacket?'

It was uncomfortably humid in the Everglades, even on a spring night, and panic had made me sweat even more. Lily and I both said no to the jacket offer, so Seb put it on the ground, for us to sit on.

'I'm so sorry,' I said. 'Do you have insurance?'

'Not the kind that will pay for a British chick running it off the road. It's my fault for making you drive.'

'I'll pay for it,' I said. 'Just tell me how much.'

'Forget it.'

'Well, at least we're not freezing our arses off,' Lily said, determined to look on the bright side. 'I bet it's practically arctic in Cornwall.'

I ignored her and turned to Seb again, touching him on the arm.

'I said I'll pay.'

'Sure you will,' he said, with no conviction whatsoever. 'And tomorrow I'll put on a cape and save a girl nose-diving into Niagara Falls.'

chapter forty-three

We walked back up the bank to the road, Lily illuminating the way with Seb's flashlight and Seb carrying his spare tyre, which he was going to leave as a marker, so he'd know where the truck left the road, in case we had to walk miles before picking up phone reception. He placed it on the edge of the carriageway and we heard a scratching noise behind us.

Lily shone the torch and there, grievously injured, was my victim. Not, as I had thought, a baby alligator. Some sort of lizard. I had run right over its tail and there was blood. It seemed dazed, but as we walked nearer it began to come around, hissing violently, its red mouth gaping.

It appeared to want to run away but had trouble moving.

'Shit, I'm sorry,' I said to it. 'I didn't mean to hit you, lizard.' Then, 'Lily, it's really hurt. It won't die, will it?'

'Tegu,' Seb said. 'Invasive species. Those little guys

eat a million bird eggs before they're through living. You just did the Everglades a favour.'

'Well, not really. It's still alive,' Lily said, kneeling from a safe distance to look at it.

'It might be all right,' I said. 'Do you think it'll be OK?'

'Are you kidding me?' Seb said, trying to stick his hands in the back of his suit trousers and realizing there weren't pockets there.

'It can't even walk,' Lily said. 'This is no place for animals that can't run, let alone walk. Some alligator's probably got a nice breakfast coming his way.'

'Bloody hell, Lil! I don't want it to be eaten alive. That's well harsh.'

'What do you think it does to other animals?' Seb said. 'What we have here is basically a sociopathic killer.'

'It's suffering. Look at it,' Lily said. 'Poor little thing. Maybe it was just out getting some food for its baby tegus.'

Seb scoffed at this sentiment and I tried to focus on his sociopathic killer comment.

'Tell me what to do, and I'll do it,' I said.

'I guess put it out of its misery,' Seb said.

'Kill it? We can't kill it. I was thinking we get it to a vet.'

'You've sort of half-killed it already,' Lily said.

'Yeah, we're gonna have to go the whole nine yards.'

'Bloody hell, Seb!'

'It's gonna die anyway,' Lily said. 'Why put it through more pain?'

'Then you'll have to do it, Lil,' I said.

'Why should I? You knocked the poor thing down.'

'You have previous form. Remember you killed a frog that time. With your bike.'

'That was an accident. Seb will do it, won't you? You'll be better at it than we will.'

'What — because I'm Cuban?' Seb said, eyes wide open.

'No. That wasn't what I meant at all,' Lily said, looking awkward.

I knew what she meant. What she meant was, *You're a boy with decent arms, so you'd probably be better placed to wring its neck or whatever needs doing.*

But that didn't exactly sound great either, so I said, 'Haven't you killed rats and stuff?'

'I'm living in a house with rats?'

'No. No! I just heard that they have a lot of rats in Florida.'

Then I had a brainwave. What I thought was a brainwave, but actually turned out to add insult to injury. 'I thought you lot went shooting ducks and stuff.'

'*You lot?* What does that even mean?'

'You know, Americans,' Lily said, backing me up. 'Like Dick Cheney.'

Seb looked horrified. 'I am not Dick Cheney.'

'Well, look,' Lily said, 'there's no good way to say this, but do you have a gun in your truck?'

'A *gun*? Uh, who exactly do you think I am?'

'Trust us to find a man in the two-thirds,' Lily said, rolling her eyes at me. 'How about a knife?'

'Jesus-fuck, lady! No, I don't have a knife. How about you go find a rock,' Seb advised her, walking a few paces down the road, his back to us, as if he really, really didn't want to see this little tegu get a lethal dose of rock medicine. Not that I did either, but the situation was excruciatingly awful and had to end. 'Do me a solid, yo, and make sure you hit it hard.'

Seb checked his phone, which had thankfully picked up a weak signal, and he made the call to roadside assistance.

'Recovery vehicle should be here within six hours.'

'What? That's ages! We can't stay here that long.'

'There's been some kind of pile-up. Not my idea of a fun time either,' Seb pointed out.

We looked around, sweeping the area with torchlight to see if there were any rocks that would do the job, but we couldn't find a stone bigger than a tangerine, which didn't seem capable of inflicting the sort of damage required.

'Seb,' Lily called down the road to his retreating form.

'You done it yet?'

'We can't find any good rocks.'

He said something in Spanish under his breath.

'Keep looking.'

'We've looked. There aren't any big ones.'

'Awesome,' he said, walking back towards us.

He stroked the stubble on his chin in a meditative way.

'Your shoes have a stiletto heel?'

I hadn't taken my shoes off, because even though they were undeniably stupid and wobbly, the tarmac was tacky and would stick to the soles of my feet. Lily's shoes had spongy platform soles, which wouldn't exactly serve our purpose.

I looked at the tegu's tough leathery skin and then at my flimsy shoes.

'Go on, Iris,' Lily said. 'One good whack.'

I went so far as to take a shoe in my hand, but I just couldn't.

'Won't work,' I said, even though it might have. I was furious with myself that I didn't seem to have it in me to end the suffering of an animal that was clearly in pain.

I heard Seb cursing but couldn't make out the distinct words.

'What are our options?' Lily said. 'I guess we could grab it by the tail and swing it at a tree a few times?'

'Lily! No! Look at its little face. It's trusting us.'

As lizards went, our tegu was pretty beautiful, with its spotted markings and elegant feet.

'Hang on,' I said.

I walked to Seb's pile of belongings, every millimetre of my body running with sweat in the humidity and my

300

slinky dress sticking to me like cling film. I grabbed Seb's jacket, along with a roll of duct tape he had in his toolkit. I wasn't exactly sure what I was going to do with the duct tape, maybe tape a splint to the tegu's tail if it would let me. This admittedly seemed unlikely, but I didn't have any better options.

When I got back, Seb was staring at the tegu, his mouth a hard line, maybe gearing himself up for an act of merciful death, and Lily was on her knees again, talking to it.

I walked up to the tegu and threw Seb's jacket over it. It went bananas and started fighting, but I got it under my arm, and, using every ounce of my strength, held on to it.

'Tape,' I shouted to Lily. 'Get the bloody tape before it has my hand off.'

Lily picked up the duct tape from the tarmac and looked at me dopily.

'Wrap it round its mouth, Lil!'

She had a good go, I had to give her that much, but the tegu had found its last resources of fight and was giving it everything it had. It wouldn't keep still for long enough for Lily or Seb to get anywhere near its mouth.

'It's not working,' she shouted.

Finally Seb took the roll and wound the tape over his jacket and around the tegu, which instantly soothed it.

I looked at him, then I looked down at the tegu wrapped in his jacket and couldn't think of a single thing to say except, 'Lil, please don't put this on Facebook.'

Any attraction that Seb had ever had to me, and me to him, had well and truly evaporated, and Lily started giggling.

The tegu made a weird noise.

'This shit is so messed up,' Seb said.

I said, 'Pass me my phone.'

chapter forty-four

There was only one person I could call. My mum was in a different country and all she'd be able to do was stress me out. Zeke wasn't an option, and Saskia was still annoyed with me, so I called the person who had a reason to keep this quiet.

I had to call Anders five times before he picked up.

'You havin' a giraffe, Iris? It's the middle of the bloody night.'

'So sorry. But, it's a – um – emergency. There's been a car crash.'

'Zeke all right?'

No great surprise to hear Anders prioritize Zeke.

'Zeke's not here.'

'He's not? Well, thank God for that. Wait, whose car are you in?'

'Seb's. And it's a truck.'

He paused.

'Am I supposed to know who that is?'

'A boy I know. A friend.'

'*A boy you know?* I thought you didn't have any friends outside of Cornwall. That's what Zeke said.'

I couldn't believe Zeke would say that. No matter if it was true.

'My sister's here too.'

'So it's your sister's chap?'

Anders seemed to be getting sidetracked from the point I was trying to make, which was: *For God's sake, help me out here.*

'No, it's just a lad I met in Miami.'

'And you went off with him in his truck? I see. You know, messing around with another bloke was not quite what I had in mind when I asked you to watch Zeke like a hawk.'

'I'm so sorry, Anders. It's really not as bad as it looks. But we need a lift. Seb's truck is out of action.'

'So get a cab.'

'We're too far outside of Miami for a cab.'

'What? Where the hell are you?'

'I'm not totally sure, but it's somewhere in the Everglades.'

'What did you just say?'

'Everglades.'

'What the FUCK are you doing in the Everglades?'

'I just really wanted to see it . . .' I said, completely aware of how pathetic I sounded. 'I'll put you on to Seb.'

304

I stood there, mortified, as Seb did his best to give Anders directions. He handed the phone back to me.

'I took a cab from the airport, so I'll have to borrow a car. It's gonna take me a few hours to get there,' Anders said, 'so stay put and don't go wandering off anywhere.'

A few hours would be torture, but by this point I was too exhausted to argue. 'Thank you. Also, can you bring some water? Enough for all three of us.' I didn't want to push my luck by asking for snacks.

Anders didn't answer that. His mind was already on to something else, 'Now, for Christ sake, don't go calling Zeke. As far as he knows, you're tucked up in bed in a massive huff with him. Got it?'

'But he's bound to hear about this sooner or later.' A car crash seemed like too big a thing to keep hidden.

'He won't. I checked him into the Fontainebleau, and he thinks you're at Lily's hotel, since you told him you needed some space. When you mentioned a car crash, I assumed you'd sorted things out with Zeke and were with him. Obviously not.'

'Oh.'

I couldn't help wondering if Zeke was alone in that hotel room in the Fontainebleau.

'Really sorry about all this, Anders. Thanks for coming to the rescue.'

Then, completely exhausted, I put my arms around my knees, sat down next to Lily, and thought about the time I went to Hawaii with Zeke. If only I could turn the clock back, I thought, to before it all went wrong.

chapter forty-five

On the Big Island, we'd juddered down a dirt track on the way to see Zeke's grandfather. The countryside was rugged and black with only a few houses and thorn trees to punctuate the desolation.

'I didn't realize Pop lived so close to the volcano,' I said.

'Yeah, his house is basically in the middle of a lava field.'

'And he likes it here?'

'Sure. He digs the isolation.'

'What if lava popped up and swept away his house?'

'This is Lava Zone 2, so that probably won't happen.'

'But it could happen?'

'No one can predict lava, and there are three active volcanoes on this island.'

'Why on earth does he live here then?'

'It's his home. Just like Oahu is mine. Just like Newquay is yours.'

Eventually we came to a house that had been constructed on poles. 'Termites,' Zeke said, before I could ask him about it. 'Termites are a huge pain in the ass here, and Pop has a thing for wood.'

'A thing for wood?'

'You'll see.'

He parked up and I expected someone to come out to greet us, but all was still and silent. The whole front of the house was open, without even a wall between the armchairs and the great outdoors. I'd never seen anything like it.

We went up the steps and looked around, Zeke pointing out home-made pieces of furniture made from exotic woods like acacia, coconut and koa, but there was still no sign of Zeke's grandfather. I was starting to worry that we'd find him dead in his bed or possibly the victim of some terrible crime. We walked through to the back of the house and stood on a balcony that Zeke called a lanai. In the yard was a brownish green pool, and in that pool, floating on his back, surrounded by koi carp and eye-wateringly naked, was Zeke's granddad.

'POP,' Zeke shouted, not seeming at all bothered by this spectacle. Pop's ears were submerged and he didn't move a muscle. His eyes were wide open as he surveyed the morning sky.

Zeke took my hand, guided it down into the water and sent some small waves across the pool.

The water was really warm. 'Geothermal pond,' he said.

The ripples hit the side of Pop's face and he righted himself and stood up.

He saw Zeke and saluted, the same sloppy salute that Zeke so often used. It felt strange to see it, to understand where it originated.

'Hey, it's my favourite grandkid!' Pop said, with a huge grin.

'You say that to all your grandkids. Want this?' Zeke said, holding up the goldfish-print towel that Pop had left folded at the edge of the pool.

'I think I oughta, seeing how you've brought a lady.'

I smiled. 'I'm really not much of a lady,' I said, without fully considering the implications Pop might draw from this sentence. 'Uhh, I mean, I don't have much in the way of airs and graces,' I added, blushing and turning away.

'A regular Ursula Andress, ain't I?' Pop laughed.

'Is it safe to look yet?' I whispered to Zeke.

'Sure,' Pop said, with the hearing of a bat. 'But, you know, it was safe to look before the towel. You kids hungry?'

'Starving,' I said.

'Right this way.'

Because of the cost of groceries on the Big Island, which were mostly imported and super-expensive, Pop tended a garden.

'I planted everything; even hauled in the dirt myself.'

It was about eight by ten metres and every inch was crammed full of vegetables and fruit. He even had pineapples growing there.

Zeke and I helped him pick some fruit and then he banished me from the kitchen, where geckoes were roaming, unhindered. 'They eat the roaches,' Zeke pointed out, when I made a face at one that ran up the cabinet right in front of me.

'What can I do to help?' I said.

'Nothing,' Pop said. 'Visiting ladies don't do any chores. Not in my home. Go, take a walk. Relax.'

I looked around, found an enormous catchment tank, plus an outhouse with a compost toilet. Pop's place had solar panels, and a wind turbine, on account of twenty-five-mile-an-hour winds every day of the year, and no sealed walls, to make the most of the island breezes.

I'd never seen a house like it, and it seemed so weird to me, so alien.

I followed the garden path, dotted with fallen thorns, down to a cave, which contained a bed and two tubs of soapy water.

'Also for the roaches,' Zeke said, appearing behind me. 'They come for a drink and the suds get them.'

'This is amazing,' I said, looking around at the cave.

'Yeah, it's the end of a lava tunnel. Pop loves it down here. It's like, literally, his man cave.'

There were internal pillars made of lava rock fragments, and totem poles carved and painted with animal faces.

That night Zeke and I slept in the cave, and in the morning he helped his grandfather paint the wooden house with creosote, which stank to high heaven, but which neither of them complained about.

Before we left, Pop shook my hand and said, 'He never brought a girl to meet me before.'

'Really? I'm the first?'

'The first and the last,' Pop said, looking straight into my eyes.

'Well, I don't know about that,' I said, embarrassed.

'Iris,' he said, shaking his head, 'I *know*. You're it.'

Zeke joined us then, carrying our bags, and for a long time afterwards I wondered about his grandfather's words. What was I? Zeke's true love? Or the only gamble he'd ever make on a girl – the one that would make or break him?

chapter forty-six

I must have dozed off, and I woke to the memory of Pop's face. I remembered the words he'd spoken to me, heard them in my head as if he was right there with me.

The sun came up and Seb was right, it was spectacular. We watched a flock of birds circle around us, a million of them, it seemed, and I breathed in the beauty. The trees behind us exhaled their pure oxygen and it gave me a head rush to finally be in this place, even if it was during one of my most terrible screw-ups to date.

But, within an hour or so of sunrise, the heat intensified and soon the rays were beating down. I wanted to stay by the road so that Anders would see us when he passed, but the road didn't offer much shade. In my sticky dress, with no water, I could feel my skin begin to prickle with heat rash. As a further indignity, my tampon needed changing, but I'd already used up my two spares and I knew it wouldn't be long before it started leaking.

Seb had run out of words, I had run out of words, and

Lily was asleep. We just sat there in silence with the angry noises of a grievously injured tegu for company. A couple of hours into the wait, Seb turned to me and fanned me with his hand.

I was so thirsty I had vivid daydreams of swimming underwater through a reservoir with my mouth open; half girl, half basking shark.

Seb had a banging headache, which I suspected was a migraine, as he felt sick and faint and even had a five-minute spell where his vision had gone funny.

Eventually Anders drove past in a top-of-the-range BMW at what seemed like a hundred miles an hour. He reversed to our position and I waited for the onslaught.

'Oh, hello there!' Lily said, as if this were a perfectly normal occasion.

'Only you would come to the Everglades in a cocktail dress,' Anders said to me, and then, 'What the fuck is that under your arm?'

The tegu chose this moment to hiss, but it was a sad, lethargic noise that just made me feel even worse for it.

'It's a tegu. We're taking it to a vet,' I said. 'I ran it over.'

'That beast is not coming into this car,' Anders said firmly. 'No bloody way.' He passed me a bottle, and two more to Seb and Lily. We drained them in seconds and I felt giddy with the relief of pure joyous water.

'This isn't even yours,' I said.

'Get in the bastard car before I change my mind about this,' he said.

I'd never heard Anders swear so liberally, and then I zoned in on the thing I'd noticed, but hadn't processed: his breath smelt of whiskey.

I didn't ask. I didn't want to know. All I wanted was to get back to Miami.

'Righty-ho,' Lily said, getting into the back.

'You know what, Iris?' Seb said. 'Now I know you guys have a ride, I think I'm gonna wait for roadside service.'

'But it could be hours yet and you're not well,' Lily pointed out helpfully. 'I'd cancel it. You can figure out what to do about your truck later. It's not going anywhere.'

Anders said, 'Lover boy, get in the fucking car.'

Seb shrugged and did as he was told.

'*In the back.* Iris, give him that prehistoric abomination, and you get in the front.'

Anders did what had to be an eight-point turn and we set off back towards Miami.

After about ten miles, Lily asleep again and Anders still scowling, I turned back to Seb and said, 'What are you gonna do about your truck?'

'Well, I'm sure as shit not gonna be driving it any time soon.' He sounded as if he was going to add some choice personal insults, when Anders surprised me by saying, 'Lay off her. Can't you see she's half-dead with heatstroke?'

I looked at my chest, where red streaks of heat rash were undeniable.

'It's all right. I'm fine.'

'I've scraped better-looking Hubba Bubba off my shoe,' Anders said.

'Thanks.'

Even in the midst of so much crap and chaos, I couldn't help feeling embarrassed about how bad I looked. About the fact that Zeke would have to see me like this; Zeke and the entire surf world.

All the girls were expected to manage without wetsuits for the tropical contests, as the water was so warm. At New Smyrna, I'd be the lesser-striped Cornish lobster.

'You should probably get something on it,' Anders said. 'We'll stop by Walgreens.'

'I'm burnt too, y'all,' Seb said.

'You can all share your calamine lotion like good little children.'

'It's fine, Anders. Really.'

I was playing it down, but I wanted to cover my body with cool cotton and stay in a cool, dark room for a week. The very next day, however, I'd have to put on a tiny bikini, walk across a baking beach and step into saltwater in front of the world's surf press, and my family, watching at home.

In the convertible, my hair flipped around and Anders handed me his Panama hat, which I pulled low over my face.

Anders was never great at respecting speed limits, or any limits for that matter, but maintaining fifty-five in a fancy BMW, while pissed, was absolutely beyond him.

Not even an hour later, I was jolted out of a doze by the wail of sirens.

chapter forty-seven

That morning we learned that Florida state police do not appreciate drunk Englishmen speeding on their roads while transporting a coat-wearing lizard.

In short order, Anders was booked, the car was seized, and Seb, Lily and I found ourselves nestled up with the tegu in the back of a police car.

Lily was making notes on her smartphone for her upcoming Facebook post, despite my protests, and Seb was silent, too exhausted to speak.

At the police station I watched through the glass door as Seb used the small change in his wallet to pull various drinks and snacks out of the vending machine. He shared them with us and we feasted in a silence that had at least become companionable. This was a fiasco, we'd accepted it as such, and now we just had to ride it out.

Lily used her credit card to book an Uber that would take us to Miami. It would cost a packet, but I said I'd reimburse her. Anders would be in the system for a little while before he could be released, and we'd hatched a plan to tell Zeke that he had been called away on urgent family business and would join us the following day for the contest.

'I have to tell him,' I'd said. 'I don't want to lie to him.'

'Don't you dare. He's already in a state without you making things even worse.'

'He'll find out eventually.'

'Well, we'll cross that bridge when we come to it. But for now, zip it.'

I tried to argue the point, but he was absolutely adamant that Zeke was not to hear a word about this.

We gave the tegu some water, then fed it a Cadbury's Creme Egg, which it devoured. I was astonished that Creme Eggs were even a thing in America, but they were, and apparently tegus loved them; them and the eggs of endangered bird species. It revived a little after that and I made a call to a local veterinarian, who agreed to pick up the animal and administer whatever care it needed and then arrange transfer to a local wildlife shelter – for a small fee of fifteen hundred dollars, which would severely deplete my current account.

But I didn't care – I just wanted that animal fixed and in the condition it had enjoyed before meeting the front wheel of Seb's truck. 'Are you sure?' the vet said. 'Euthanasia is eighty dollars.'

She took payment over the phone, and I could have sworn as I read out the digits of my card that the tegu looked at me in gratitude, still licking Creme Egg off its face.

True to her word, the vet came to collect the tegu, and I reflected that I'd just had the most expensive driving lesson imaginable, before I even factored in the cost of Seb's truck, which would take all my savings.

Finally the Uber arrived, we climbed in, rolled down the windows and I stuck my head out into the fifty-mile-an-hour wind.

chapter forty-eight

When I arrived at the hotel, Zeke had still not got back. The room smelled musty and I opened the balcony door to let in some air. I drank some water, took a long cool shower, changed into tracksuit bottoms and a T-shirt and flicked on the television to wait for him. I didn't know how I'd keep my Everglades trip a secret, or how we'd smooth over what had happened at the party, but I knew I couldn't face another row.

I flaked out on the bed and tried to distract myself with a reality-TV show, but I couldn't get comfortable – my head was aching and my heat rash was painful. I searched through my toiletries for Ibuprofen, but could find none. Eventually, I found some Advil in Zeke's bag. He also had a bottle of his vile-tasting vegetarian multivitamins, which I grabbed too, as I thought they might help with the skin-healing.

I popped the cap, tapped a few out on to my hand, and was confronted by two different types of pill. One a huge, green vitamin that I recognized; the other a small, white oval tablet.

It took me a while to figure out what I was looking at. Aspirin, I told myself. Paracetamol. Because I didn't want to see what I already knew was true. It had been so much easier to stuff my head in the sand and forget what my instincts had been telling me over and over.

He'd hidden them in with his multivitamins, which I'd bought for him, and which he'd assumed I'd never take, on account of me trying one and declaring it tasted like vomit.

I held the white pills up to my eyes, and that's when I knew for sure. There was no drug name. The place where the drug name should have been was filed down. He, or the person who sold him these, had gone to the effort of hiding this information.

All the sleeping. The drinking. His surfing performance being so up and down. I had known something was wrong. Why had I just let it go?

Zeke was using again.

But using what?

I sat down, put my head in my hands and tried to think.

Zeke had promised me he was done with drugs, but he had a secret stash of mysterious pills. If he was on drugs, again, he'd lose his sponsors, his career, his main reason to live. His joy. The time of his life as a successful pro-surfer would be over.

He'd have made himself a hypocrite. He'd been out on beaches the world over with DFS scrawled large on his surfboard: Drug Free Surfer. And he'd been secretly chucking down pills?

What the hell was he thinking? How could he let his fans down like that? His family? Anders?

How could he do that to me?

I left him a note. One word, surrounded by pills.

Liar.

And then I packed my rucksack and walked to Lily's hotel.

chapter forty-nine

After six hours of talking it through with Lily, she convinced me to go back and confront Zeke. My head was still in bits, but I'd left my passport in the room safe and had to go back for that if nothing else.

'Where the HELL have you been?' he said.

'Road trip.'

'A road trip, huh? Who with?'

'Like you even care.'

'No, I clearly don't care about you at all, which is why I've been going out of my mind all day, while you ignored my calls and didn't return my messages.'

'You just care about you. Oh, and drugs.'

'Shut up already. They're not even real drugs.'

'What the hell are they then, Zeke?'

I chucked a handful of his pills at him, which I'd taken to show Lily, and they scattered at his feet.

'Nothing.'

'Yeah, they're definitely something.'

'You can't even call those drugs. Zoloft. It's, like, hardly stronger than an Advil.'

'Why are you taking them?'

'To help me relax.'

'Who gave it to you?'

'A doctor.'

'A doctor prescribed you something to relax? What doctor? When did you go and see a bloody doctor?'

'In Steamer Lane, while you were busy with the contest.'

'You snuck off to get stress medication?'

'I didn't sneak anywhere. I just didn't tell you.'

'Why doesn't it have the brand name on it?'

'OK, the doctor was actually a med student. I guess he was trying to cover his tracks, in case his roommate found his stash.'

'If you don't tell me what Zoloft is, Zeke, right this second, I'm going to google it.'

'It's nothing. Like some antidepressant that a million people take.'

'You're on antidepressants? *Why?*'

His face was contorted and I could tell this conversation was excruciating for him.

'Because . . .'

'Because you're depressed? Brilliant.'

'No. I don't know. The med student thinks maybe. I couldn't sleep. These help me sleep.'

'You've done nothing but sleep since we arrived here! Now I know why.'

'Iris, I've been thinking maybe we should take a break.'

'You're *dumping* me? Now? The minute I find out you're on pills?'

'I love you. You know I do. I love you so much. But we have to change things up; we can't keep doing this. All this arguing is too much. It's gotten way too intense.'

'You're blaming ME for this shitstorm? I had nothing to do with it.'

'No, I don't blame you. How could I? But I think we need some time out. From dating.'

Dating? It was weird to hear him call it that. Because I thought what we had was a relationship. A serious one.

'There's an article about me coming out. It's gonna be bad.'

So after all of Anders's plotting to keep even the rumour of this article from Zeke, he knew.

'Methsurfing,' I said.

'How long have you known?' he said, looking at me as if I'd betrayed him.

'Only last night. Daniel told Kelly.'

'So everybody knows. Perfect.'

'Not everybody, and most people won't even care.'

'My sponsors will care. Iris, it's not working. I can't handle all this fighting. We need some time apart to figure things out.'

'*You* need time apart, you mean. You're making out that this is for me, but you're the one who just got caught with illegally prescribed drugs, and now you want to run away.'

'It's not just me I'm thinking of. You're so young to be in such a big thing. And I'm not in a good place right now. I'm a total screw-up. All of this will wash back on you if you don't get away from me. Your career shouldn't suffer too.'

'I'm perfectly capable of deciding what's best for me.'

Zeke stood up, twitchy and tense, and avoided looking me in the eye.

'So we're splitting up?' I said. 'Just like that?'

'I'm sorry – I just don't know what else to do.'

saturday

chapter fifty

At 5 a.m., when the alarm on my phone started screeching, the argument was still raging on. He was standing with his back to the window, his eyes flashing with anger. He set his mouth into a hard line and started breathing deeply through his nose. Yoga breaths. He was trying to calm himself down.

'We shouldn't be talking about this right now. You have to get Zen for the contest,' he said, opening the blinds. The sun hadn't come up, but the night was clear and the lights of Miami were beautiful. We had come to one of the coolest cities in the world, and we still couldn't be happy.

Shame and regret vied for pole position; I thought I'd been ready for this relationship, but I wasn't. Zeke wasn't either. It was too much. Neither of us could handle it.

My mum had seen it coming, I was sure. She had been reluctant to let me chase my dreams, but I'd worn her down, convinced her that this was my big chance. Maybe she knew that in these circumstances my relationship with Zeke would burn out, but that she had to let it run its course. I was stubborn, and maybe she thought if she'd stood in my way I'd have left home anyway, at the first opportunity. She'd have been right.

'I don't care about the frigging contest! I'm not even going to it!'

He turned away from the window, alarm in his eyes.

'Yeah, you are.'

We took the coach to New Smyrna, and by the time we arrived Zeke was pale and his eyes were shining wet. I could feel the tears in my own eyes too.

He handed me my bag from the overhead storage. 'You have to go compete. Try to shake this off and we'll figure it out after.'

'I don't care about any of this shit. It's just a contest. Tell me what's going on so I can understand it. Why are you on pills? JUST TELL ME!'

'Don't you get it?' he said gently.

Yeah, I got it. My throat ached and my voice, when it came out, was a whisper. 'It's me, isn't it?' I said, feeling as if my heart was being clawed out. 'I've caused you nothing but hassle since the day you met me. I've made you depressed.'

'It's not about you.'

'It obviously is!'

'It's fucking not! Aargh! I saw the blue stars. I heard Nanna's voice singing the lullaby she sang us when we were little.'

I stared at him, wondering if he'd somehow slipped some LSD without me noticing.

'I don't—'

'My brain was shutting down. I had no air. I felt myself die.'

chapter fifty-one

Blue stars. Someone, and I couldn't even remember who it was, had once told me that was one of the stages of hypoxia. Oxygen deprivation.

Zeke was talking about the Cribbar. He'd almost drowned.

But he never talked about that. He said he didn't think about it, didn't dream about it; said that he was fine.

And then, with a realization like acid splashing out of my stomach and burning through the rest of me, I saw just what I'd missed.

Everyone was off the coach now, except us.

His voice was strained when he said, 'I've been held down by waves before, been beaten bloody on coral reefs in three different continents, but every one of those times I felt strong. Knew I'd be OK. It was different at the Cribbar. I couldn't hold on. My lungs were on fire, and I kept my mouth shut until I couldn't any more, and then I felt them fill with water. Man, that pain . . . and I couldn't do a single thing to stop it. I never felt more powerless in my whole life. My head's a fuckin' mess – I think I maybe have some kind of PTSD.'

Zeke had post-traumatic stress disorder?

'Oh God, Zeke,' I said, holding his hand. 'I'm so sorry. I didn't . . .'

Didn't what? Notice? Why? Because I was too busy stressing about the number of girls he'd slept with in the past? The number of contests I had left? The rank I'd make on the board?

My mind flipped back to an old argument we'd had before we left Newquay. I wanted to go to the Headland Hotel to have lunch, but he'd said he couldn't bear to look at the sea if the waves were good, because he'd need to be out there surfing – that view was torture, he'd said.

The windows of the Headland Hotel looked out on to the reef where the Cribbar waves broke.

How had I not seen it? I'd focused on all the wrong things; missed the important stuff right in front of my nose.

'Oh God, Zeke,' I said again. 'I don't know what to say, except I'm so sorry I haven't been there for you.' I cupped my face in my hands; wished I could disappear.

'Stop,' he said. 'It's not your fault. I love you, Iris.'

'I love you too.'

Standing in the aisle, Zeke wrapped his arms around me and I felt the weight of him.

'Maybe it'll be OK,' he said, swinging from despair to hope. 'We love each other. We gotta be able to fix this, right?'

The coach driver cleared his throat, tapped his mic, and said, 'Hey. Lovebirds. Get off my damn bus.'

three days later

chapter fifty-two

From forty thousand feet in the air, I looked at the cloudscape far below and listened to the deep breathing at my shoulder. Within a few hours, we'd be descending, pulling up on the runway, queuing to collect our luggage, walking through customs and into arrivals, where people would be waiting for us.

I thought about a time a few weeks after Zeke and I got together. I was wrecked from a very late night at his apartment, when we'd talked non-stop until dawn broke around us and we'd watched it set the windows of Newquay aflame. By midday I was shattered, so I sat on the beach with Sephy, while Zeke went off coasteering with a group of little kids and their parents, and Sephy started talking about Zeke's past. She said that when he and his brothers were growing up on the North Shore of Oahu, she always tried to dress them in the exact same T-shirt and board shorts.

'Like triplets?' I said, smiling as I imagined Zeke,

Garrett and Wes all dressed identically. They were really close in age, so it must have looked pretty cute. When I said as much, Sephy scoffed.

'Cute had nothing to do with it. I dressed them that way so that when one of them ran off and got lost on the beach, I could point to his brothers and tell the lifeguard, "This is what he's wearing."'

And then she'd squint through the binoculars, alternating with the lifeguard, until finally she'd hear, 'How about this one? Is *that* him?' and at last, with incredible relief, she'd look through the binoculars and say, 'Yeah, that's him.'

Zeke, though he was the littlest, was always the biggest worry to her, because he had the most to prove.

'He wanted to be the last surfer to come in at night and was out there even after the older guys had gone home.'

'Zeke,' she went on, 'was this little tow-headed grom of seven or eight, always determined to do his best, and he'd still be out there in the water when the sky turned black, and I would call him and call him, and sometimes he'd hear and he'd holler back, "Just one more wave, Mom," and I'd pray he'd get a good one, so he'd get out of the water.'

'He's still like that now,' I said.

'Zeke,' she said, 'never had moderation. Whatever he did, he dived in so deep it was hard for him to see the surface. It's just the way he's built. Oftentimes I'd have to get in there and haul him out myself, even when Pipeline was super heavy. Some days I'd have my own board with me, so I could paddle out, but not always, and then I'd have to swim out to him. Swimming out after dark when there's big-ass sharks cruising around is never a whole heap of fun.'

And she told me about a time when Garrett and Wes were visiting their grandfather on the Big Island, and it was just her and Zeke. The waves had been unusually poor that day, and all the other surfers and the lifeguards were gone, but Zeke was still out there, in the dark.

She'd called for him until she was hoarse, battled the impact zone, swum out to the second reef and she still couldn't see him in the water. She got out and patrolled the waterline in case she'd somehow missed him, pacing up and down the beach, panicked out of her mind, thinking the worst. He'd been taken by a current. Or a tiger shark. Or had smashed his skull on coral and drowned.

But at the same time she couldn't truly believe such a terrible thing had happened, because life without Zeke was unthinkable.

She'd just decided to call in the coastguard when she saw him walking towards her through the darkness, a buckled board under his arm.

'Zeke?'

'Hey, Mom – I broke my board.'

He'd had a nasty wipeout, and had got disoriented enough to walk off in completely the wrong direction. By the time he got his head together and found her, Sephy said she'd died a thousand times.

'You know, Mom,' he said, looking spooked, 'that was real scary just now.'

'Tell me about it!' she said, hugging him again.

'Yeah, I was walking up the beach and it sounded like someone said *shhhh* in my ear.'

Sephy was so emotional that it took her a moment to process what Zeke was saying.

'*That* was scary? Someone saying *shhhh* in your ear? Kid, I thought you were dead!'

She told me that afterwards, even when Zeke started travelling alone and surfing giant waves, she never worried about him the same way again, because her panic sensors were burned out.

'I hope I stop worrying about him,' I said, 'because otherwise I'm going to drive myself mad with all these mental waves he has to surf next year. He's already talking about Cortes Bank.'

'You'll be good with it,' she said, 'in five or six years.'

And it seemed so odd that Zeke's mum spoke that way, because everyone else's parents, including mine, were adamant that summer romances should end with September and none of us teenagers should settle down too early, but Sephy actually thought it was possible that

Zeke and me could make it in the long run, and that had blown my mind.

An air hostess walked past, pushing her trolley, and I looked down at the clouds again, and then over to Lily, who twitched in her sleep, and I thought about the other flight, carrying Zeke.

Our planes had taken off and flown in different directions, ours to Heathrow, his to Honolulu, and the last words we'd spoken to each other swirled through my mind.

'You said you wouldn't leave me.'

Hundreds of strangers had been bustling around us, dragging suitcases and shouting at their families to hurry up; we were standing in the centre of it all, facing each other.

'Please,' he said, 'I need you. Come with me.' He gripped my wrists, his hands sweaty and his blue eyes wild with panic.

'Zeke,' I said, loosening my hands from his, 'I can't come to Hawaii. You know I can't.'

'Sure you can – I'll buy you a ticket right now!'

He ran his hands over his shorn scalp, a habit from a lifetime of long hair, and I felt my resolve begin to weaken. The temptation to reach up and kiss him, to give in and say, 'Fuck it – I've changed my mind – I'm coming with you,' grew stronger by the second. Because life without Zeke was unthinkable.

My very soul urged me to say yes to him, to do whatever it took to make him happy. But there was also the thin vein of self-preservation at the centre of me, which knew better.

'Don't leave me. Not like this. Please, Iris.'

It was then I locked eyes with Lily; she looked so sad, because she knew how much pain I was in, and she nodded gently.

'Zeke . . .' I said, dreading my next words, because once they were said, I'd have to turn and somehow force myself to walk away from him, 'I love you. So much. More than anything else in this amazing world you've shown me, but we're hurting each other and we have to stop.'

'So we stop,' he said, brushing away tears with the back of his hand. 'We can totally do that. We'll treat each other right again.'

My face was tight with the effort of not crying, but my voice, when it came out, was firm and clear. The moment I'd said it, I saw the last flicker of hope in his eyes die.

'I don't want this any more — I want to go home.'

Acknowledgments

I would like to thank the following people, who have helped
and encouraged me so much over the past two years:

Jon and our girls.

My parents, Alicia and Geoff.

Ben Illis of the BIA.

Roisin Heycock, Niamh Mulvey, Rachel Faulkner and
Talya Baker.

Leighton Lloyd, John Duigan and Emma Adams.

Big-wave surfer Tom Butler and his mother, Sue Butler.

Pro-surfers Oli Adams, Tassy Swallow, Chris del Moro,
Chris Bertish, Jaide Lowe, Tina Beresford and Jessie
Tuckman.

Stevie Davies and Nigel Jenkins.

Eve Harvey.

Nicole Grant and Jon Grant of Whiskers, Newquay.

Rhys John, Max Hepworth-Povey and Christopher Hunter
of Errant Surf.

Laura Ward, Karl Michaelides, Rachel Lamb, Marci Pearce, Victoria Edge, Tristan Edge, Francesco Rigolli, Catherine Brealey, Lindsey Campbell, Amanda Handley and Alison Brazier.

Maia Garner and Nikita Jenkins.

The writers of YAT.

Jenny Davies.

Sarah Clarke of Checkered Photography.

Daniel Stapleford, Aimee Stapleford and Kristin Becker.

Margaret Cann, Steve Cann, Rich Boyes and Victoria Boyes.

Paul Glass, Laura Glass, Hilary Ely, Moira Briggs, Leena Heino, Kirsty McCluskey, Katherine Neal, Deb Stainer, Claire Beney, Beki Jenkins and Rosy Barnes.

Is this really it for Iris and Zeke?

Find out in

RIDE

COMING JUNE 2016

www.quercusbooks.co.uk

@quercuskids